"Since when do you carry handkerchiefs?"

Phoebe dabbed at the corners of her eyes.

Cash shrugged. "We're at a wedding. I came prepared."

"How very Boy Scout–ish of you."

"And you always cry. I figured it'd come in handy."

He'd noticed. Phoebe wasn't sure if she felt mortified or flattered.

"Contrary to what you may think, I pay attention." He stared ahead at the bride.

"Hmm. Yes. It's our job to be observant."

"Not that." He lowered his mouth to her ear and whispered, "I pay attention to you. I always have."

A burst of warmth radiated though her. Did he like her? Romantically? Was that what he was really saying?

"I don't want to," Cash continued, "and given the chance, I'd rather not. But you kind of demand it."

Her mind emptied, and she clenched her mouth shut rather than ba

Cash *did* like her...

Dear Reader,

I love starting a new series. My first step is creating my community. My newest series, Wishing Well Springs, is a place I filled with all kinds of interesting and compelling characters. Stories revolving around a wedding barn has been an idea of mine for a long, long time, and I'm so happy it's finally come to life!

The Cowboy's Holiday Bride is one of my favorite kind of books to write—a cowboy story (of course) and a holiday story and a wedding story. This time, I pulled a little bit from Charles Dickens's classic tale *A Christmas Carol*. Cash co-owns the wedding barn; Phoebe is the wedding and event coordinator. He's commitment shy, having been engaged and dumped three times. She's been secretly in love with him since high school. Rather than being visited by three ghosts, Cash's three former fiancées all get married at Wishing Well Springs within weeks of each other during December, the wedding barn's busiest month. And like Scrooge, Cash learns a valuable lesson from each of his "visitors."

I had so much fun with this book. I hope you enjoy reading about Cash and Phoebe finding their way to a happily-ever-after. Welcome to Wishing Well Springs!

Warmest wishes,

Cathy McDavid

PS: I love connecting with readers. You can find me at:

CathyMcDavid.com

Facebook.com/CathyMcDavidBooks

Twitter: @CathyMcDavid

Instagram.com/CathyMcDavidWriter

HEARTWARMING

The Cowboy's Holiday Bride

———

Cathy McDavid

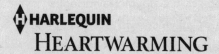

HEARTWARMING

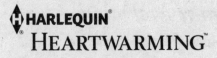

ISBN-13: 978-1-335-88994-2

Recycling programs for this product may not exist in your area.

The Cowboy's Holiday Bride

Copyright © 2020 by Cathy McDavid

This edition published by arrangement with Harlequin Books S.A.

For questions and comments about the quality of this book, please contact us at CustomerService@Harlequin.com.

Harlequin Enterprises ULC
22 Adelaide St. West, 40th Floor
Toronto, Ontario M5H 4E3, Canada
www.Harlequin.com

Printed in U.S.A.

Since 2006, *New York Times* bestselling author **Cathy McDavid** has been happily penning contemporary Westerns for Harlequin. Every day, she gets to write about handsome cowboys riding the range or busting a bronc. It's a tough job, but she's willing to make the sacrifice. Cathy shares her Arizona home with her own real-life sweetheart and a trio of odd pets. Her grown twins have left to embark on lives of their own, and she couldn't be prouder of their accomplishments.

Books by Cathy McDavid

Harlequin Western Romance

Mustang Valley

Having the Rancher's Baby
Rescuing the Cowboy
A Baby for the Deputy
The Cowboy's Twin Surprise
The Bull Rider's Valentine

Harlequin Heartwarming

The Sweetheart Ranch

A Cowboy's Christmas Proposal
The Cowboy's Perfect Match
The Cowboy's Christmas Baby
Her Cowboy Sweetheart

Visit the Author Profile page
at Harlequin.com for more titles.

To Michelle Grajkowski. Thanks for being my sounding board and taking all my phone calls when I needed to talk through ideas. Also for reading and commenting on version after version of the synopsis. Champagne's on me this time!

CHAPTER ONE

No ONE IN their right mind climbed a fifteen-foot extension ladder in flaming red three-inch heels—which, in Cash Montgomery's mind, explained a lot.

He strode through the barn's wide entrance, removing his denim jacket first, then his Stetson, and tossing both onto the nearest table. While bare now, it would soon be sheathed in a linen tablecloth, set with fine china and silver flatware, and surrounded by happy guests. That was, if Phoebe Kellerman didn't accidentally kill herself first and cause the wedding to be canceled.

Reaching the foot of the ladder, Cash's gaze traveled up to the top rung, where Phoebe stood attempting to hang a Christmas wreath the size of a tractor tire on the wall.

He should have been glad she'd worn pants today rather than those silly little skirts she tended to favor—not that he noticed her clothes. Much. Her legs, however, were an entirely different matter. Cash was human, after all, and Phoebe had what his late grandfather used to call spectacular gams.

"You're not wearing appropriate footwear to be on a ladder," he called, his voice echoing off the walls in the enormous empty space. "You could hurt yourself, and we can't afford an increase to our workman's comp premium. Or the cost of hiring your replacement while you're at home recovering."

Even at that height and while wrangling a heavy load, she managed to crank her head around and fire a laser stare down at him. "Your concern is touching."

"How much did that behemoth cost?"

"The invoice is on your desk."

"Am I going to be unhappy?" he asked.

"When aren't you unhappy?"

Grumbling under his breath, he gripped the base of the ladder with both hands and steadied it. What had made her think she could manage a clearly two-person task all by her lonesome?

"Get down from there. Let me do it."

Her answer was to draw back slightly and examine the wreath.

His blood pressure spiked. "For Pete's sake, Phoebe. Hold on, will you?"

Sighing, she obliged him. "Do me a favor. Go to the middle of the room and tell me if this thing is centered and hanging straight."

"Promise not to let go."

"I'd cross my heart, but I'd have to use my hand."

Against his better judgment, he did as she requested—only because he'd learned long ago that arguing with her was a waste of time. They'd been picking fights with each other since grade school. For over twenty years, she'd been underfoot, in the way and a thorn in his side. Initially because she and his younger sister, Laurel, were best friends and these last two years because she, Laurel and Cash were in business together.

On second thought, maybe Phoebe wasn't the only one lacking common sense. Cash, apparently, suffered from the same affliction.

Except, no denying it, she was the best wedding coordinator in Payson and one of the best in the state. Without her, Wishing Well Springs wouldn't have been recently ranked ninth on a list of Arizona's top ten wedding venues. Cash had to admit, he and his sister were lucky to have Phoebe—even if she did irritate the heck out of him on a regular basis.

Reaching midroom, he turned and evaluated her handiwork. "It's straight."

"You sure?"

What did he know? "Straight enough."

"The Pendergrass-Sloans are paying top

dollar for this wedding. They expect perfection."

"It's a wreath. I doubt the placement will have any effect on the wedding's perfection or the couple's fifty-fifty chance of not divorcing."

"Ha. For someone in the business of happily-ever-after, you have a pretty negative attitude."

"Comes with the territory," he said dryly.

"Right. I forgot for a second."

She sent him a glance that managed to be both guilty and amused before turning back to the wreath. She was well acquainted with Cash's history and knew he preferred not to talk about his three failed engagements.

"Hey, I booked a holiday family reunion this morning," she said in that effervescent way of hers. "For the week of Christmas. That's twenty-eight total weddings and events between today and New Year's. Nearly one every day of the month."

"Cha-ching!"

She rolled her eyes. "I swear, Cash. You're hopeless. Wishing Well Springs isn't just about the bottom line. We bring people together and make their dreams come true."

"Hmm." He ignored her in favor of running numbers in his head.

"I recognize that tone. You're already spending the profits."

"Right again."

Twenty-eight weddings and events, Cash mused. More than double the number they'd had last December. And with their planned mock Western town expansion, they'd increase that number next year.

It was almost enough to dim the painful memory of his family losing the ranch and going bankrupt.

Phoebe tilted the wreath a few inches to the right, the movement causing her long curtain of pale blond hair to resettle between her slim shoulders. "How about now?" she asked.

"Looks great to me. The wreath," he clarified.

"You sure? You don't want me to have to climb up here again, do you?"

She was smiling; he could hear the mirth in her voice. Darned if she wasn't an expert at jerking his chain.

"It's fine." He started back across the room toward the ladder. "Now get down from there before you break your scrawny neck. I mean it, Phoebe."

She fiddled with the wreath for another minute before gingerly climbing down the ladder. Cash waited at the bottom, steadying it. With each step, her bright red high heels drew nearer and nearer until they were at Cash's eye level.

"Are those bells?" he asked.

"Cute, huh?" A delicate silver chain circled her right ankle from which hung a pair of matching bells that jingled softly with each movement. "My sister gave them to me."

Cash didn't ask which sister. She had four; all of them older than Phoebe and carbon copies of each other. From the time they were young, the Kellerman girls had been a force to be reckoned with, and he'd diligently avoided them. Nowadays, unfortunately, that proved impossible.

Phoebe's parents owned and managed Joshua Tree Inn, which, besides their four-star accommodations, offered one of the best dining experiences in Payson. They frequently catered wedding receptions at Wishing Well Springs, and the two neighboring enterprises enjoyed a mutually beneficial relationship, regularly referring customers to each other.

All the Kellerman sisters, save Phoebe, worked for Joshua Tree Inn and showed up regularly at the weddings they catered. Cash could only tolerate them in small doses. Just like Phoebe.

He let go of the ladder and retreated, giving her room as she descended the remaining rungs. Reaching the floor, she pivoted, a bright, happy smile on her face—which was a mere four inches from his. How had that happened? And when had he started noticing every tiny detail about her?

Taking another backward step, he studied what had to be the newest addition to her ugly sweater collection: a Christmas tree decorated with cat-head ornaments.

"Tell me you're not wearing that to work," he said.

"The clients love my sweaters."

They loved *her*. Unlike Cash, she related well with people and developed instant rapports. That was why he much preferred being the long-distance member of their partnership.

Once or twice each month, he traveled from Phoenix, where he worked as a project architect at Strategic Design, and spent the weekend in Payson. Cloud file sharing and video meetings allowed him to easily handle the majority of his duties as Wishing Well Springs' chief financial officer from afar.

Usually. Thanks to his sister, Laurel, and her pending trip to Palm Springs, that arrangement was temporarily changing as of today.

"You're here early," Phoebe commented as they left the barn together, Cash retrieving his denim jacket and cowboy hat on the way. "It's barely ten o'clock."

"I wanted to make a few sketches before heading to the house."

"New idea?"

He was constantly revising the drawings for their Western town expansion. "Been thinking about adding a bank."

"I love it." Phoebe quickened her already clipped pace. "Imagine the fun photo ops. The bride holding up her banker dad for money to pay for the wedding—" She stopped short. "Okay, maybe that last part's not such a good idea. But the bank is wonderful. I approve. It should go between the general store and the livery stable. Leave the sheriff's office-slash-jail on the end."

Cash started to say something about running the numbers first only to change his mind. "You're right."

"Did we really just agree for once?" Phoebe gawked at him in mock alarm. "And thunderbolts didn't appear out of nowhere to strike us down?"

"Not yet." He grinned and peered at the sky.

Rather than any sign of a storm, bright sunlight ducked in and out of picture-postcard billowy clouds. Cash had a habit of checking the local Payson weather every day, even when in Phoenix. Rain, wind and occasional snow wreaked havoc with weddings and events and ran the staff ragged executing a plan B.

"Did you notice the well?" Phoebe asked.

He hadn't and looked now. "You put a wreath on it. And a red bow on the bucket."

She gazed admiringly at her work. "I'm going to create a holiday spectacle. Lights. Garland. Animated figurines. Paper lanterns. No, luminaries."

"We talked about this."

"I promise not to blow the budget."

Cash hated being the scrooge in their partnership, but one of them had to maintain a close watch on the finances. It wasn't that Phoebe had no concept of money. Rather, her priorities were different. She believed in sparing no expense, whereas Cash watched every penny.

"If we're not careful," he said, "we'll run out of money halfway through our expansion."

"I get that you're not a fan of borrowing money, but companies take out loans all the time. My parents did to start the catering operation, and they increased profits enough to pay off the loan early."

"Overextending is what bankrupted my family and forced Grandpa to sell off the ranch."

"With a loan, we could finish the expansion early and do some other improvements around the place."

"No."

"Interest rates are down."

"Phoebe."

"All right, all right. It was just a suggestion." She must have accepted she'd hit a brick wall, for she changed the subject. "We really need to showcase the well more for the holidays. It's key to our marketing campaign, not to mention the history behind it."

She was right about that.

The original well, dug by Cash's great-grandfather, had been nothing more than a hand pump mounted on a pipe driven four-hundred feet straight down to the exact spot where the property's two subterranean springs converged. Cash had decided to construct a fieldstone well complete with a shingled peaked roof and bucket and pulley system.

Everyone who visited the barn raved about the well, and many tossed in a coin. A wire net suspended beneath the water's surface collected the coins, which, as the posted sign announced, were collected twice a year and donated to a local charity.

"What are you thinking?" Cash asked.

"Off the top of my head, stack a bunch of fake wrapped presents in front of it."

He kicked at the dry ground. "They'll get dirty. And what if it rains or snows?"

"Killjoy," Phoebe muttered.

"Just being practical."

"Like always."

"How about I drag that old pony sleigh out of storage from above the carriage house? You can sit it next to the well and decorate it with… I don't know what."

She instantly brightened. "Mr. and Mrs. Inflatable Santa Claus! Like they're riding in the sleigh. And those lighted reindeer could be pulling it. Oh, Cash. That's perfect!"

What had he gotten himself into?

"But will you have time?" she asked. "We're really slammed this weekend. Three weddings, remember?"

"I will on Monday."

"You're staying longer?"

Too late, Cash realized his mistake. "Actually, I'm—"

He was spared having to explain by the arrival of a white panel van that pulled up beside the golf cart. The van's side door slid open with a whoosh, causing half of Wishing Well Springs' logo, their phone number and slogan—We Make Your Wishes Come True— to disappear. Three workers piled out, along with the driver. Each was dressed in jeans and a gold sweatshirt, on the back of which was printed the same logo, phone number and slogan as on the van.

Waving and hollering greetings, the workers

immediately started unloading crates, boxes and cases onto a pair of handcarts. Before long, the barn would be ready for the Pendergrass-Sloan 4:00 p.m. wedding.

Assuming Phoebe would be overseeing the crew, and eager to execute a hasty retreat, Cash excused himself to start on his sketches. "See you at the office."

"Don't go yet." She hooked him by the elbow, her grasp firm yet gentle. Was that even possible?

He stared at her fingers on his jacket sleeve and found himself wondering how they'd feel on his bare skin.

The next second Cash came to his senses. He and Phoebe had long shared a mild attraction, true. But they couldn't spend ten consecutive minutes together without disagreeing about something. Usually money.

"What?" he asked, striving to keep his tone neutral.

"You didn't finish earlier." She studied him expectantly, her hazel eyes searching. "I asked if you were staying longer."

Cash cleared his throat and silently cursed himself. He'd hoped to postpone this conversation until he and his sister were both free to talk to Phoebe.

"Is something going on?"

Left with no choice, he admitted, "Um, actually, I'll be here for the next three weeks. I'm covering for Laurel while she's in Palm Springs," he finished with less conviction than he would have liked.

"You're covering for your sister," Phoebe repeated slowly.

"Yeah. We—you and I—are going to be working together. Well, more than we usually do." He produced what he hoped passed for an affable smile. "I'm your new able-bodied assistant."

"You're…joking."

"Afraid not."

Gone was the perpetual twinkle in her eyes and the upward tilt of her Cupid's-bow mouth. "We agreed to bring Georgia Ann on full-time to help me while Laurel's gone." Her glance cut to the crew unloading the van and the lone gray-haired woman.

"We were considering bringing on Georgia Ann. The fact is, we don't have any extra money in the budget. Not if we want to start construction for the expansion on schedule. You read last month's financial reports." Cash tamped down his impatience. He'd explained this to Phoebe before. "As least, I assume you did."

"What about your job at Strategic Design?"

"I have enough accrued vacation days."

She stood there, tapping the toe of one

red shoe, her hands crossed over her middle. "Nope. Won't work. We have to figure out another solution. Find the money for Georgia Ann's wages somewhere else in the budget. Move a few line items around."

"I'm sorry you found out this way, Phoebe, but the decision's made. Laurel and I were planning on telling you together."

"Without me being consulted?"

"The vote would have been two to one even if we had."

Her features hardened. "That doesn't give you the right to cut me out. I'm a partner. An equal one. Not merely an employee."

And here, he thought, was the real reason for her anger. He and his sister had unfairly excluded her.

Before Phoebe could justifiably lay into him, Georgia Ann called out with an urgent, "Hey, we have a problem."

"We'll talk more later," Cash said.

"We most certainly will." Phoebe spun on her heels and stormed off.

He watched her go, his thoughts less on his sketches and more on the next three weeks, which, no thanks to him, were off to a lousy start.

PHOEBE STUDIED THE wooden floor where the shattered crystal candleholder lay. Each of the hundred glittering slivers was a perfect reflection of her current emotional state in the wake of Cash's announcement: jagged and sharp and disconnected.

It wasn't that he, and not Georgia Ann, would be…what had Cash said? Her new able-bodied assistant. Phoebe would survive, frustrating and nerve-racking as the arrangement was bound to be. No, what bothered her most was being cut out of the decision process entirely.

Granted, Cash and Laurel owned the property. The main house, wedding barn, carriage house and twelve acres were all that remained of the once thriving and sprawling quarter horse ranch that had been left to them by their late grandfather. And Laurel's custom wedding dress boutique was hers and hers alone. But the business side of Wishing Well Springs was an equal three-way partnership. Phoebe deserved to be included regardless of whether Cash and his sister had planned all along on sticking together.

She rolled her shoulders in an attempt to shed her annoyance. To be fair, Phoebe and Laurel usually sided against Cash. But they *included* him in their discussions. There was a big difference.

"Chicken," she murmured under her breath,

convinced he'd chosen to avoid what would doubtless be a heated debate.

"What'd you say?" Georgia Ann asked. She stood across from Phoebe on the other side of the shattered candleholder, fretting and fussing.

"Nothing."

"I don't know what happened. The darn thing just slipped from my fingers. I know the bride was very specific about having holiday candlesticks, and this was our only pair."

An oversight Phoebe would soon correct. "Don't worry. Accidents happen."

"I'll be glad to explain the situation to her and take full responsibility."

There was no hint of insincerity in Georgia Ann's voice, another reason why the two of them got along so well. Both were convinced that the couple's wishes, regardless how unusual or outrageous or costly, were important and deserved to be honored to the best of Wishing Well Springs' abilities. If the bride wanted holiday holders for the unity candles, she'd get holiday holders for the unity candles.

"Hang on." Phoebe lifted her ever-present phone dangling from a lanyard around her neck and speed-dialed her sister Trudy, head of catering at her family's inn.

"Hey, sis." Phoebe called all her older siblings by the same endearment. With four of them, it made things simpler.

"If you're worried about the lobster crepes, don't be. Everything's under control, and we'll be there by three sharp."

"I'm not worried. We have another problem." She explained about the shattered holiday candleholder. "Can you bring that pair from the front window when you come?"

"Mom won't be happy."

"Don't tell her."

"She'll notice. She doesn't miss a thing."

Phoebe sighed. "Please. I'll have Georgia Ann drive them back over as soon as the bride and groom walk down the aisle."

Beside her, Georgia Ann nodded vigorously. She'd fetched a broom and dustpan and had swept the crystal shards into a tidy pile.

"Fine, fine," Trudy grumbled.

Phoebe swore she could hear her sister's eye roll through the phone. "Thanks. I owe you."

"I'll trade you for babysitting."

"Done."

Trudy was six months along with her first child and their parents' seventh grandchild. Phoebe remained the sole offspring not married and not producing future generations—a fact that was brought to her attention on a regular basis. Not in a you're-a-disappointment way but in a we-just-want-you-to-be-happy way.

Had things gone differently, she'd be celebrating her third anniversary this spring and bouncing one or even two babies on her knee. But it wasn't meant to be, and the enthusiasm she'd once poured into making her own wedding plans come true she now poured into others'.

"Cash arrived earlier than usual. I saw his pickup drive past."

Trudy's comment shook Phoebe from her mental wanderings. "He did."

"What's wrong, sweetie?"

It was just like her sister, *any* of her sisters, to correctly guess Phoebe's mood after hearing only a few syllables. "He's not just here for the weekend. He's staying for three weeks. The entire time Laurel's in Palm Springs with her VIP client."

"The wealthy art gallery owner?"

"Yeah. That one."

"Ooh. Really?"

"What does that mean?" Phoebe was less adept than her sister at interpreting tones and inflections.

"Just that… Well, come on. You. And Cash. Together…"

"So what?" *Don't say it. Please.*

"You…like him—"

"I do not," Phoebe insisted with enough vehemence that Georgia Ann sent her a curious look.

"You always have." Trudy was either mixing batter or running a blender, for a whirring sound filled the background. "Since you were kids."

"I had a crush on him for maybe two months in high school."

"Oh puhleeze."

"I'm not going to dignify that with a response." Neither was she giving herself away to her astute sister.

Phoebe had harbored a crush on Cash for a lot longer than two months or even two years. But he'd barely noticed his younger sister's best friend except to demand she make herself scarce. She'd hung on arena fences, gawking, when he'd competed in junior rodeo, and bought tickets to see him compete professionally during his college days.

She'd visited him in the hospital when he blew out his shoulder bulldogging at the National Finals Rodeo, attended his graduation from Arizona State University, had lunch with him during her periodic excursions to Phoenix, followed his career at Strategic Design and kept up with the latest happenings in his life from his sister.

She'd secretly cried when, during his junior year at ASU, he'd gotten engaged for the first time. She'd emerged from the despair brought on by his second engagement vowing enough was enough and eagerly pursued the first man to glance twice in her direction—a mistake that had ultimately wasted the best part of her twenties and left her with nothing to show for it except a refusal to repeat past mistakes.

At least one big positive came out of it— she'd been too immersed in her own failed love life to feel much when she'd heard about Cash's third engagement. Thankfully, she'd sufficiently recovered by the time Laurel's idiot boyfriend dumped her, so she was able to be a supportive friend. Not long after Cash's third fiancée bailed, he and Laurel converted their ramshackle house and falling-down barn into the present day Wishing Well Springs, bringing Phoebe in as a partner.

The irony didn't escape her. One of the most popular wedding venues in Arizona was run by three people with a history of broken engagements and failed relationships. Go figure.

"Hey, I gotta run." Trudy's voice sounded muffled, as if she'd entered the walk-in cooler.

"Me, too. See you at three."

Phoebe disconnected and assessed her surroundings. While she'd been on the phone, her crew had worked their magic and transformed the room into a winter wedding wonderland.

White wooden folding chairs were arranged in rows to resemble church pews, complete with an aisle down the middle. The chairs faced the rear of the barn, where an altar and lattice arch had been set up beneath the empty hay loft. Rather than storing sweet-smelling alfalfa and providing a playground where children's imaginations could soar, the loft was now used for additional seating, overhead photography and filming, storage, a dance floor or, for one wedding, choir seating.

On the far wall, two of Phoebe's workers were hanging red and green silk streamers that stretched out from the enormous wreath like long arms. Georgia Ann attached red and green bows to the backs of the chairs while the other two workers set up the tall space heaters.

"Everything looks great," Phoebe called to Georgia Ann. "If you need me, I'll be outside. I have another call to make."

"Okeydokey."

Phoebe walked and dialed at the same time. If not for being sidetracked by the broken candleholder and her sister, she'd have placed this call the second Cash was beyond earshot.

Laurel answered almost immediately, mumbling around the pins perpetually shoved in her mouth. "Hiya. What's up? All set for the Pendergrass-Sloans?"

"Why didn't you tell me Cash was covering for you while you're gone?"

A long span of dead air followed. Phoebe pictured Laurel removing the pins from her mouth one by one as she considered what to say next. She had no less than three custom wedding dresses in development at any given time, each one in a different stage of production. "You heard."

"Cash let it slip. I'm pretty sure unintentionally."

"We were going to tell you together."

"So he said." Phoebe cleared her throat in an effort to erase the whine waiting to escape.

Laurel sighed. "We can't afford to bring on Georgia Ann full-time. Temporarily or otherwise. I get that you and Cash don't always agree and he isn't your first choice for a helper. But the fact is, he's capable, organized and won't cost us any extra wages."

"He's not good with people."

"He can be when he wants to."

"He's too serious," Phoebe insisted. "Couples like over-the-top enthusiasm. Especially the brides. And he's not sympathetic enough. Can you see him comforting a distressed bride or calming a nervous groom?"

"Actually, he's a good listener."

He was. Phoebe pushed aside a long-ago memory of Cash patiently sitting with her while she'd cried and lamented about her brutal breakup with her ex, Sam. She remembered wishing Sam had been half as good a listener as Cash.

"Not with strangers he isn't."

"Send him on errands," Laurel said. "He excels at manual labor."

"He's bossy."

"And you're not?"

"Laurel." The whine escaped and Phoebe clamped her mouth shut.

"We have two days to train him before I leave."

"Is that enough? Excellent customer service is our trademark."

"Be honest. What's really bothering you?"

She stared at Cash, leaning against a pine tree in the empty field beside the barn, and frowned. "You two made a pretty big decision without including me."

"I swear, it was last second," Laurel insisted. "Cash came up with the idea and got approval for his vacation time without talking to either of us. He informed me literally an hour ago. We agreed to tell you after my appointment.

I didn't realize he was heading to the barn first. My bad."

"He should have called us before putting anything in motion."

"Him helping out isn't a bad idea," Laurel cajoled. "He does know the business and has a personal stake in things going well."

"Says the person who'll be gone and doesn't have to work with him."

"You're right."

"This isn't how we agreed to run our partnership." Phoebe pouted and then caught herself.

"I'll have a chat with him later today."

"Forget it. No big deal." The last thing she wanted was for Cash to think she'd tattled on him. They weren't kids anymore.

"No, it is a big deal," Laurel insisted. "And it won't happen again. I was wrong to go along with Cash when he called this morning."

Phoebe blew out a long breath. What she'd wanted most was to be heard, and she had been. "Apology accepted."

"Shoot. She's early. See you later."

Phoebe heard the distinctive chime of the front door in the background. Laurel's appointment had arrived.

"I'll be heading your way in a bit."

"Again, hon, I'm sorry. Won't happen again. I swear."

Not intentionally, thought Phoebe, but it would happen. Blood was thicker than water. She and Laurel were close. Cash and Laurel were closer.

Losing pretty much everything save the shirts on your back either drove a wedge between people or strengthened their relationship. It had done both to the Montgomerys. A dynamite blast couldn't sever Cash and Laurel's bond, while their parents had divorced less than two years after filing for bankruptcy.

Cash had changed in the wake of his family's personal and financial tragedies. Very little of the carefree, impetuous, fun-loving teenager remained in the ambitious, focused and cautious man today.

That hadn't altered Phoebe's feelings for him. Her sister Trudy was right. She liked him. Too much for her own good.

Besides his not reciprocating her feelings, which, face it, was a big obstacle, they were in business together. If they started dating and things soured, the result could have a disastrous effect on them *and* Wishing Well Springs. She didn't want to risk that. She *wouldn't* risk it. Her position here was too important, and she'd be devastated to lose it.

CHAPTER TWO

CASH TRIED. He did. But he couldn't help himself and glanced up from his tablet every few minutes. As a result, his sketch of the Old West bank wasn't much more than a rough outline with a door and window.

Phoebe remained outside the barn's looming entrance and staring into space, not moving after her phone call ended. He guessed she'd been speaking with his sister. Who else? He'd deduced from Phoebe's intense pacing and constant tugging on her sweater hem that the conversation hadn't gone well. More than once she'd stopped to jab the empty air in front of her.

Had she been imagining stabbing his chest with a sharp object? Probably. That was the thing about Phoebe. Her emotions were always at one end of the spectrum or the other, almost never in the middle. And she could bounce between happy and sad, or bubbly and angry, at the speed of light.

All at once she went back inside the barn. Marched, actually. Phoebe rarely walked.

Deciding his creativity was shot for the day, at least until they settled this latest skirmish, he powered off his tablet and headed around to the back of the barn. There, stored out of sight, were stacks of reclaimed lumber and steel beams purchased for construction of the mock town.

Cash was nothing if not a perfectionist. Like the wedding barn and main house renovations, the town would be built from as much reclaimed material as possible to produce an authentic and appealing aesthetic. That, and he liked the idea of leaving a smaller carbon footprint. It was a practice he employed not just with Wishing Well Springs but at Strategic Design, too.

Satisfied with the condition of the material, he returned to his truck and, yes, checked on Phoebe's whereabouts. She and Georgia Ann were visible through the barn door, rolling out the gold carpet that would line the center aisle.

All at once she straightened and turned, her gaze landing hard on Cash. Seconds passed, neither of them moving, neither of them smiling.

What now? Hadn't he sufficiently apologized? He shrugged. *I don't know how to make this better.*

She raised her chin, her mouth compressed into a very flat line. *If you don't know, I'm not going to explain it to you.*

He raised his palms in surrender. *I give up.*

She rolled her eyes. *You're hopeless.*

He hitched a thumb over his shoulder. *Meet you at the house for our appointment.*

She nodded brusquely—*Fine*—and then ignored him in favor of Georgia Ann.

Cash drove slowly along the dirt road to the main house, which, since the restoration, closely resembled the home of his and Laurel's idyllic childhood. Before his grandmother had died from a rare cardiovascular disorder that first drained the family's resources. Before the economy had tanked a year later and purchasing expensive, quality quarter horses for reining and roping and endurance riding became a luxury fewer and fewer people could afford. Before his grandfather had been forced to sell most of the ranch just to keep the lights on and put food on the table. Before bankruptcy had driven his parents to divorce a week after Cash's sixteenth birthday. Before his dad had become someone Cash spoke to a few times a year and saw less often than that.

With a role model like that, he should have run from marriage. Instead, he'd popped the question three times and to the wrong women.

A therapist would no doubt have a field day with him.

Rather than pull his truck into the garage, he continued driving a short distance to the old carriage house. There, he came to a stop and climbed out of the cab, taking in the dilapidated structure—his next project at Wishing Well Springs after the mock Western town expansion.

A pair of wooden doors sat askew, in danger of being ripped from their rusted hinges by the next strong wind. Decades of grime coated the panes on the small square window above the doors, reducing visibility to zero. A rooster weathervane sat atop the roof. Once a proud guardian of all it surveyed in any direction, it now tilted at a forty-five degree angle, a broken and useless reminder of what the house and barn had resembled before Laurel had changed their lives by proposing the idea they turn their inheritance into a wedding venue.

Cash had readily agreed with his sister's idea. It made sense on many levels. She already had an established wedding dress business with built-in clientele. Payson was a popular tourist town and honeymoon spot. They were conveniently next door to Joshua Tree Inn. And last, Cash had been ready to try something different. He'd been growing steadily dissatisfied with being an underappreciated cog in the large machine known as Strategic Design.

Shielding his eyes from the sun's glare, he peered through a wide crack in the carriage house doors. The last time he'd been in there, the pony sleigh was stacked on top of the old hay wagon. Now? Who knew. Sometime during the weekend, he'd risk stepping on mouse droppings and being bit by a black widow just to get the sleigh for Phoebe. He owed her that much after this morning.

Hearing a friendly nicker, he followed the sound to the paddock beside the carriage house. Elvis and Otis ambled over from their covered enclosure to greet him.

"Hey, you two. How you been?"

The half-quarter, half-Percheron horses lifted their big, shaggy heads over the top fence railing and snorted. Cash obliged the pair, giving them a thorough scratching between the ears.

"You been taking care of the place for me while I'm gone? How are your feet doing?" He bent to examine their enormous hooves through the railings for any sign of trouble. "Okay. No cracks. No foundering. Though you both could use a trim." He'd have to call the farrier. "Coats are growing out, aren't they?" He stroked Elvis's neck, the thick hair two inches longer now that winter had set in. "Think I'll still put blankets on you. It's supposed to snow in a couple weeks."

At twenty-two and twenty-three years old, the long-in-the-tooth pair were the only livestock left from the days when Cash's entire family resided on the ranch. They'd been a favorite of his late grandmother's, and Cash refused to sell them even though the horses no longer earned their keep.

"Maybe I'll take you out for a drive while I'm here." He grabbed the top railing and tugged, noting the board wobbled loosely. "And do a few repairs around the place."

He was about to return to his truck when a diminutive gray tabby popped out from a hole in the corner of the carriage house and padded over.

"There you are." Cash smiled. "Right on time."

His late grandmother had also fed every stray cat to wander onto the ranch. Cash didn't continue that tradition. He had his limits. But Stubby had appeared last spring, delivering her litter in a secluded corner of the carriage house. Cash had found homes for her kittens when they were old enough and then used a humane trap to capture her and have her spayed. His sister checked on Stubby and filled her food bowl daily when Cash was away, but the cat only came out of hiding for him.

Feeling his jacket pocket vibrate, he dug out his cell phone and released a low groan when he read the number. His first day off in over six months, and he'd barely made it to noon before getting a call from the office.

"Hello? It's Cash."

"Hey, man. You busy?"

He recognized the voice of his associate Travis. "Just checking on the horses. What's up?"

"Nothing. That's the problem. The building schematics for the Horizon Bank Tower are giving me grief. I could really use your insight."

"I'm off the clock, pal."

"I know, I know. But you left without any warning and stuck me with the heavy lifting."

"You ask Marguerite?" Cash's immediate supervisor had agreed to cover for him.

"She wasn't any help. Said to call you."

Cash groused under his breath. This had better not be a preview of things to come for the next three weeks.

"Give me the condensed version," he told Travis and listened while the other man explained. "It sounds like an error with the elevations. Email me the file and I'll look at it."

"That's great. Not to be pushy, but when?"

"Not until later today." Cash glanced over his shoulder in the direction of the main house. "I have a meeting at one."

"On the expansion?"

"I wish. Nope, this is with wedding clients. I'm sitting in."

Travis erupted in laughter. "Sorry, man, but it's funny, thinking of you planning a wedding."

"Assisting," Cash emphasized.

"You're not exactly the type."

"What type is that?"

"Come on." Travis finally managed to control his laughter. "You used to rodeo. Professionally, right? Not a whole lot of cowboys plan weddings."

"I'm covering for my sister. Not considering a career change."

Little did his coworker know how much firsthand experience Cash had at wedding planning. No guy engaged three times came away without a fair amount of education. That didn't include what he'd gleaned from his sister and Phoebe.

"Well, don't have too much fun," Travis said. "We'd hate to lose you."

"Not a chance."

Not much of one, anyway. If he ever quit

Strategic Design, it wouldn't be to work full-time for Wishing Well Springs. No, in his wildest dreams, he'd have his own architectural practice. A small one-man operation in Payson where he'd pursue his recently discovered passion for renovating old barns and houses.

But that was a long, long way off, if ever. Twenty percent of Cash's paycheck went directly into Wishing Well Springs' coffers. In the past, to get them started. These days, to fund the expansion. If all went as planned, he'd earn a nice return on his investment. Until then, leaving Strategic Design was only a long-off dream.

"I'm sending the file now," Travis said.

Cash heard his phone ping. "Got it."

"Thanks again, pal."

Cash disconnected. While he'd been talking with Travis, Stubby had climbed the fence post to the top. She sat there batting Otis on the nose. The old horse wasn't deterred and continued sniffing her, earning himself another angry swipe.

Hmm. Their relationship reminded Cash a little of his and Phoebe's.

"Play nice, you guys. I'll be back tonight at feeding time."

Parking in the garage a few minutes later, he shut off the engine, grabbed his duffel bag from the floor of the passenger side and took the creaky set of wooden stairs up two flights to the attic room he bunked in during his stays. Laurel had taken over the entire second floor, including Cash's boyhood bedroom, for her personal quarters and workspace.

He didn't stay long after unpacking his duffel. Returning to his truck, he retrieved his briefcase and entered the main house through a connecting door. A short hall opened into a large country kitchen. There, he helped himself to a cup of coffee from the machine on the counter before winding his way to the first floor's spacious entryway.

To his right was Bellissima, his sister's custom wedding dress boutique. Cash started that way only to reverse direction when the sound of voices reached his ears. She must be with a client.

Instead, he wandered into the seating area for Phoebe's wedding coordinating clients. Her desk, currently unoccupied, and its two visitor chairs faced the twin couches and a side chair. Cash used a small desk in the back, hidden behind a partition. He neither needed nor wanted more.

As he crossed the highly polished hardwood floor, several large objects stacked haphazardly on one of the couches caught his attention.

What the...? No way!

Cash bore down on the couch. Grinding to a stop, he stared at the fabric sample books as if daring them to be a figment of his imagination. They weren't, and his blood pressure skyrocketed.

Despite his explicit instructions not to, and with no regard for their budget, Phoebe had gone out and done exactly what she wanted. And she was mad at him for making a decision without consulting her? Dropping his briefcase on the coffee table, he grabbed his phone, fumbling to unlock the screen in his haste.

The chime sounded a split second before the front door could be heard opening and then closing. It was followed by a familiar *clack, clack* that could only be produced by a pair of ridiculously inappropriate red heels.

Cash pocketed his phone. She was here. Even better.

Phoebe didn't keep him waiting and appeared a moment later. Surprise widened her eyes, and she ground to a halt. "What are you doing here? Danielle and Marcus aren't due for a while."

He pointed to the fabric sample books. "You care to explain?"

"I doubt that's necessary." She skirted past

him and proceeded to her desk. "You're a smart man." She heaved herself into her desk chair.

"Phoebe." He spoke her name through clenched teeth.

"Cash," she said, attempting to mimic him.

"We're not reupholstering the office furniture."

"Calico Cover Up is having a sale."

"I don't care. The expansion comes first. All available money is designated for that." Money that, at the moment, was coming from Cash's paychecks—which Phoebe knew.

She pushed back her chair and stood, waving her arm expansively to include the couches and side chair. "This old furniture is an eyesore. If we hope to attract more clients, we need to spruce up the place. The offices and *not* the mock Western town are what will make a positive first impression on people."

"Take the sample books back." He advanced on her. First one step and then another. Enough to, in his opinion, press the advantage of his greater height.

She also advanced two steps, putting them practically toe to toe. "Laurel and I agreed. You're outvoted."

A small victory smile pulled at the corners of her mouth. Her very pretty mouth. That wasn't far from his. Cash had leaned in and kissed women farther away than her. This was the first time he'd wanted to lean in and kiss Phoebe.

"You can't get blood from a stone," he said, struggling to concentrate. "And you can't have furniture reupholstered with money that doesn't exist."

"I'm merely obtaining a quote. What harm is there in that?"

He lowered his head. Toe to toe had become nose to nose. Game on! "You're wasting time we can't spare. Like you pointed out earlier, we have almost thirty weddings and events between now and New Year's and may book more. With Laurel gone, you and I have enough on our plates."

"We need to get the furniture reupholstered before February and the Valentine's Day rush." Her eyes twinkled. She liked the game, too.

"I'll authorize new throw pillows." Had he really just said that? Good grief. Travis would bust a gut laughing if he heard Cash.

"Throw pillows? Talk about a waste of money."

"Take it or leave it."

She stilled and narrowed her gaze at him. He stared in return, enthralled and excited by her intensity.

"Enough, already! I can hear you from Bellissima."

They both spun at the warning. Laurel stood at the entrance to the business offices; her fists were braced on her hips and she was wearing an annoyed scowl.

"Oops," Phoebe murmured and flashed a guilty grimace.

Cash groaned. He could kick himself. His little exchanges with Phoebe were increasing in frequency. And enjoyment. What was with that?

As THE YOUNGEST of five children, Phoebe had gotten into her fair share of trouble and been forced to endure countless lectures. Cash, too. The getting-in-trouble and listening-to-lectures parts. His parents had been even stricter than Phoebe's.

Laurel obviously took after them. For someone yet to have children of her own, she was impressively skilled at scolding and finger wagging.

"Thank goodness my client left before you two really tore into each other. I don't like having to explain that my business partners are incapable of acting professionally in each other's company. Yeesh."

"Sorry," Phoebe said for the third time. "We got carried away."

Cash muttered something about it not happening again.

Laurel released a martyred sigh. "Maybe I shouldn't go to Palm Springs, after all."

"No," Phoebe and Cash blurted simultaneously.

"This job is too important," Phoebe added.

"Yes," Laurel agreed. "It is." Flopping down on the nearest couch, she rubbed her temples. "Not only the money—there's the possibility for future client referrals and future bookings. This woman has some major connections."

She didn't need to explain. The art gallery owner boasted a large network of people in high places. Her wedding to a prominent sports figure would be well publicized with photos appearing in numerous publications. The potential exposure for Bellissima and Wishing Well Springs was not to be taken lightly.

For those reasons, Laurel had agreed to spend three weeks away from Wishing Well Springs during their busiest time of the year. Plus, she was making a simplified version of the gallery owner's gown for the flower girl and a tasteful ensemble for the mother of the groom. Despite extensive preparation, Laurel would be lucky to finish in the allotted three weeks.

Phoebe crossed to the couch and perched

beside her best friend, leaving Cash to take a seat on the adjacent couch alongside the fabric sample books.

He aimed an accusatory stare at her. *Are you trying to send me a message?*

She shrugged. *Perhaps.*

"Please don't worry." She placed a hand on Laurel's arm. "Cash and I promise to behave while you're gone."

Laurel's gaze zigzagged between the two of them. "I'm annoyed that we're even having this discussion."

"Did you vote with Phoebe to have the furniture reupholstered?"

Phoebe frowned. Cash would ask that.

"I agreed she could get a quote," Laurel said.

"That's not how she put it." His stare intensified.

To call his eyes brown would be a disservice. Not that she was one to wax poetic about a man's looks. But even if she'd been born with a heart of stone, she'd still go all gooey inside at the sight of Cash's eyes.

Cocoa. Brandy. Chestnut. Raw umber.

Ugh. She needed to stop studying fabric samples. That last one was too absurd even for her. But chestnut? Yeah, that worked.

The thing about Cash's eyes, though, it wasn't just their incredible color. He had a way of looking at people that drew them in and made them want to know him better. Intimately. No wonder so many women had fallen for him. Present company included.

"You implied Laurel fully supported you," Cash continued.

"I'm hoping you both will," Phoebe countered. "If the price is right. That fact is, we need to spend money to make money, and our seating area is screaming for a refresh."

"We *are* spending money. A lot of it. On the expansion." He half stood and reached for his briefcase on the coffee table, setting it on his lap as he resumed his seat.

Phoebe tried not to openly admire his long, muscular limbs and natural athleticism, preferring to wait until he wasn't paying attention.

A lifetime of riding horses and rodeoing had endowed him with strength and agility and a masculine grace that turned heads when he passed. What Phoebe found most appealing, however, was Cash's complete obliviousness to his effect on people. He had no idea of the charisma he exuded. Phoebe sure did.

Releasing the briefcase's latch, he withdrew a slim stack of paper-clipped reports that he then distributed three ways.

Phoebe's shoulders slumped. Not the monthly financials. She took the report, wishing she were elsewhere. Talking about money was like having dental work done—a highly unpleasant necessity.

"Danielle and Marcus are arriving soon." She made a production of looking at her phone. "Do we have time for this now?" The couple were planning an elaborate Christmas-themed wedding and pulling out all the stops.

"You said one o'clock." Cash checked his watch. "That gives us twenty minutes."

More than long enough for Phoebe to be bored out of her skull. She skimmed the reports while he translated their meaning for her and Laurel's benefit, her mind drifting. As she often did, she pondered how someone like Cash could be fascinated by numbers and calculations and measurements. It wasn't just that he looked like someone who belonged sitting in a saddle rather than behind a desk, staring at architectural drawings or financial reports.

He'd loved rodeoing and riding and camping out under the stars with his grandpa and dad. She knew for a fact he'd often spent the night in the barn, staying awake to tend a sick horse or pregnant cow. He'd been the first to volunteer for a game of backyard football and spent endless hours practicing his lasso skills until he could rope a practice dummy blindfolded.

Loss changed a person, she supposed. Poor

Cash had suffered more than anyone deserved and at such a vulnerable young age. Not just his late grandmother's death and losing the ranch and his father's abandonment. He'd lost his security and with it the confidence everything he had today would still be there tomorrow. She was no expert, but that had to account for his failed engagements to some degree.

Phoebe understood the changes in him. That didn't stop her from missing the young Cash, and she relished those rare glimpses of him. That probably accounted for why she was constantly egging him on. Whenever he was annoyed with her, he most resembled his former self.

"Is that a good enough compromise for you?" Laurel asked.

Phoebe blinked herself back to the present. "Say again? I was reading the budget projections." She flipped to the last page that, fingers crossed, contained the projections.

"If we can reduce our December expenses by ten percent, Cash will consent to having the furniture reupholstered in January."

"But you'll need to really curb your spending," he cautioned.

Phoebe straightened, certain she'd heard incorrectly. "It's the holidays. I don't think we should curb our spending. If anything, we should spare no expense."

"Find ways to economize. I can help you with that while I'm here."

She massaged her throat, feeling an awful lot like a dog on a very short leash. "Cash, please." She didn't often plead with him. "Won't you reconsider?"

"I think what he's offering is fair," Laurel said in her adult-disciplining-children tone. "The reupholstering will cost twice that. He's taking the rest out of the expansion budget."

He was? She'd missed that part. "Thank you, Cash."

"Congratulations!" Laurel applauded. "That wasn't so hard, now, was it?"

Phoebe managed a smile. Her friend was a nervous wreck and worried sick about leaving. She wouldn't add to that by playing hardball.

"About the rising cost of our office supplies." Cash flipped a page. "There's been a significant spike this past quarter—"

The chime sounded, announcing visitors. Phoebe nearly shouted with relief at being set free.

"That must be Danielle and Marcus." She jumped off the couch and hurried toward the entryway, hearing only Laurel bringing up the rear. Cash had evidently stayed behind, preferring not to mingle with clients. That would have to change if he was going to be her helper.

The couple were stripping off their bulky sweaters when Phoebe greeted them with an exuberant "Hello!"

"We're a little early," Danielle said. "Hope that's not a problem."

"Of course not." Phoebe hugged the other woman warmly and shook Marcus's hand. Laurel followed suit, exchanging pleasantries.

"My bride-to-be couldn't wait," Marcus said, grinning sheepishly.

"Not just me." Danielle gave him a playful punch.

He responded by drawing her close. "Guilty as charged."

Phoebe loved, loved, *loved* this part of her job. Nothing pleased or satisfied her more than working with couples so obviously happy and devoted to each other. Unless it was watching them walk arm in arm down the aisle after the ceremony. That was always when she cried a little. Not when the bride first appeared, which was when most people shed tears.

She held out her hands. "Let me take those for you." Hanging their sweaters on the nearby coat tree, she said, "I thought we could go over your wedding and reception plans first, and then you can head to your final fitting with

Laurel." This arrangement worked well, as fittings could be unpredictable and frequently ran longer than anticipated.

Danielle's eyes glittered with excitement. "Yes. That's perfect."

"Great." Laurel motioned toward Bellissima. "I'm going to leave you in Phoebe's capable care while I ready your dress."

"I can't wait!"

"Me, either. I think the changes we decided on last time came out gorgeous."

Danielle pulled on Marcus's hand. "You'll have to wait outside. You can't see the dress. Not before the wedding."

"We have plenty of reading material and a TV in the groom's lounge to keep you occupied," Phoebe said, and led the way to the client seating area, remembering at the last second that she'd forgotten to remove the fabric sample books.

Shoot. Well, too late now. She doubted Danielle and Marcus would cancel their wedding just because the waiting area was a bit untidy.

Except it wasn't. Cash hadn't remained behind to avoid client contact. He'd carted off the fabric books and the financial reports. How about that?

"Have you met Cash Montgomery?" She nodded toward where he waited near her desk.

Both Danielle and Marcus answered no and shook their heads.

"He's Laurel's brother and our partner in Wishing Well Springs."

"Nice to meet you." He came forward and shook hands.

"Cash is actually going to sit in on our meeting," Phoebe said, watching Danielle and Marcus in an effort to gauge their reaction to someone new. "He's assisting me while Laurel's in Palm Springs."

"Oh." Danielle's brows rose, her expression one of mild disconcertment.

"If you'd rather I didn't, I can leave," Cash offered. He understood she might not want a stranger intruding.

"No, it's not that."

"I'll be sitting on the couch over there and taking notes." He placed his hands on the back of the visitor chair in front of Phoebe's desk and turned it slightly, inviting Danielle to sit. "You'll hardly notice me."

"We just want to provide you with the very best service," Phoebe gushed. "With Laurel gone, I recruited the next best person. Cash has assisted with countless weddings." A slight exaggeration.

"All…right," Danielle conceded.

"Come on, babe." Marcus tweaked her chin

between his fingers. "Relax, will you? They just want us to be happy."

"Yes, ma'am," Cash agreed.

Danielle laughed, visibly less nervous, and sat in the chair. "I'm such a goof."

"No, you're not," Phoebe reassured her and then addressed Cash. "Would you mind getting Danielle and Marcus some peppermint hot chocolate? It's her favorite."

"Absolutely," he replied smoothly, avoiding her glance as he left for the kitchen.

Phoebe didn't let the snub get to her. Yes, she'd dispatched him to perform a menial task, but wasn't that what assistants did?

"I thought we'd start with the flowers first. You mentioned earlier that you prefer white peonies. I'm worried we may have trouble getting them during the holidays. What about white lilies as a backup? They're also gorgeous. Or champagne roses?"

She went around her desk and pulled out her chair, only to stop short. Cash had dumped all the fabric sample books beneath her desk, hiding them from view while also making it impossible for her to sit there.

Her initial annoyance dissolved into admiration. She'd have done the same thing herself in his place.

CHAPTER THREE

"So WE ATTENDED this wedding last year," Danielle said, turning toward Marcus and then back to Phoebe. "At the end of the ceremony, all this confetti fell from the ceiling. It was…" She closed her eyes. "Magical!"

"I bet." Phoebe imagined the bride and groom being showered with confetti. "I've seen that done with balloons."

"What are the chances we could have fake snow instead of balloons?" Danielle asked hopefully. "It is a Christmas wedding, after all."

Phoebe thought a moment. "It's possible. We could rent a machine and blow the fake snow from the hayloft." She glanced over at Cash sitting on the couch. "Can you look into that for me?"

He gaped at her as if she'd spontaneously sprouted a pair of antlers and a red nose. "Won't that make a mess when it melts?"

"Actually, they have party machines that produce particles resembling snow. The particles evaporate on contact and are much less messy. Though I don't know where to get the machine or how much it costs."

Danielle clapped her hands. "That'd be awesome. It won't, you know—" she pointed to herself "—ruin my dress or anything?"

"I'll find out."

"Might be expensive," Cash muttered.

Phoebe rested her elbows on her desk, having moved the fabric sample books so she could sit. "We'll get the details and call you," she said in her most congenial tone.

"Wonderful!" Danielle glowed.

"If not, we can always substitute red and green confetti." She nodded at Cash, who, after a long moment, made a note on his tablet. Just like when he sketched drawings or ran numbers, lines of concentration furrowed his brow. She remembered that same expression from back in high school when he was studying for a test or sizing up the competition during a steer-wrestling event. Like then, she found herself captivated.

Good grief. Enough already! Shaking her head, she refocused on Danielle and Marcus. "You were saying?"

"About the centerpieces…" Danielle reached into her oversize tote and removed a magazine clipping. "I know we agreed on white candles and holly and red berries. But I came across these adorable nutcracker wedding cake toppers the other day, and I was wondering if there's a larger version we could use instead." She passed the clipping to Phoebe, who studied it front and back.

"Did they by chance mention the name of the manufacturer?"

"Argh!" Danielle clamped a hand to her head. "I should've thought of that."

"No problem. I'll do some research."

Phoebe opened her mouth to tell Cash, but he was already typing into his tablet. Okay, one small point in his favor.

"The last thing I need to mention before your fitting is the string quartet." Phoebe scanned her notes. "The best price I was able to negotiate is three hundred dollars per hour with a two-hour minimum charge."

Danielle looked worriedly at Marcus. "What do you think? Too much? I know Mom and Dad said they'd pay, but I don't want to empty their savings account. Dad's planning on retiring in a few years."

Phoebe noticed Cash frowning. Fortunately, the bride and groom couldn't see him from where they sat.

"I could always ask my parents," Marcus offered.

"No, no. They're already paying for the honeymoon. Two weeks at a resort in New Zealand," Danielle told Phoebe and then flushed prettily. "I mentioned that already, didn't I?"

"Sounds incredible," Phoebe concurred. "The trip of a lifetime."

Over on the couch, Cash worked his jaw. He was probably thinking about the cost of the trip.

"I can wait on the string quartet," she told the bride and groom. "But understand they may take another booking."

Danielle's features fell. "I guess we can do without music. I just always wanted a string quartet to play at my wedding."

"Hire them," Marcus insisted. "We'll find a way to cover the cost. We're bound to get money for wedding gifts. And we can have one of those dollar dances at the reception."

"That feels like begging. I mean, people will be bringing gifts. To ask for money, too…" She made a face.

"We'll dip into our house down payment fund."

"We can't!" Danielle protested. "That'll set us back three months."

Marcus captured her hand and drew it to his mouth, kissing her palm. "Big deal. We wait a little longer."

She squealed with delight. "Really?"

"Anything for you."

Phoebe heartily approved. Weddings should be what every couple always wanted, even if they spent more than originally planned.

From where he sat on the couch, Cash coughed. Or did he snort?

They quickly finished up, and Phoebe escorted their clients to Bellissima, where Laurel waited with Danielle's stunning dress. Phoebe had to admit, her friend had outdone herself. Then again, she had the exact same thought with almost every dress. She also secretly compared each dress she saw to the one she might have worn at her own wedding if she and Sam hadn't parted ways.

The memory still stung even after all this time. She hadn't been wrong to assume they'd eventually marry and to start making wedding plans without him. After three-plus years of dating, what woman wouldn't expect her boyfriend to pop the question?

Only Sam hadn't proposed. Worse, he'd accused her of pressuring him into marriage and eventually used that as an excuse to break up. When asked, Phoebe always said they'd realized they weren't right for each other and she'd dodged a bullet.

In truth, she'd desperately wanted to get

married, and Sam had fit the bill. She'd loved him and had seen herself spending the rest of their lives blissfully married. If anyone had dodged a bullet, it had been Sam. Phoebe would've made him miserable.

She freely admitted her faults, high-maintenance topping the list. She needed a self-assured man with a backbone of pure steel who wasn't intimidated by her. Someone like—

Entering the client seating area, she nearly collided with Cash. A small tingle skittered along her spine. "Um, excuse me."

"Danielle and Marcus could afford the down payments on three houses with the money they're spending on this wedding," he announced. "Isn't buying a home far more practical?"

"Yes, they could buy a home." Bye-bye, tingle. She cut left and retrieved the empty hot chocolate mugs from her desk. One in each hand, she started for the kitchen. "But they want a big splashy wedding."

Cash trailed after her. "An expensive wedding. Who needs a string quartet and fake snow?"

"Particles. And I refuse to keep having this same conversation over and over during the next three weeks. Your job is to assist me, not criticize or even comment on the couples' choices."

"You're right."

She paused. "I am?"

"What do I care? The more our clients spend, the more money we make."

The mugs clinked as Phoebe put them in the kitchen sink. "That's a pretty callous attitude."

"I'm a callous guy."

"Well, you're going to need an attitude adjustment. If only while Laurel's gone."

He appraised her with those compelling chestnut eyes of his that always set her heart aflutter. "Not sure it's possible."

"I have an idea where to start."

"Yeah?"

Glad for a distraction, she said, "Grab your jacket and let's go."

"Where?"

"The barn. It's three-ten now. The Pendergrass-Sloan wedding starts at four sharp and the caterers just arrived. Starting right now, it's all hands on deck."

"And how is this supposed to adjust my attitude?"

"Quit dawdling." She gave him a shove. "I dare you not to be happy at a wedding."

"Challenge accepted."

"Ha, ha, ha." They exited through the front

door and jogged down the porch steps to where Phoebe had parked the electric golf cart.

Cash held out his hand for the key. "I'll drive."

"Not on your life."

She slid in behind the steering wheel and powered up the vehicle. They zipped along the dirt road at a jaunty clip.

"You're stirring up dust," Cash complained while holding on to the side bar.

"Oh. Sorry." *Not.* "By the way, I need you to go with me to the nursery tomorrow."

"What for?"

"More poinsettia plants and a Christmas tree for the barn. Maybe a second one for the main house."

"It's only December first. Trees won't last until New Year's."

"Correction." Phoebe accelerated around the last turn before climbing the small hill to the barn. "Our first trees. We'll have to buy fresh ones in a couple of weeks. It's in the budget," she interjected before he could protest. "Be ready at ten."

Cash shoved his right foot into the floorboard as if slamming on the brakes. "Can't. I have a meeting then."

"With who?"

"The contractor. We're meeting at Mountainside Building Supply to go over prices and scheduling and look at some material. Excavation of the land starts right after the first of the year."

"By noon, then. No later." She slowed to a stop behind her family's catering van. "We have a wedding at seven, and I promised the couple a fully decorated Christmas tree in the barn for their ceremony."

"I should meet you at the nursery. To be on the safe side. Not sure how long my meeting will run."

"Good idea."

They piled out of the golf cart. To Phoebe's satisfaction, the barn and grounds hummed with activity. Trudy was there and barking orders at the catering staff like a drill sergeant. She spotted Phoebe and Cash and waved before hurrying over.

"Hey there, you two." Her six-month pregnancy belly stuck out adorably from her uniform, a crisp white apron over a matching white shirt and hunter-green slacks. When day stretched into evening and temperatures dropped, she and the other catering staff would don green pullovers. "Cash, welcome home. Good to see you."

"Hi, Trudy."

She threw herself at him, leaving him no

choice but to hug her. Peering at Phoebe over Cash's arm, Trudy waggled her eyebrows. Phoebe pantomimed a gag.

"Where's the ice sculpture?" she asked, happy to interrupt her sister's fun.

Trudy extracted herself from Cash. "In the van. It's a work of art, in case you were wondering. Two doves forming a heart on top of a bell."

"Nice."

"No, not there!" Trudy scurried off to intercept one of her crew lugging a champagne fountain.

Cash turned to Phoebe. "What's first on the list?"

Before she could answer, Georgia Ann flagged them down. "Phoebe. Where did you put the extra Christmas bulbs? Two have burned out."

"Check the storage closet." She fell into step with Georgia Ann. "I'll help. Did you set up the ladder?"

Cash materialized beside her. "I'll change the bulbs. You aren't climbing a ladder again. Not in those shoes."

"You're no fun."

After that, everything became a blur. Family members and friends arrived with their own list of needs: a station for the guest book, a table for gifts, a projector to cast photos on the wall. The minister was next to show, along with the groom, the groom's parents, his best man, the ushers and the photographer. Just as everything was coming together, Phoebe received a text. The bride and her entourage were five minutes out.

"Let's go, people," she announced loudly. "It's showtime."

She and Cash went outside to welcome the small caravan of vehicles. Georgia Ann remained behind to handle any last-minute problems.

The bride emerged from the first sedan, a gorgeous vision in snow-white taffeta and lace.

Phoebe let out a soft gasp. To her utter shock, her throat closed and her eyes stung with tears.

How could this be? She never cried until the end of the ceremony. And yet a soft sob escaped. She wiped her damp cheeks.

"Here."

Feeling a nudge from Cash, she looked down. He held out a folded handkerchief.

She hesitated.

"Take it."

She finally did and dabbed at the corners of her eyes. "Since when do you carry handkerchiefs?"

"We're at a wedding. I came prepared."

"How very Boy Scoutish of you."

"And you always cry. I figured it'd come in handy."

He'd noticed. Phoebe wasn't sure if she felt mortified or flattered.

"Contrary to what you may think, I pay attention." He stared ahead at the bride.

"Hmm. Yes. It's our job to be observant."

"Not that." He lowered his mouth to her ear and whispered, "I pay attention to you. I always have."

A burst of warmth radiated through her, halting her breathing and curling her toes. Did he like her? Romantically? Was that what he was really saying?

"I don't want to," Cash continued. "And, given the chance, I'd rather not. But you kind of demand it."

Her mind emptied and she clamped her mouth shut rather than babble incoherently. Cash *did* like her! The next instant, her mind filled, this time with a dozen thoughts and images. Her and Cash cuddling. Canoodling. Kissing. Sweet-talking. Discussing future plans.

"Sort of like watching a charging bull," Cash continued. "You know the poor guy's going to get stomped, and it'll be bad, but looking away is impossible."

Not the most flattering comparison, Phoebe mused.

"Or a rash you can't stop scratching."

The burst of warmth promptly cooled. She'd been wrong. Way wrong. The mortification she'd wondered about earlier set in and the tears threatened to return.

"Are you okay?" Cash asked, utterly ignorant of her distress.

"Splendid," she quipped and marched forward to greet the bride, chiding herself for being such a fool. When in heaven's name would she learn?

"QUIT CROWDING ME, you two."

Cash used his elbows to nudge Otis and Elvis away as he carried several thick flakes of alfalfa across the paddock to the wrought-iron feeder. The old horses weren't easily deterred and snatched quick bites from the flakes as they ambled along beside him.

"If I hadn't fed you myself last evening, I'd think you were starving."

Otis nipped at Elvis, who squealed in protest.

"Knock it off." Cash dumped the hay into the feeder. Particles flew everywhere and he wiped his nose and eyes with his jacket sleeve. "That should hold you until dinner."

After a brief battle for choicest spot, the horses settled in, burying their noses in the hay and snorting with contentment.

While they ate, Cash called the farrier and set up an appointment for the following Tuesday. When he was done, he headed into the tack shed, where he removed the thick blankets from storage and located the grooming caddy. Taking his load outside, he got to work, brushing coats and combing manes and tails until every tangle and trace of dirt had been removed. He then put on the blankets, which would not only keep the horses warm at night but also clean for a wedding photo shoot later that day.

With its country setting and rustic barn, Wishing Well Springs was the perfect venue for country- and cowboy-themed weddings. Docile-natured Otis and Elvis were a nice addition, and today's couple had requested them to be in some of the photographs. Just last month, a couple had used the horses in their engagement photos. Cash insisted on only charging enough to cover costs. He figured Otis and Elvis were a good advertisement and brought in new clients.

"Hmm," Cash murmured, adjusting one of the straps circumventing Elvis's belly. "One of us has put on a few pounds since last winter."

Elvis paid him no attention and instead searched Otis's side of the feeder for any last stalks of hay that might have been missed.

Cash retrieved a pick from the caddy and began cleaning all eight hooves. Bending over while bracing a heavy hoof on his knee put a strain on his back. The work, however, felt good. It had been too long since he'd spent time outdoors engaged in physical labor.

"Am I getting soft?" he asked Stubby, rubbing his lower back.

The tabby had emerged from hiding while he'd been busy with the horses and perched on her favorite fence post. Cobwebs clung to her whiskers and a layer of dust coated her fur. She must be taking a break from her favorite pastime: keeping the carriage house free of rodents.

Cash joined her at the fence post. "I think I'm spending too much time in the company of women and helping with weddings. Not that I don't like women." He pushed an unbidden image of Phoebe's shapely legs from his mind. He'd been thinking of her a lot lately, and it seldom concerned business. "What I need to do is get out and chop some kindling or break a green horse. Manly stuff that'll help bolster my faltering ego."

Stubby gave him some serious side-eye.

Cash leaned his sore back on Otis's enormous hindquarters. "I'm really looking forward to meeting with the contractor this morning. If I never hear another discussion about lilies versus pansies or posies or whatever flowers those were, it'll be too soon."

Stubby suddenly leaped from the fence post and scampered toward the carriage house. A second later she disappeared through the same hole she'd appeared from yesterday.

"See." He pushed off of Otis. "Even the cat can't stand talking about flowers."

"Morning. You're here early."

Hearing Phoebe's perpetually sunny voice, he turned, adjusting his cowboy hat in an attempt to mask his embarrassment. Had she heard him conversing with Otis and Stubby? "Yeah, I wanted to get the horses ready before my meeting with the contractor."

"Which reminds me, Laurel texted last night. She scheduled a last-minute fitting and meeting with a client this afternoon and wants us there. We need to be back from the nursery by three at the very latest so the crew can unload the Christmas tree and plants before tonight's wedding. So don't let your meeting run long."

"Yes, ma'am."

"And no filling the bed of your truck with

equipment and material. I know how you are at these meetings. We need room for the tree and poinsettias."

"Got it." He let himself breathe easy. She either hadn't heard him talking to the animals or was doing an excellent job of feigning ignorance. Odds were on the latter. "I won't be late, and the truck bed will be empty."

"Okay. Good." She hugged herself and stomped her booted feet, shivering slightly from the cold.

Today's ugly sweater, a 3D Santa face with tufts of white yarn for the beard, clearly wasn't warm enough. She'd added a pair of Santa earrings with blinking eyes that would be really annoying if he stared at them long enough.

"Is something wrong?" she asked.

"No." Cash shook his head, breaking the spell she'd been casting on him more and more often. "Other than I didn't sleep well last night. Sleep enough," he amended.

The wedding reception hadn't ended until well after 11:00 p.m. It was well past one when Cash fell into bed, losing consciousness the instant his head hit the pillow.

"Welcome to my world," Phoebe quipped cheerily. "You're going to have to develop some stamina if you plan on doing this full-time."

"Trust me." He walked around to the paddock gate and let himself out. "I'm escaping to Phoenix the second Laurel gets home."

"What about Christmas? Your mom will be expecting you."

"I'll be here."

His mom tried her best to keep the flagging family tradition going. Turkey and stuffing, sweet potato casserole, pumpkin pie and exchanging gifts—all of which she transported from her home in Globe to Payson and then prepared with loving care in the main house kitchen. But with both his grandparents gone and his father's glaring absence, the dinner tended to leave Cash feeling empty and morose. He participated solely for his mother's and sister's sakes and a desire not to disappoint them.

He looked forward to the day when he'd celebrate the holidays with his own family. That was a long way off, however. He couldn't consider settling down until the mock Western town was complete, his investment was recouped and Wishing Well Springs was operating well in the black.

"Wouldn't miss it," he added.

"Good grief, Cash. You looked happier when the state audited our sales taxes."

He stretched his mouth into a grin. "Better?"

She held up a hand as if to ward him off. "Now you're scaring me."

He was glad to see she'd returned to her usual self and that whatever had upset her yesterday afternoon at the Pendergrass-Sloan wedding appeared to have passed. They had trouble enough getting along without Phoebe crying at brides emerging from cars.

"As much fun as I'm having, I need to scoot." She patted Otis's nose over the fence before hurrying off.

Cash resisted for five seconds before checking out her legs. She was wearing a skirt—bad choice for a shopping trip to the nursery. Then again, she was wearing bright red tights that he supposed made it all right.

He was about to holler that she should change, only to clamp his mouth shut. Looking at her legs might be the singular highlight of their errand together. Why ruin it?

On his way to the main house, he stopped first at the attic room to grab his wallet and keys. While there, he paused to study his surroundings.

The cramped and shoddy room could definitely use an update. He'd be staying here more than usual once construction on the expansion started and could really use some extra space. With Laurel using the entire second floor for her workroom and living quarters, Cash had nowhere to go short of getting his own place.

He envisioned an older home, nestled in the wooded foothills, in need of a complete remodeling. One he could design to his particular liking. Then again, he'd been toying with the idea of converting another barn, only this one into a house rather than a wedding venue.

Wait. Scratch that. He wasn't moving to Payson. He'd have to leave Strategic Design and, as much as he craved a change, he was stuck at his job until the expansion was complete and fully funded.

Until then, he'd feed his creative drive with projects around here. Like the mock town and carriage house and, yeah, this sorry excuse for a room. Built-in bookcases would make a difference, he mused. And a Murphy bed rather than the ancient twin studio bed. No, an elevated double bunk like in those tiny homes. Then he could add storage drawers beneath the bunk.

Cash roamed the attic room, considering and discarding various ideas. In the compact bathroom built by his grandfather, he knocked on the wall behind the sink and was rewarded with a hollow sound. The wall was shorter than the other three because of the sloping ceiling.

Two feet of empty space behind it was filled with insulation.

If done correctly, the bathroom and adjoining closet could be expanded into the empty space, increasing the size of both by potentially twenty percent. While not a huge amount, it would make a difference. He wasn't too worried about the loss of insulation. Heat rose, and the attic room was surprisingly warm in the winter. Summers, however, would be unbearable. He'd have to figure out a way to increase cooling to the room. A challenge but not an impossibility.

"More trouble than it's worth," he murmured, backing away from the wall. "You aren't here enough."

On second thought, if he remodeled the room and made it more livable, they could rent it out to a boarder for additional income or to an employee as part of their compensation. Laurel would like that.

Step one would be to get rid of all the old junk. His grandfather had used the attic room to store his grandmother's belongings after her death. Then Cash and Laurel had used it to store *his* belongings when he'd moved in with their aunt. They'd cleaned out much of the stuff when they began work on the house and barn so that Cash had a place to crash. They'd used what antiques they could to decorate Bellissima and furnish the business office.

The rest had remained, collecting dust and slowly deteriorating. Cash wandered over to his grandmother's old cedar chest. He hadn't seen the contents for several years, avoiding the memories they evoked.

Drawing a deep breath, he lifted the lid, the hinges squeaking their complaint at being disturbed. Most of what he found were rodeo mementos—plaques and trophies and ribbons going all the way back to his grammar school days. Intermingled here and there were photos and certificates. A torn cardboard box held a collection of belt buckles. More than twenty by his estimation.

Laurel must have put them there. The last time Cash had seen them, his grandmother was still alive.

He picked up first one buckle and then another, reading the rodeo name and the event. He was about to close the box when his fingers landed on a gold buckle from the Gilbert Days Rodeo. The first-place win for bulldogging had qualified him for the National Finals Rodeo a few weeks later, where, on day two of the competition, he'd blown out his shoulder.

He'd been with Melanie then, his first fiancée. They'd joked about having a quickie Vegas wedding to celebrate what they were certain would be a championship title for Cash. But they were young, still seniors in college and up to their eyeballs in student debt. They'd reasoned it was better to wait a couple of years until they were both earning decent wages and had saved a little money. Cash hadn't wanted to end up in the same position as his parents.

Just as well they'd decided against a quickie wedding. Cash had wound up spending months recuperating after his surgery and was forced to drop his classes. With professional rodeo no longer a career option, he'd changed his major to architecture, requiring him to complete yet another semester in addition to the one he'd missed, and putting their marriage on further hold. One day, Melanie announced she'd accepted a job in another state and left Cash alone and heartbroken and feeling like a failure.

A wiser person might have closed the chest. Not Cash. He kept digging, eventually discovering a gold watch his second fiancée, Hannah, had gifted him their second Christmas together. Turning the watch over in his fingers, he examined the memories it stirred from a safe emotional distance.

She'd been everything he'd ever wanted in a woman, or so he'd thought. They had met during his first year at Strategic Design when Cash was determined to prove his worth by climbing the corporate ladder. He'd fallen fast and hard for her and couldn't wait to marry her and start a family—which they'd planned on doing the second Cash was promoted to project manager and given a decent raise.

His being passed over once, then twice, had delayed their plans. Hannah had grown discontent and kicked Cash to the curb. Like Melanie, with very little warning. Licking his wounds, he'd sworn to himself he was done with relationships and buried himself in his work.

Setting the watch aside—he should probably have donated it—he rummaged around the very bottom of the trunk. Beneath a pair of worn and cracked child's cowboy boots—Cash's first pair—a thin strip of material caught his eye. It took a moment for his brain to recognize the black formal bow tie. How had that gotten in there? The last time he'd worn a tux was to the Arizona Theater Gala he'd attended with Silver.

And, like that, the face of his third fiancée lit up his memory's motherboard. They'd originally met at Strategic Design's holiday party. She'd been there with another man but had flirted outrageously with Cash. Not being made of stone, he'd responded, and they'd started dating. In those days, she'd been a model with aspirations of becoming an actress.

Cash had promptly forgotten all his vows to avoid a serious relationship. Silver, he'd been adamant, was the one. Yet again, he'd gotten down on one knee and proposed.

Except Silver had coveted a certain affluent lifestyle that went along with being a model and, as their relationship progressed, an actress in local TV shows and national commercials. Cash had decided he'd needed to work harder and save even more money. When she'd landed a part in a Hollywood movie, off she'd gone. Confused, angry, heartsick and once again unsure what he'd done wrong, Cash was more than ready for a distraction. It wasn't long after that Laurel had suggested they convert their grandfather's inheritance into Wishing Well Springs.

Why, Cash wondered, had he held on to these reminders of his past mistakes? Pushing to his feet, he grabbed the belt buckle, watch and bow tie and stuffed them into his jacket pockets. At the bottom of the stairs, he hit the button to activate the garage door opener and trudged outside. Around the corner of the house he found two large dumpsters, a black one for waste and a blue one for recycling.

Opening the lid of the black dumpster, he

dropped in the buckle, watch and bow tie. When Laurel's boyfriend had stupidly dumped her, she'd burned the gifts he'd given her, calling it a cleansing ceremony.

Cash wasn't about to go that far. Throwing away the belt, watch and bow tie was plenty cleansing for him.

As he walked through the connecting door to the house, there was a lightness to his step missing since Silver had driven away in her, yep, *silver* Mercedes.

CHAPTER FOUR

CASH STOOD IN the middle of Mountainside Building Supply's large material yard and inhaled deeply. The pungent, tangy scent of fresh-cut lumber filled his nostrils. Across the yard, a pallet truck beeped in warning as the operator reversed to relocate a stack of siding. Two employees wearing ball caps and neon-orange safety vests carried on what appeared to be a friendly conversation while busily loading concrete pavers onto a customer's flatbed trailer.

"Ah!" Cash broke into a wide satisfied grin. "Yes."

He'd missed this environment. Wherever his gaze landed, men were hard at work lifting and lugging, using tools and running equipment. Not a wedding dress or throw pillow in sight. He felt like beating his chest and roaring.

Not since he'd finished renovating the barn and house had his mood been this elevated. Could it be because he'd discarded those useless reminders of his former fiancées earlier this morning? More likely, it was because of his upcoming meeting with the contractor. Besides reviewing the excavation plans and finalizing the construction schedule, they were inspecting a new delivery of reclaimed beams and timber. The manager of Mountainside knew Cash was always on the hunt for material and would call him whenever he got something in that might fit Cash's needs.

During his brisk walk across the loading dock, his phone rang. He reached into his pocket, read the phone's display and put it to his ear. "Hey, Lex."

"I'm running a little late," his contractor said. "Ten minutes. Fifteen tops. One of the kids has the flu, and we were up half the night with him. I finally hit the sack around three and then overslept." Lex groaned. "Just what we need for the holiday season. The flu making the rounds."

"No rush. Take your time. I'll be inside."

Disconnecting, Cash entered the sales office and showroom from the side door. He stopped at the beverage station and poured himself a cup from the dispenser. The coffee was dark and aromatic and strong enough to eat a hole through metal. Just the way he liked it. No peppermint hot chocolate for Mountainside customers.

"Morning, Cash."

He turned to greet Mac, the owner and manager. "How's it going, sir?" He didn't remember a time when Mac wasn't running the place.

"You here for the beams and timber I called you about?"

"Lex is on the way."

"Good, good." Mac rummaged in the pocket of his carpenter's apron, which he was never without, and extracted a pencil. In colder weather like today, he wore the apron beneath his flannel jacket. "I think you'll be pleased. Stuff comes from an old mining operation on Blue Ridge."

"Not too weathered?"

Mac stuck the pencil behind an ear. "Some pieces are better than others. You want to see?"

"I'll wait for Lex."

"Hey, Mac," a customer called. "You got any more of this number 5 rebar in stock?"

"Be right there." He waved to the customer and then said to Cash, "Find me after Lex shows."

"Will do."

Cash leaned an elbow on the end of the counter and sipped his coffee while perusing emails on his phone. There were three from Strategic Design. The only one he responded to was from Travis, who'd thanked him profusely for his suggestions on the Horizon Bank Tower project. Cash had finally gotten around to looking at the schematics.

The task had proved harder than anticipated. Not because the drawings were problematic. Rather, Phoebe had also been at her desk, and he could hear every word of her numerous phone conversations over the partition that separated them. In between calls, she'd fire questions or instructions at him. Had he found a party machine yet for Danielle and Marcus? What about the name of the nutcracker bride and groom manufacturer? Don't forget he needed to have Elvis and Otis ready by two tomorrow for the wedding photo shoot. Perhaps they should meet with Laurel one last time tomorrow morning. She'd bring breakfast.

It had occurred to him that Phoebe may be taking this temporary side hustle of his a little too far. Well, two could play at that game, and Cash had refused to let her irritate him. He'd replied to each of her questions with monosyllabic answers. Nope. Soon. Won't. Fine. Thanks.

Rather than be annoyed with him, she'd laughed and called him stubborn. The partition hid his smile. She didn't just irritate him, she amused him, something considerably harder to resist.

Two deep voices interrupted his thoughts.

"Someone had better talk to Mac. He'll let just about anybody in this place."

"Appears so, son."

Cash glanced up from his phone at the approaching men and leveled a finger at them. "He will. You two are proof of that."

"Good to see you, stranger. Been a while." Channing Pearse grabbed Cash's outstretched hand and pulled him into a back-slapping hello that rattled Cash's teeth.

"Same here." He squirmed loose from Channing's killer grip to shake the other man's hand. "How have you been, Burle?"

"Can't complain." Channing's father made a miserable face. "On second thought, I can."

"Don't listen to him," Channing joked. "Mom has him on a diet and now he's in a perpetual bad mood."

"She's a cruel woman. So what if my blood pressure and cholesterol are a little high? It's the holidays. You can't make a meal fit for a king and then insist the king eat only greens and broiled fish."

The three of them chatted for several minutes, catching each other up on what was new in their lives. Cash told them about staying in Payson for the next three weeks, downplaying the part about helping Phoebe and emphasizing the part about readying for construction to start on the mock Western town.

"Lex should be here any minute," he said.

"Your expansion idea is right smart," Burle told Cash. "Your business will double, mark my word."

"Let's hope."

The vote of confidence meant a lot to Cash. Burle owned Rim Country Rodeo Arena. Cash had spent a good portion of his teenage years there, learning the sport of rodeo and occasionally getting into trouble with his buddy Channing. They'd both suffered their first broken bones at the arena, celebrated their first wins and kissed their first girlfriends.

Those were the only good memories from his high school days. After his family filed for bankruptcy, the rodeo arena became the one place where Cash was respected and not taunted. No sixteen-year-old kid should have to endure being called Cash-less by his fellow students when he walked down the halls. The fact he'd had no control over what had happened to his family made no difference. Cash had been tainted by association.

"Hey, as long as you're going to be in town awhile," Burle said, "any chance you'd be willing to consult on a project?"

"What kind of project?" Cash asked, instantly intrigued.

"It's why we're here today. To get some prices. You remember that old cabin of ours?"

"I do."

How could he forget? Cash and Channing had gotten into trouble there, too. Once, they'd nearly burned it down when a lit log had rolled out of the fireplace during a sleepover. Then there had been the time they'd driven Cash's dad's truck to the cabin, without permission, and buried the truck's front end fender-deep in the storm-swollen creek.

He exchanged glances with his former cohort, who grinned conspiratorially before saying, "We're thinking of fixing it up."

"Someone moving in?"

"Nah. Dad wants to turn the cabin into a vacation rental. With the way this town is booming, thanks in part to you and your sister, we might be able to make some money off it."

"Better than letting it slowly bleed us dry," Burle added. "Taxes and insurance and maintenance are sky high. The darn place has to be winterized every year and mucked out every spring."

Cash's interest grew. "What kind of consulting did you have in mind?"

"Frankly, we don't know where to start."

"You could meet us there one day," Channing suggested. "Give us some suggestions. Make a few drawings."

"Naturally, we'd compensate," his dad said.

"I wouldn't charge you," Cash insisted.

"Nonsense. You provide a service, you get paid. I wouldn't have it any other way."

"Let's meet at the cabin first," Cash said. "Then, after I've had a look, we'll talk."

"Fair enough."

"What about next week?" Cash opened the calendar app on his phone.

The three of them decided on the following Wednesday. Cash figured he could slip out at lunch without having to provide Phoebe with an excuse. She may not like him taking on another project during their busy season while he was supposed to be focused on helping her.

Cash's fingers abruptly stilled, and a frown pulled at his mouth. He wasn't accountable to Phoebe. He could spend his free time doing whatever he wanted and without having to concoct excuses.

"While you're plugging in dates—" Channing tapped Cash's phone "—pick one for coming out to the arena. Our new calves are a frisky bunch."

Cash laughed. "I haven't roped in years."

"Like riding a bike, my friend."

Not exactly. He'd still be able to throw a rope. Whether it'd land correctly was another matter.

"I'd hate to embarrass myself."

Channing slung an arm around his shoulders, reminiscent of when they were younger. "What I'm hearing is you're too citified for us country folks."

Cash winced. "You really know how to insult a guy."

"Prove me wrong."

"Gotta be during the week." He scrolled through his days, searching for a free one. "I'm slammed on the weekends."

"How 'bout after our meeting at the cabin?"

Cash debated. He'd have to be back to the ranch by midafternoon for that evening's wedding. Even then, Phoebe was bound to pitch a fit if he took off for several hours in the middle of the day.

"Move our meeting at the cabin up to 11:00 a.m. and we have a deal," Cash said.

"Great." Channing grinned.

Cash did, too. At the moment, nothing appealed to him more than consulting on a new renovation project and spending time with his old buddy calf roping—even if he was rusty. Next Wednesday was shaping up to be a stellar day.

All of a sudden the front entrance of the showroom whooshed open and a petite woman entered, bringing with her a blast of cold air that instantly neutralized every molecule of heat in the vicinity. Despite her diminutive size, messy ponytail, worn jeans and faded hoodie, every pair of eyes in the place fastened on her.

Female customers weren't uncommon at Mountainside. This particular gal, however, tended to command attention. She could work alongside any man, regardless of his size and strength, and match him hammer swing for hammer swing.

"Morning, Lexi." Cash raised a hand and waved.

Spotting him, she hurried over. "Sorry I'm late." She acknowledged Channing and Burle. "Happy holidays, gentlemen. Hope the world's treating you right." Rim Country Rodeo Arena was one of her regular clients.

"My wife is trying to kill me with this new diet—" Before Burle could finish, Channing dragged him away.

"Enough already, Dad. Let's go. They've got business to attend to and so do we. See you next week, Cash, if not before. Give our regards to your sister and mom."

"Will do. And the same to your family." Cash turned his attention to Lexi. "What's first on the agenda?"

"Let's look at the reclaimed material. Then, if you don't mind, can we run across the street to Coffee Calamity? I haven't eaten yet today or had near enough caffeine. We can review the excavation drawings and construction schedule while I refuel."

"Sounds good." Cash gestured for Lexi to precede him, and they went out the same side door Cash had used to come in.

As they searched for flaws in the beams, he realized that he found himself working with a lot of women. Seemed he couldn't avoid being surrounded by the opposite sex if he tried.

Most guys would probably love to trade places with him. Well, they didn't have to work with Phoebe Kellerman.

As if his thoughts had traveled the fifteen miles to the ranch, his phone pinged with a text from her.

See you at the nursery noon sharp. Laurel's dropping me off ☺

He didn't reply. Not only that, he shut off his phone.

PHOEBE PICTURED THE front porch of the main house, the entryway, the client waiting area, the wishing well, the entrance to the barn and, lastly, the altar inside the barn. Tapping her chin with the tip of her finger, she mentally calculated. "Fifty at least. Maybe sixty."

Cash choked as if he'd swallowed a flying insect. "Not happening," he said when he could speak. "Besides the cost, we can't fit fifty poinsettia plants in my truck along with a tree."

"Hmm. Good point. We'll have to make a second trip."

She sighed with contentment. With all those plants and the tree, Wishing Well Springs would never look better or more Christmassy. She should call the *Payson Herald* when they got back to the office and set up a time for the photographer to come out and take pictures. The local newspaper frequently ran stories on Wishing Well Springs. Phoebe and the features editor were on a first-name basis. The advertising manager considered her a friend.

"Phoebe," Cash said, his tone firm. "We aren't buying fifty poinsettia plants. Not in two trips, not in one."

Her face fell. She actually felt her muscles droop. "You don't understand."

"No, *you* don't understand. There isn't enough money in the budget."

"I'll give up…"

What was she saying? She didn't want to give up anything.

"The Christmas tree?" Cash suggested.

"Our clients are expecting a tree, along with all the other holiday decorations. It's on our website." She tapped her chin some more. "I know! The throw pillows."

"You already gave up the throw pillows, remember? When I agreed we could have the furniture reupholstered. And only if you found a way to trim expenses. Buying fifty poinsettias isn't trimming. You can have twenty-five."

She crossed her arms and narrowed her gaze. "What happened at your meeting with the contractor? She throw a wrench into your plans?"

"Nothing happened. In fact, we accomplished a lot."

Phoebe led the way through the holiday section of Green Rock Nursery. Christmas trees in various sizes, shapes and types stood in orderly rows, everything from eighteen-inch table-toppers to ten-foot giants.

Wouldn't one of those be nice for the barn? Phoebe eyed a gorgeous Douglas fir. She couldn't resist running her fingers over the tree's deep green branches and inhaling its rich, tangy scent.

The entire rear half of the nursery had been

reserved for wreaths, swags and evergreen garlands and plants, including an impressive array of poinsettias. Phoebe made a beeline in that direction.

Mr. Grumpy kept pace with her, his hands shoved in his pockets.

When he didn't elaborate about the meeting, she said, "Details," and bent to meticulously examine an especially lush poinsettia.

"Excavation is scheduled to start January seventh and will take about a week," Cash said. "Then we can begin constructing the permanent wood foundation."

"Not a concrete foundation? Wouldn't that be, like, more durable?"

"We're building a mock Western town resembling those from the late 1800s. Concrete wasn't in wide use then."

"Would anyone notice?"

"I'd notice."

"Fair enough." Realism was important to him. She got that. He was an architect. "Is wood more expensive than concrete?"

"The cost of the expansion has nothing to do with our operating budget or how many plants you get to buy."

She harrumphed, well aware she was being a poor sport. "Tell me the excavation won't interfere with our weddings." She imagined massive earth-moving machines and the ruckus they would surely create. "Won't there be a lot of noise?"

"Some. Yes."

"And debris. We don't want any complaints from couples and guests who are coughing their heads off."

"The excavators will spray water to control the dust."

"Sounds messy."

"Trust me, Phoebe. Our clients' satisfaction is my highest priority. The week after New Year's is slow for us. But just in case, excavation work will be restricted to the mornings. Lexi gave me her assurance."

"Okay. Good."

"If not, I'll shut down the expansion."

"You'd do that? Seriously?" She wanted to believe him.

He moved closer. "I promise."

"Um, thanks."

His voice had curled around her like a warm cloak. She didn't move right away, letting herself luxuriate in the sensation for just a moment.

"Phoebe?"

"Right. Plants."

While he stood by, she culled the twenty-five choicest poinsettias and set them aside.

"Are we done?" he asked. "I'll get a cart and be back."

"Wait, wait."

"For?" He straightened.

Phoebe peered over her shoulder at him. "I want to—"

She'd intended to send him a lethal stare. Instead, she fell silent.

Two women shoppers in the vicinity had stopped in their tracks as if trapped by an invisible force field, their gazes riveted on Cash. The next instant, they broke free and moved on, arms linked and conversing in hushed whispers. No doubt they were discussing his dreamy good looks.

She'd noticed, too. How could she not?

His jacket's upturned collar emphasized his chiseled jaw and tanned complexion that openly defied winter's lack of sunshine. Square, broad shoulders narrowed down to lean hips. Muscled legs strode forward with confidence and purpose. And to top it off, a short lock of hair two shades lighter than his chestnut eyes had casually fallen over his strong, masculine brow.

Cash, darn him, had absolutely no clue of his attractiveness, making him all the more adorable. Rather than noticing his surroundings, he scrolled through his phone while waiting for Phoebe to finish whatever it was she'd been planning to say.

"Be strong," she murmured, entranced by the attractive two-day stubble darkening his jaw. "Resist."

"What was that?" he asked, glancing up and pocketing his phone.

"Nothing. Thinking out loud."

She was suddenly fifteen again, pining after him in secret. Except, rather than wishing he'd notice her as more than his little sister's dorky friend, she prayed he remained oblivious. If he had any idea of her romantic inclinations toward him, it would be the end of their already shaky working relationship. It might even be the end of their partnership, something she refused to let happen.

"The tree," he said and pointed.

"I beg your pardon?"

"Pick out a tree and let's go."

Nothing like a reminder that they were here on business to help her pull herself together. "First, I'm going to make a case for more plants."

He shook his head. "You're wasting your breath."

"Hear me out, Cash."

Starting with the plants she'd already chosen, and ignoring the other customers who watched in puzzlement, she lined the plants up in twin rows, forming an aisle.

"What are you doing?"

"Imagine we're in the barn and these plants are placed along the center aisle." She then went over to the display rack holding the swags and grabbed one with a long gold ribbon that reached her knees. Holding it in front of her like a bouquet, she went to the end of the makeshift aisle and started walking forward in slow, measured steps while softly singing, "Here comes the bride."

"And what's your point?"

"Cash!" She stopped midstep, groaning with exasperation. "Stop being obtuse for one second, will you, and try to picture this. We're in the barn, the chairs are filled with happy guests holding lighted candles. The tree over there is decorated with lights and ornaments and garlands. Glittering snowflakes are suspended from the ceiling. Music is playing. The besotted groom is at the altar, watching the love of his life walk down the aisle toward him." Phoebe resumed singing and walking, her heart overflowing with joy at the magical scene she'd created.

"Okay. I get it."

She spun to face him. "Do you? Because a

wedding is the highlight of people's lives, and it's our job to see their every wish is fulfilled."

"Not sure twenty-five versus fifty poinsettias will make the wedding more or less of a highlight."

"You're hopeless."

"Are you crying?"

"No." She blinked, distressed to feel tears at the corners of her eyes. "It's the cold. They need heaters in here."

"Heaters would cause the trees to dry out."

"Why am I wasting my time?" Grumbling, she marched to the display rack and rehung the swag she'd borrowed. To her surprise, Cash was there when she turned back around.

"I'm not as hopeless as you think I am. Or as callous," he said softly. "I know probably better than most guys how important the perfect wedding is for a woman. Not only am I a partner in a wedding business, I've had three fiancées tell me in minute detail exactly what they wanted and why it mattered to them."

If there were other people in this section of the nursery with Phoebe and Cash, they melted into the shadows. She saw only him. That face. Those shoulders. The silly lock of rebellious hair. He stood close enough she could step into his embrace if she dared. Except she couldn't move. Her bones had turned to mush, just like her insides.

"Yes, ah…" Her thoughts once again deserted her. She struggled to collect them. "Thirty plants. We'll compromise."

"On one condition."

"What's that?"

His hand was suddenly cradling her cheek, the pad of his thumb wiping away a tear. "You tell me what happened between you and Sam."

"You know the s-story," she stammered, her legs on the verge of collapse.

"I know the basics. I'm curious about the details."

A very attractive smile tugged on his lips. Lips she'd pictured kissing often in her younger days. All right, as recently as yesterday. Who could blame her? He had an incredible mouth.

"Since when?" she asked skeptically.

Turning from her, he bent and picked up four plants, balancing two in each arm as easily as if he were carrying empty plastic jugs.

"Since you showed me the kind of wedding you would have had if things had worked out with Sam."

CHAPTER FIVE

"I DIDN'T MEAN to embarrass you earlier."

Cash pushed the flatbed cart loaded with poinsettias away from the register and toward the nursery entrance. There, he and Phoebe waited for the salesperson to bring around the seven-foot tree she'd selected.

"You didn't," she insisted.

If that was the case, why had her cheeks flushed a vivid red and her attention become fixated on everything but him? And why did she still refuse to look at him even now, ten minutes later?

He let the subject drop, temporarily, while he jogged to his truck and then drove it to the curb. The tree had yet to appear, leaving him and Phoebe no choice but to continue waiting.

"They must be busy." He checked his watch.

"I hope we're not late getting back to the office." She pulled out her phone from between the folds of her coat and began scrolling through messages. "Laurel texted. The couple with that last-minute meeting called. They're due in forty-five minutes."

Cash got the hint—she was done discussing her former boyfriend. He wasn't, however. "You met Sam at your parents' inn, right? Six years ago?"

"Give or take."

"He worked there?"

"Really?" She peered up from her phone to stare him down. "We're going to talk about this?"

"We are. And it seems we have some time to kill."

She dropped her phone, which dangled from the lanyard around her neck. "He worked for the inn's beverage vendor. On his sixth sales call, I asked him out. The rest, as they say, is history."

"You asked him?" That was news to Cash.

"He was shy," she said.

"And you're..."

She bristled. "I'm what?"

He chuckled. How could he not? "Phoebe, come on. You have a big personality. That can intimidate some men."

"My. How flattering."

"I'm sure Sam liked being in a relationship with a woman who—"

"Don't you dare say *wears the pants.*"

"—knows what she wants and isn't afraid to go after it," Cash finished.

Her demeanor softened.

"He obviously liked that about you. You dated a long while."

"He didn't like it that much." She coughed, probably to cover a hitch in her voice. "If he had, we'd be married."

"What happened?"

"He wasn't ready. I wasn't ready."

"You were pretty determined to become Mrs. Sam, as I recall."

"What difference does it make? But if you must know," she blurted, as if to get the words out before they had a chance to sting, "he contracted an incurable case of cold feet and sent me packing."

Cash winced. "That had to hurt."

"It did."

"He wasn't the right guy for you, Phoebe."

"You think?" she bit out.

"Because the right guy would have realized what a catch you are and married you before some other lucky guy stole you away."

Her breath stilled. "You think I'm a catch?"

"You're smart and talented. Funny when inclined. You're ambitious and you're great at your job. People like and trust you. And—" he shrugged "—you're not ugly."

"Another compliment." She pressed a hand to the base of her throat. "I'm touched."

"Sam didn't deserve you."

A wobbly smile appeared. "That's about the nicest thing you've ever said to me, Cash Montgomery."

"My oversight. I'll try harder to say nice things to you more often."

She studied him for several seconds. The mask she'd been keeping in place since he'd raised the subject of Sam momentarily slipped. Longing and hope bloomed in her eyes as if written there with a neon-colored marker.

"Phoebe."

He felt it then, a shifting inside him. No, more like a tiny crack in his carefully constructed defenses. She was getting to him slowly but surely.

Before he could say more, a teenaged salesperson arrived with their tree, bound with twine and ready for transport. While the kid and Cash secured the tree in the truck bed, Phoebe loaded plants, filling in the empty spaces on each side of the tree. The end result resembled a picture in a storybook Cash's mother had read to him as a child—Gulliver staked out and surrounded by tiny Lilliputians.

When they were done, the salesperson returned to the nursery. Cash and Phoebe climbed into the truck, and he drove to the exit, mindful of the many customers coming and going. While they waited for an opening in traffic, Phoebe pulled out her phone and became instantly engrossed.

Cash ignored her second hint to drop the subject. "I'm surprised you haven't met someone else."

"I'm picky," she murmured.

"As you should be."

Dropping her phone, she turned the tables on him. "Why haven't you started seeing someone new? It's been—what?—two or three years since you and Silver called it quits."

"I learned my lesson."

"You don't want to get married anymore?"

"No. I still do. One day. And have a family. But I refuse to make the same mistake my parents did." The all-too-familiar tightness formed in his chest.

"What mistake is that?" she asked.

"Not having enough money saved for when life takes a bad turn. Because sooner or later it will."

"Your parents couldn't help what happened to them."

"They couldn't, you're right. But they could help how they reacted, and they darn sure could have prepared better. Not skimped on health insurance. Bothered to save for retirement. Made well-informed, better-researched decisions. Put family first, not take the easy way out by filing for bankruptcy." The shame Cash had felt returned, burning his skin from the inside. "Not split at the first opportunity."

"You're talking about your dad."

Cash gritted his teeth, tamping down the anger rearing its ugly head. "I put myself through college with scholarships and rodeo winnings."

"I know. Laurel told me."

"Yeah, well, she never had a chance to go. She worked her way up from the bottom at a Phoenix fashion house and started Bellissima on her own without anyone's help."

"That speaks very highly of the two of you."

He tapped the brakes as they took a corner, not wanting to lose any of the plants they'd just bought. "Good thing neither of us took after our dad."

"You were young at the time," Phoebe gently cautioned. "You may not know everything, and what you saw was from a teenager's perspective."

She reached over the console and touched his arm, her slim fingers applying a light pressure. The anger coursing through him lessened and he marveled at her effect on him. None of his former fiancées had ever worked that kind of magic.

"I know everything," he said, memories shooting to the surface. "All I had to do was listen to the arguments. And there were plenty of those. All night long."

"That must have been awful."

"My dad was a quitter." Cash couldn't keep the bitterness from invading his voice. "And before you argue that with me, remember he left town rather than repay the money he legitimately owed. Try living with everyone in town knowing that about you. I haven't been inside Payson National Bank or Duke's Auto Repair since he split."

"I can't imagine anyone holding you responsible for your parents' debt."

He went on as if not hearing her. "Not responsible. But like I was contaminated by them and what they did. My last two years of high school were the worst of my life. I couldn't walk down the hall or enter a classroom without someone making fun of me."

"Teenagers can be cruel." Phoebe remembered. Laurel, either because she was younger than Cash or a girl, hadn't been treated as poorly.

"My grandfather and dad were responsible for every bad decision and losing the ranch.

But my mom's also to blame. She just stood by and did nothing. I've never gotten over that. Or forgiven her. She and my dad were both oblivious to how their actions affected their kids."

"I'm not defending your family. But sometimes people wind up in situations they simply can't get out of. I'm sure your parents cared. But maybe they were too absorbed with their problems and…"

"Forgot about us? Ignored us? Left us to fend for ourselves?"

"They were preoccupied."

"Same thing." Cash took his foot off the gas pedal, letting the truck slow. He'd been going too fast again. "I will never do that to my wife and kids. Wind up in the position where we're living on a shoestring. I guarantee you, I'll have resources to spare. Money in the bank. Decent health insurance. Equity in my property. Low debt." Conscious of his tightening grip on the steering wheel, he forcefully relaxed his muscles.

"Oh, Cash." Phoebe's fingers tightened reassuringly on his arm. "It wasn't my intention to stir up bad memories."

"It's probably hard for someone like you to understand. You've had a pretty comfortable life. Parents who stayed together and had money to spare."

She stiffened and withdrew her hand. "I realize we had different experiences growing up, and I can't claim three engagements that ended in disaster. But I've known hurt and disappointment." She turned her gaze toward the passenger window. "We all have our own wounds to bear and our own scars."

He reined in his temper, instantly regretting his outburst. Phoebe deserved better from him. "You're right. This isn't a competition. I'm sorry."

"I suppose that's what we get for digging up bones."

It was always like this with him and Phoebe—playful, joking and teasing one minute to bickering the next. Try as they might, they couldn't stay on an even keel. The recent tender moments and intimate contact, however, was brand-new. He wasn't sure what had prompted him to cup her cheek or her to squeeze his arm. Those kinds of gestures could be easily misinterpreted, and he should nip them in the bud before he started liking them too much.

"I didn't intend to dump on you, either," he said.

"We're friends." She beamed at him. "And friends get to dump on each other. It comes with the territory."

Fortunately, the ranch appeared in the distance. Cash couldn't wait to get back to business. Discussing his family always soured him. Though being with Phoebe lifted his spirits much faster than usual.

"Did you call Georgia Ann and tell her to meet us at the barn with the crew?" he asked.

Phoebe nodded. "She texted on the drive here. They're waiting for us now."

At the barn, the crew helped them unload the tree and the poinsettia plants, except for a few Phoebe planned to display on the front porch of the main house. The crew had already brought out boxes and crates of decorations from storage and began stringing lights the moment Phoebe selected the perfect spot for the tree. The poinsettias were lined up in rows on each side of the center aisle.

Cash was reminded of the holiday wedding Phoebe had tried to create in the nursery. He could see her walking down the aisle on her father's arm, radiant in her gown, her luxurious blond hair wound into an elegant twist. Her groom waiting for her at the altar. He tried envisioning the man's face. Slowly, pixels resolved and the features clarified into... Sam.

A sharp pang sliced into Cash's gut and he rubbed the spot. What was that all about? Surely not jealousy. Must be indigestion. Except he hadn't eaten since breakfast. Maybe hunger was the problem.

"We'd better hurry," Phoebe called, letting her phone drop to swing from her neck. "Our appointment just arrived."

She and Cash left the rest of the decorating to Georgia Ann and the crew, driving quickly to the main house. There, they met up with Laurel, the bride and her sister in Bellissima. Sister? Cash had been expecting the bride and her groom.

"This is a color consultation," Phoebe explained in a whisper. "Grooms often skip it."

Powering up his tablet, Cash joined the ladies in the viewing circle. While the four women talked, he made notes. A color consultation, he learned, was to create a palette for the wedding, including the bride's dress, the men's tuxes, the bridesmaids' dresses, the flowers, decorations, cake, table linens, centerpieces, invitations and whatever else.

Plump-cheeked and with a high-pitched giggle, the bride found enormous delight in even the most mundane of her wedding details and debated each decision as if the fate of the world rested on it.

Her sister seemed less interested in wedding details and more interested in Cash. Several times, he glanced up to meet her fixed stare and flirty smile. When he turned his head, Phoebe was staring, too. At the woman. Not him.

"I really love the idea of periwinkle tuxes," the bride said. "One of the gals at my gym said it's a trending color this year." She giggled. "Kyle would probably pitch a fit, but he'd look so handsome. And we could use periwinkle trim on my dress and some kind of blue flowers in my bouquet and the boutonniere."

"Periwinkle is a lovely color," Laurel said, demonstrating incredible patience. "However, it may not go with your lilac dress. Take a look at these fabric swatches."

The bride, Cash had learned, was bucking tradition. She'd chosen lilac for her dress because her future mother-in-law liked the color.

"Really?" The bride pouted. "My favorite dress when I was six was purple and blue."

"I think that's Laurel's point," the bride's sister said. "A little girl wears those colors." She winked at Cash.

Phoebe sat straighter and cleared her throat.

"Might I suggest tuxes in either charcoal or stone," Laurel said. "Gray's also a trending color and goes well with lilac."

The bride sighed long and loud. "Let me think about it."

The discussion continued for another ten

minutes until Cash's skin started to itch. For crying out loud. How hard could it be to pick a few colors? They had a wedding scheduled to start in two hours, and he still needed to groom and ready the horses for their photo shoot.

He was at the point of concocting an excuse when Laurel said, "I happen to have a gray tux jacket in my workshop I use for matching dress fabrics. I could go get it."

"Yeah. A visual might help." The bride crinkled her brow in thought. "I wish I could see it on a…you know, guy." She shifted her attention to Cash.

Her sister stared at him as if he were on display. "What a fabulous idea."

His itching skin intensified and he glanced at the door.

"Cash, would you mind modeling the jacket for us?" Laurel asked, a hint of pleading in her voice that probably only he noticed.

He almost said, "Anything to get this meeting over with." A warning glance from Phoebe stopped him. Instead, he smiled accommodatingly. "My pleasure."

Phoebe nodded approvingly. Laurel dashed upstairs to her workroom and returned a few minutes later, tux jacket in hand. Cash slipped into it, expecting the sleeves to be too short and the shoulders too tight. To his surprise, the jacket didn't fit half bad.

The bride's sister lit up like a kid on Christmas morning as he stood in front of the four women. "My, my. Very handsome." She jabbed her sister in the side. "Gray, definitely, don't you think?"

Normally, Cash didn't mind a woman's attention. Modeling for these women, however, made him uncomfortable. While Phoebe maintained a neutral expression, the gleam in the bride's sister's eyes bordered on feral.

"I do like it," the bride mused. "What about you, Phoebe?"

She gave Cash an impersonal up-and-down. "Gray is a good choice for a winter wedding. When it's paired with lilac, you'll look like a princess."

That instantly tipped the scales and the bride made her choice. Glaucous, whatever shade that was.

Cash shrugged out of the jacket and handed it to Laurel. "You ladies will have to excuse me. I need to get our horses ready for the photo shoot at the barn."

She took the jacket and flashed him a grateful smile. "Thanks for being such a good sport."

He said his goodbyes, first to the bride and

then her sister, who complained about his leaving. Rather than head straight out, he detoured to the business offices and his desk, where he dropped off his tablet.

As he reemerged, he drew up short when he heard the bride's sister mention his name, her voice carrying across the entryway.

"It's probably rude to ask, but is he single?"

The bride gasped. "You're terrible."

"No harm in asking. Nothing ventured, nothing gained."

"Cash is single," Laurel admitted.

"Oh goodie. Will he be at the wedding?"

"He's not looking for a serious relationship right now," Phoebe interjected.

Her clipped tone bothered him. Had he hurt her earlier? If so, he couldn't imagine how, and that certainly wasn't his intention.

"How do you know?" the bride's sister asked. "Are you and he, like, together?"

"Cash doesn't mix business with his personal life," Phoebe replied flatly. "Clients or coworkers."

"Hmm. Too bad. For the both of us."

"Us?"

"I saw the sparks, girlfriend."

"I assure you," Phoebe answered crisply, "there's nothing between us."

"If you say so." The bride's sister let out a loud hoot.

The next second, the topic returned to color selection.

Phoebe was right, of course, Cash thought as he headed out the front door, down the porch steps and toward the horse paddock. He didn't mix business with his personal life. Nor was he looking for a relationship. Hadn't he made that clear as recently as an hour ago?

But what if circumstances were different? Would he ask Phoebe out?

He didn't need to look deep for the answer. It was yes.

PHOEBE UNLOADED COVERED food dishes from the soft-sided cooler and set them on the counter. She'd arrived early for Laurel's send-off breakfast meeting, bringing goodies from the inn as promised.

Trudy had insisted Phoebe take an entire spinach-and-Brie quiche, some freshly baked sweet potato muffins, and a fruit salad made with Trudy's special-recipe dressing. She'd also packed a lunch for Laurel, saying the poor girl needed energy for the grueling six-hour drive ahead of her, first down the winding mountain roads and then across the desert.

After placing the quiche and muffins in the

upper oven to warm and the salad in the refrigerator to chill, Phoebe grabbed forks and napkins and paper plates, laying them out on the kitchen table. Lastly, she brewed a fresh pot of coffee.

Two loud thumps coming from the vicinity of the front door announced Laurel's arrival—her suitcases being deposited on the floor for Cash to carry out to her SUV.

A minute later, she strolled into the kitchen and dropped her oversize purse on the counter. "Don't forget to call me the second the pearl heart buttons are delivered. And I left a message with Valley Wide Sewing Machines and Vacuums. My old serger is acting up again. They're supposed to send a technician tomorrow. If he's not here by the afternoon, can you follow up?"

Phoebe smiled affably. "Good morning to you, too."

Unfazed, Laurel rattled off three more items from her to-do list, stopping only to pour herself a mug of coffee when the red light turned green. Taking a sip, she closed her eyes and moaned with delight as if the mug contained nectar of the gods rather than plain old coffee. The next second, her eyes snapped open. "Promise you won't forget anything."

"I'll text you hourly updates," Phoebe said.

"Updates for what?" Cash asked, breezing into the kitchen via the hall.

Phoebe wished her heart wouldn't instantly launch into a cha-cha-cha at the rich timbre of his voice. When was this going to stop? Their conversation yesterday had made it crystal clear he wasn't entertaining romantic notions. Certainly not about her.

"Laurel has a to-do list," she said, opening the door to the oven.

Coming up behind her, he peered over her shoulder and inhaled. "Smells great."

For a crazy second, Phoebe thought he was talking about her, and her tummy began shaking maracas in time to her cha-cha-cha-ing heart.

"Are those your sister's sweet potato muffins?"

Not her. Of course. How could she have been so stupid?

Adopting a light tone, she said, "Quit crowding me," and removed the quiche, setting it and the remaining food on the table. Gesturing to the mouthwatering bounty, she announced, "Dig in, everyone."

Cash wasn't shy. Filling his plate, he sat and began stuffing food into his mouth at breakneck speed. When he caught her staring at him, he slowed down. "I'm hungry."

"Laurel." Phoebe grabbed a serving spoon. "Trudy packed a lunch for you. It's in the fridge."

"How nice. Tell her thanks." Laurel sat across from Cash. "For breakfast, too. This is wonderful."

"Yeah," Cash mumbled, slathering butter on a sweet potato muffin.

Two empty chairs remained at the table, one next to Laurel and the other next to Cash. Phoebe considered before choosing the chair next to Cash. She wanted to give the impression that everything was status quo between them, which it was, and that nothing had changed in the last twenty-four hours, which it hadn't.

All her careful deliberation was for nothing. He didn't spare her even the tiniest of glances when she settled in beside him. Laurel did, however. She sent Phoebe a what's-up-with-you head tilt that went unanswered.

While they ate, Laurel reviewed her Palm Springs' schedule yet again with Phoebe and Cash. The three of them next ran through every wedding and event between now and the twenty-first, when Laurel would be returning. Most notably, they had a Christmas Day vow renewal ceremony to celebrate a fiftieth anniversary, complete with Santa and elf costumes and a mini stage production, and they would need Laurel's help. There was also a super secret wedding on the twenty-third. Many of the specifics were still under wraps, including the identity of the couple. Phoebe was convinced they were A-list celebrities or some other high-profile individuals.

"I'll call both of you every day at lunch and in the evening." Laurel helped Phoebe stow the leftover food.

"Is your car unlocked?" Cash started for the doorway leading to the front entrance. "I'll carry out your suitcases."

"Wait." Laurel chased after him. "I have a system."

"For suitcases?"

"Plus all my garment bags and notions cases and sewing machines. It's critical nothing gets damaged or wrinkled during the drive."

Phoebe followed them, their mild bickering reminiscent of their youth. How often she had watched from a distance, an outsider gazing into Cash and Laurel's private world.

Did they feel the same about Phoebe and her sisters, on the outside gazing in? Probably not. Neither Cash nor Laurel harbored a secret longing to be included in Phoebe's world.

Going into partnership with them was a great opportunity for her. It allowed her to pursue her dream of being a wedding and event coordinator while helping to build a business from the ground up. Along with planning her own unrealized nuptials to Sam, she'd been in charge of all four of her sisters' weddings plus those of several cousins. Phoebe had known from the time she was fifteen what she'd wanted to do with her life.

The partnership also afforded her the opportunity to work alongside Cash and maintain a connection to him. It wasn't emotionally healthy, something she continually told herself. But like many addicts, she regularly fell off the wagon, thrilling to the too brief highs and then hating herself in the morning.

Thirty minutes later, Laurel's SUV was loaded to her satisfaction and the route to her Airbnb programmed into her phone's navigation. On the passenger seat sat her lunch sack along with two bottles of water. A travel mug of coffee had been tucked into the cup holder.

"Tell Mom hi for me," Cash said.

Laurel was planning to stop at their mother's house in Globe for a quick visit on her way to Palm Springs. Phoebe knew that, in addition to Christmas, Cash visited his mother a few times a year and always took her out to dinner on her birthday. Laurel saw her more often—she had less resentment toward her mother than Cash did, and their relationship was friendlier.

Phoebe waited while Cash pulled his sister into a brotherly embrace. "Drive careful. No speeding."

"Me?" Laurel kissed him on the cheek. But rather than withdrawing, she rested her head on his chest. "Thank you for covering for me. It means a lot."

"Go get 'em, sis." He gave her forehead a light peck.

What would it be like, Phoebe wondered, to be held by Cash and feel his lips on her skin? She imagined being held by Cash. In her scenario, his strong arms didn't stop at her shoulders but wrapped completely around her, drawing her so close she could feel heat radiating off him and hear his heartbeat drumming in time to hers. Instead of her forehead, his mouth would seek her lips and find them warm and responsive in return.

"Phoebe. Phoebe. You in there?"

Fingers snapped in front of her face, rousing her.

"What?" She opened her eyes. The fingers belonged to Laurel, whose face filled her vision. "Sorry. I was…" No excuse came to mind, the residual effects of her imaginary kiss with Cash having caused her brain's neurons to misfire. "Momentarily distracted."

Laurel took hold of Phoebe's upper arms. "No fighting with Cash while I'm gone, okay? It's imperative that you two get along. Crucial. Vital. Paramount."

"We will."

"The entire success of my trip depends on it."

"The *entire* success?"

"I won't be able to concentrate if things here are falling apart. And if I can't concentrate, my creativity will evaporate."

"Got it."

"I'm serious, Phoebe. This job is important for all our futures."

"Cash and I will get along. Didn't we manage a productive trip to the nursery yesterday and both returned unscathed?" She shot him a glance.

"We did," he concurred.

Laurel pulled her into a hug. "Cut him some slack. Please?"

"Did you have the same talk with him?"

"In the shop." She grinned, dropped her hands and stepped back. "While you were carrying out my dress forms."

At least Phoebe wasn't the only one being chastised, she thought glumly. "We understand how important this job is to you. We won't screw up. We promise."

Perhaps to demonstrate his willingness to cooperate, Cash moved to stand beside Phoebe and slung an arm over her shoulders. She jerked in response. The gesture too closely resembled what she'd been imagining mere minutes before. And the way she fit against him—her shoulder into the crook of his arm—they might have been two halves of one whole.

He leaned down and murmured sultrily, "Relax. I don't bite. Not hard, anyway."

"Stop it," she hissed.

"What's wrong?" Laurel frowned at them.

"Nothing." Not wanting her friend to fret, Phoebe slipped her arm around Cash's waist, decreasing the distance between their bodies to a hair's width. "Everything's fine."

"We'll behave," Cash said, and then gave her arm a playful pinch.

"Quit it!" Phoebe squawked and shrugged him off. How old was he, six?

Grinning, he retreated. She instantly missed the pleasant weight of his arm and the tingles it had elicited. Twice now in the last twenty-four hours he'd touched her. First in the nursery when he'd tenderly cradled her cheek, and now this. She felt like a dieter biting into a decadent dessert after a long abstinence.

The need to flee overwhelmed her. The recent and subtle changes occurring between them defied explanation and, truthfully, were not welcome. The next time he touched her, if he did, she wanted it to be an expression of care and affection. Not because he was joking around or felt sorry for her.

"I'd better hurry if I want to make Palm Springs by five." Laurel yanked open the driver's-side door. "I told the bride I'd get there before her gallery showing tonight."

The art gallery owner/VIP client had invited Laurel to her monthly event. It was another great chance for Laurel to make connections. The Airbnb wasn't far from the gallery and, more important, came with a spare room that Laurel could use for a workspace.

Cash and Phoebe stood side by side, waving as Laurel pulled away from the house. The second she reached the main road, Phoebe spun to face Cash.

"I'll be back in an hour."

"Where are you going?"

"The inn."

"Weren't you just there to pick up breakfast?"

Phoebe braced her hands on her hips. The movement caused the row of candy canes hanging from her Christmas vest to clatter.

"I didn't think I needed to report my every action to you."

"Hey. I was just making conversation." He turned and jogged up the porch steps. At the door, he said, "I have calls to make and plenty of stuff to research. Finding the manufacturer of nutcracker cake toppers is harder than you'd think."

"It's business," she called after him, the lie tasting sour on her tongue. "I need to talk to Trudy about…catering menus."

"Okay. See you when you get back." He opened the door and disappeared inside.

Phoebe could have walked to the side of the garage where she'd parked her car. Instead, she set out at a brisk walk. The inn was less than a half mile away. With luck, the fresh air and exercise would restore her sunny disposition.

Unfortunately, it didn't. She was just as rattled and confused and moody when she pushed open the inn's front door. The blast of warm air hit her chilled cheeks, causing them to sting.

"Hey, Phoebe." The hostess on duty flashed her a wide smile. "Your parents are in the office, if you're looking for them."

"Actually, I'm here to see Trudy. She in the kitchen?"

"Not sure." The young woman stood on tiptoe to look past Phoebe at the group of people approaching from the lobby. The inn's buffet breakfast was popular with guests and non-guests alike. "Good morning, folks. Welcome."

Phoebe darted off. She tried not to interfere with business when she stopped by the inn.

Trudy, it turned out, was in their mom's office, along with her dad. All of Phoebe's sisters worked at the inn but in other capacities. Cora supervised the housekeeping staff. Lilly was in charge of reservations and managed the front desk. Zoë handled their marketing along with inventory and ordering supplies—currently from home, where she cared for her eight-month-old son.

"What's going on?" Phoebe asked. "A family meeting?"

"We're narrowing down entertainment options for our anniversary party."

"How's that coming?"

The inn would be celebrating its twenty-fifth anniversary in March, and the Kellermans were planning a month-long celebration that included discounted package deals and extra festivities.

"Good." Phoebe's mom came out from behind her desk to give Phoebe a hug.

"What's new, kiddo?" Her dad hauled her into a bear hug. "How's my favorite girl?" He referred to each of his daughters as his favorite girl.

"What brings you by?" Trudy didn't rise from where she sat in a visitor chair, rubbing her pregnancy belly and resting her swollen feet on a box of files.

"Nothing really." Phoebe flopped down into the other visitor chair. "I just needed a break and wanted to see my family."

"Did Laurel leave yet?" her mom asked at the same time Trudy asked, "A break from what?"

"A few minutes ago." Phoebe hunkered down in the chair. "And a break from Cash."

"Hmm." Trudy's brows disappeared beneath her soft wave of blond bangs. "You haven't even gotten through your first hour of working with him and already you need a break. Interesting."

"He can be trying," Phoebe griped.

"Well, sweetie pie." Her mom returned to her seat behind the desk. "You can't let Laurel down. She's counting on you. You'll have to figure out a way to work with him."

"That's not the problem, Mom." Trudy shook her head.

Phoebe's dad perched his stocky body on the corner of her mom's desk. All the daughters had inherited his fair hair and gregarious personality. "Our youngest has the hots for him."

"Dad!" Phoebe suppressed a cry of frustration. "I do not."

He sent her mom a look, the kind long-married people shared.

"Didn't you have a crush on him in high school?" her mom asked gently. "I seem to remember—"

Trudy cut her off. "She did. Big-time. Still does. *Big*-time," she reiterated.

"I didn't come here to be picked on." Phoebe crossed her arms and legs, squeezing the candy canes.

"Now, now," her mom soothed. "Phoebe needs our help, not our teasing. What can we do, honey?"

Phoebe groaned through gritted teeth. "I came here to get away for a few minutes. What's the big deal? Can we not attempt to analyze my life?"

"Have you told Cash how you feel?" her dad asked. "We guys can be kind of dense. We need you women to spell things out for us. 'I like you, idiot. I'm available. Quit dawdling and ask me out.'"

"I haven't told him, nor will I." Too late, she realized her mistake as all eyes focused on her.

"Because there's nothing to tell. I don't have the hots for him."

"It's kind of funny when you think about it," Trudy continued, undeterred. "Cash is such a scrooge and money burns a hole in our Phoebe's pocket."

Her dad nodded. "They say opposites attract."

"That's it!" Indignant, Phoebe pushed to her feet and marched toward the door. "I'm outta here."

"Sweetie pie, no. Come back," her mom pleaded.

"Let her go." Trudy's laughter followed after Phoebe. "She's only mad because we're right."

Phoebe hated that her family knew her so well. Really, really hated it.

CHAPTER SIX

"WHERE HAVE YOU BEEN?" Phoebe's clipped demand caught Cash just as he was turning the corner to his secluded desk.

Grimacing, he answered, "I had an errand to run."

"What kind of errand?"

Darn it. He really needed to hone his skills if he intended to keep sneaking in and out. This was the third time in the same number of days he'd been busted playing hooky from work.

Mustering an agreeable grin, he pivoted to confront his accuser. She stood facing him, her scowl identical to the one the gorilla on her Christmas sweater wore. Its Santa hat sat at a crooked angle and it squeezed a kitten in its palm. The image, in Cash's opinion, made no sense.

"Well?" she insisted when he didn't immediately respond.

Cash diverted his gaze. But not fast enough. She'd noticed him noticing her legs. It was fifty degrees outside, for Pete's sake. Most sane people would be wearing pants.

Huffing with annoyance, she bustled past him en route to her desk.

"I was meeting Channing and Burle," he admitted. Lying was useless; she'd see right through him. "They're thinking of converting that old cabin on their property into a rental or guest house and asked me to consult."

Resigning himself to a lecture, he plunked down in her visitor chair. Their two morning appointments had gone reasonably well, and their one wedding today—a small, simple affair with only twenty guests—wasn't until seven tonight. Phoebe had handled all the details long before Cash had arrived last Friday.

In his way of thinking, that had left him free to meet with Channing and Burle. As a result, his tablet was filled with notes and sketches and ideas. The cabin would make a great rental, and he'd promised to start on the drawings after the first of the year.

"You were gone three hours," Phoebe accused, her tone sharp enough to split hairs.

"We stopped by the rodeo arena when we were done."

"Another project?"

"To see the new calves. Channing's trying to get me back into roping."

Her scowl deepened. "We're slammed every day, morning till late at night. You don't have time for side projects, and you sure don't have time for calf roping."

"This job comes first. I won't let Laurel or you down."

"Did you ever get the sleigh out of storage and take it to the barn?"

"First thing this morning. Georgia Ann's already started on the decorating."

"Locate a snow machine for Danielle and Marcus?"

"The party store in town carries them. I have one on reserve."

"What about the nutcracker centerpieces?" Phoebe asked.

"I printed out the information and put it on your desk. They're pretty pricey. I also ran a month-to-date expense report. I realize we're barely a week into December, but we're right at budget, not under, like we'd hoped."

He waited to see if she understood his meaning: no furniture reupholstering if she didn't reduce costs.

She worked her jaw for several long seconds before saying, "We're almost out of coffee and those flavored creamers. You might check our hot chocolate supply."

He leaned back in his chair, thoroughly

amused and more than a little taken with her. Phoebe on a tear was interesting and, yes, captivating. "Is that my punishment for ditching work?"

"Are you above shopping for supplies?"

"What if I get sidetracked?" He tried not to grin. "The Boot Depot is having a holiday sale. They're in the plaza across from the store. The smell of leather is mighty tempting." Unable to help himself, he cracked a smile.

"This is serious, Cash. We're only going to get busier, what with weddings and events every day through New Year's."

"Yes, ma'am."

She'd been in a snit for days. At first, he'd blamed Phoebe's determination to run a tight ship in Laurel's absence. Then he'd begun to believe something else was responsible, but he couldn't put his finger on what. The change had occurred simultaneously with Laurel's trip to Palm Springs, no doubt about that.

He got up, planning to return to his desk.

"Wait. There's something I need you to do for the Rouse-Tirney wedding tonight."

Cash stumbled as if he'd blindly walked into a pothole. Not because Phoebe was making a request. Rouse had been Melanie's last name. Of course, his first fiancée was hardly the only person in the world named Rouse, but it wasn't that common. Odd that he'd been thinking of her a few days ago, and now a bride was getting married at Wishing Well Springs with the same last name.

"What do you need?" he asked, keeping his tone light.

"The bride's cousin flew in this afternoon. She's on her way here to drop off a portrait of their late grandmother. According to her, the bride adored her grandmother, and with the portrait on display during the ceremony, it will feel like she's there in spirit."

Cash nodded. Few requests surprised him; they'd gotten all kinds. "Why doesn't the cousin just bring the portrait with her when she comes to the wedding?"

"She's surprising the bride. Isn't that sweet?" Phoebe's features softened. For a brief second, she was her pre-snit self.

"You want me to get the easel out of storage?" He had a hard time looking away.

"Georgia Ann already did. What I need from you is to be here when the cousin shows. I'd do it, but I'm facilitating a video chat between Laurel and one of her clients." Phoebe checked the time on her phone. "Any minute now. I can't be both places at once."

"Can do. When you're finished, I'll run to the store for supplies."

"No rush," Phoebe said. "That can wait until tomorrow."

So she'd been punishing him, after all. They probably weren't even low on coffee and creamer. Ha, ha, ha.

Cash filled the time waiting for the bride's cousin by starting on a supply list for next week's weddings and the upcoming family reunion. Finishing with that, he balanced the November bank statement and then researched lumber prices for the mock town expansion. He was in the middle of sketching a sleeping bunk and built-in dresser for the attic room when the bell over the front door chimed. The cousin must have arrived.

As he neared the entryway, he heard voices coming from Bellissima. Phoebe and the client were on the video chat with Laurel.

A woman about Cash's age stood in the entryway, holding a large rectangular object and glancing around uncertainly.

Cash strode forward, smiling affably. "Afternoon. Is that the portrait for the Rouse-Tirney wedding?"

A look of relief spread across her face. "I assume I'm in the right place."

"You are." Cash held out his hands. "I can take that for you. We have the easel ready and waiting."

"Thanks so much." The woman reluctantly relinquished the portrait as if parting with a priceless treasure. "Melanie's going to be over the moon. I can't wait to see her face. I spent the entire flight from Cleveland with this under the seat in front of me."

Cash had trouble hearing her over the roaring in his ears. Melanie? Cleveland? Impossible! This had to be a weird coincidence.

"Your cousin's name is Melanie?"

"Yeah. We grew up together, but she left home after high school to attend ASU and then never moved back." The woman sighed. "Just as well. She met an amazing man. They've been through some rough times together. Health issues. His. She stood by him, though, and now he's in full remission. This wedding is truly a cause for celebration." Another sigh.

Cash's balance wavered. As if the portrait could restore his equilibrium, he gripped it tighter and mentally connected the dots. His former fiancée had grown up in Cleveland. She had a lot of extended family Cash had never met, including cousins. She'd loved her grandmother who, Cash had heard through mutual friends, passed away some months after they'd broken up. She'd attended ASU, which is where they met.

No, it couldn't be *his* Melanie getting married here tonight. The odds were astronomical.

Did she know about him and Laurel owning Wishing Well Springs? Eleven years had passed since he'd last seen her. Cash spent almost no time on social media, and his accounts were woefully outdated. If she'd looked him up, she wouldn't have found much.

Striving to appear cool and casual, he asked, "Did your cousin by chance major in communications and graduate eleven years ago?"

"Her degree was in business, I think. I'm not sure about the year she graduated." The woman drew back and evaluated Cash. "Why are you asking?"

"I went to ASU and knew a Melanie Rouse." He waited for the cousin to say something that would assure him the bride was someone else entirely. And waited.

"You'll have to stop by the wedding," the cousin suggested amiably. "The two of you can reconnect. I'm sure she'd like that."

Cash was less convinced. If the bride and his Melanie were one and the same, she'd have no desire to see him. Especially on her wedding day to a man she'd stood by during a health crisis.

Why him and not Cash? He'd had a health

crisis, along with a career crisis. But that hadn't stopped Melanie from walking out on him.

The answer hit him like a ton of bricks: she hadn't loved him enough. Not like she evidently loved this man.

He manufactured a disappointed groan for effect. "Wish I could stop by. Unfortunately, I have somewhere to be." Anywhere far away from the barn.

"I'll tell Melanie hi for you. What did you say your name was?"

"Nah, that's all right. I'll get in touch with her in a couple of weeks."

The young woman peered at him curiously. "Whatever." She hitched a thumb toward the door. "I'd better hit the road. Melanie's expecting me for our hair and makeup session. Thanks again for your help with the portrait."

Cash muttered something that must have been appropriate, for the cousin hurried on her way. The second he shut the door behind her, he turned the portrait around. A sharp pain stabbed him in the gut. The woman pictured could be no one other than Melanie's grandmother. He'd met her once and seen the photo Melanie had kept on her bookcase hundreds of times. The shape of the eyes and crescent scar on her chin from a childhood fall were unmistakable.

Slowly, the voices coming from Bellissima penetrated his foggy senses. The video call with Laurel's client was nearing an end. He pivoted and made for the office, having no wish to run into anyone. At his desk, he propped up the portrait and stared, his mind in a jumble.

How could Melanie be getting married at Wishing Well Springs without anyone knowing it was her? Or did they?

Phoebe came looking for him a short while later, poking her head around the side of the partition. "Oh good. You got the portrait. You mind driving it to the barn while I—"

"Why didn't you tell me the bride's name is Melanie Rouse?"

Phoebe frowned in confusion. "I did."

"No, you didn't."

"What's the big deal? Looks like the portrait was delivered safe and sound."

"Melanie Rouse is my fiancée." He pushed back and stood. "*Was* my fiancée."

Shock blossomed on Phoebe's face. "A-are you serious?"

"As a heart attack." He held up the portrait. "I met this woman, Melanie's grandmother, when she came to Phoenix for a visit."

"Cash… I…" Phoebe's mouth hung open,

and she shook her head dumbly. "I truly had no idea."

"How could you coordinate the wedding and not recognize her?"

At his harsh tone, Phoebe stiffened. "It's been... I don't know, ten or twelve years. And I only ever saw her a couple times during holiday gatherings. We didn't interact much. Frankly, I didn't *want* to interact with her."

"What are you talking about? She was always nice to you."

Phoebe glanced away, her jaw tightening. "She looks different now. Her hair's long and streaked with purple. She wears glasses."

Cash supposed it was possible Phoebe hadn't recognized Melanie.

"Her last name didn't ring a bell?"

"Honestly, no. We hear a lot of names in our line of work. And Melanie clearly didn't recognize me, either."

"What about Laurel? She'd remember Melanie."

"Laurel wasn't involved. Melanie had only the one appointment when she toured and booked the barn. They opted out of a rehearsal." Phoebe flipped the tables on Cash. "Didn't she know this was your family's ranch? The history of Wishing Well Springs is posted on our website."

Her point was well taken. It was one thing for Phoebe not to recognize Melanie, but surely Melanie must have realized Cash was a co-owner. She'd been aware he'd grown up in Payson. Also that his family had once owned the largest horse ranch in the area.

He rubbed the back of his neck, searching his memory. "Mom and Dad were divorced by the time we met, and my grandfather had moved in with my aunt and uncle. When we weren't going to classes, I was competing on the circuit. I never brought her here. No reason to."

Cash had also been determined to put his past behind him. When Melanie had inquired, he'd told her someone else owned the ranch. A stretch but not an outright lie. His grandfather had sold off everything except what he'd left to Cash and Laurel. When he'd refused to discuss the ranch and his unhappy youth, Melanie hadn't pushed.

It was possible, he supposed, she'd had no idea that he was a co-owner of Wishing Well Springs. Still, the odds of her getting married here were astounding.

"We shouldn't cancel on them," Phoebe said, "if that's what you're thinking."

"No. Of course not."

"I'll take the portrait to the barn. And oversee the wedding. You don't need to be there."

He nodded. "That's probably for the best."

"I'm sorry, Cash." Phoebe hesitated before placing a hand on his arm. "I really had no clue."

"I know." He studied her hand, the sweet gesture that of someone who cared. Despite their bickering, they liked each other. A lot, apparently. "Maybe I should start double-checking the names of the couples from now on."

"You could. But I can't imagine something like this happening again."

"I have been engaged three times." He forced a dry laugh.

Phoebe left shortly after that to deliver the portrait to the barn, and Cash retreated to his desk. Telling himself he was wasting his time, he scanned the names of upcoming weddings and events for the next three months. None was familiar, for which he was glad. He then berated himself for being an idiot.

Through sheer force of will, he kept busy the rest of the afternoon. That didn't prevent his mind from drifting to Melanie and her wedding at seven. What had become of her? Had she ever followed her dream and become a teacher? Did she remember him fondly or hate his guts? Why hadn't she stuck with him just a little longer? What did she look like with purple streaks in her hair and glasses?

He left the office at five thirty and drove to town for dinner at the local barbecue joint. Less chance of running into Melanie that way. His friend Channing, there with a buddy, invited Cash to join them. He passed on their invitation for a second beer, though, claiming he had an early morning. While pulling into the ranch's driveway, he finally admitted the truth to himself, through actions if not words.

Rather than continue on toward the main house, he turned right at the Y in the road. Mistake or not, he was about to watch his first fiancée marry another man.

A SHIMMERING GLOW poured from the barn's open doorway. Brightly colored lights strung along the roofline flashed on and off in synchronized rhythm. The sleigh, with an inflatable Mr. and Mrs. Santa Claus in the driver's seat and fake presents in the back, sat beside the gaily decorated well. The sleigh was pulled by a pair of lighted reindeer whose motorized heads rose and lowered almost in time to the flashing barn lights.

Cash didn't consider himself the romantic

type but even he had to concede the scene was straight off the front of a holiday greeting card.

He parked his truck behind the barn and climbed out. The blast of frigid air should have cleared his senses. It didn't, and he entered the barn through the small rear door. Inside, he stopped for a moment and listened to the officiant. It sounded as if the ceremony was well underway. Making as little noise as possible and ducking to keep out of sight, Cash crept up the stairs to the loft. There, he lowered himself onto one knee and peered over the half wall down onto the main room.

This was wrong and his better sense warned him to get the heck out of there. He had no business secretly observing Melanie's wedding. But he couldn't tear his gaze away if he tried.

Purple streaks and glasses aside, he'd know her anywhere. Old hurt and pain pressed against his lungs, making breathing difficult. At one time, he'd loved this woman to distraction. Seeing her with someone else, about to commit her life to him, wasn't what had Cash's emotions in turmoil, however. Neither was he jealous. Not of her groom. He might be a little jealous of the happiness the two of them had clearly found. The happiness that always escaped Cash.

When he'd met Melanie, he'd been at his lowest—alone, sad, estranged from his dad, barely speaking to his mom, his emotional wounds still raw and bleeding. He'd buried himself in his classes during the week and spent weekends away on the rodeo circuit. He'd been surprised the pretty and bubbly girl in his accounting class had even noticed him.

But she had, and she'd changed his life. Her gentle loving had filled him, lifted him and nourished him. She'd turned him into a better version of himself and helped him believe in a future brimming with potential where previously there'd been none.

Recuperating from the bulldogging injury that, according to the surgeon, had left his shoulder an ugly, useless mass of torn tendons and ligaments, required months and months. With his rodeo career over in the blink of an eye and having to take a semester off at college, Cash's morale had plummeted. His ego hadn't let him call his condition what it was: depression. He'd been convinced fate was determined to keep him down, and he'd needed Melanie's tender care and support more than ever.

It had been then, in his darkest moments, that she'd left him to take a job in another state. He'd known she was disappointed with him delaying their wedding. But it wasn't like he didn't have a good reason. Being unable to compete in rodeo had affected his ability to earn money. And taking a semester off had postponed his finding a good job after graduation. How could they have possibly married? He'd be paying off his medical bills for years, along with his steep student loans. They'd have nothing, and Cash had seen what having nothing did to a marriage.

The old wounds from her leaving bled anew as Cash watched her say her vows to another man. Once, he and Melanie had been really good together. Memories of the good times he'd suppressed surfaced one after the other. Her cheering him on from the arena bleachers. Late-night studying sessions that had always ended as late-night cuddling sessions. Her silly jokes. The way she'd pretended to be annoyed when he kissed the back of her neck but secretly loved it. Her praise and encouragement, which had made him feel ten feet tall. Her thrilled reaction when he'd proposed by hiding the engagement ring in a Christmas stocking.

Melanie had given him those gifts. As Cash watched her, for just a moment, he let himself be the man he'd been all those years ago, and his heart swelled.

The feeling didn't last. Applause and cheers

from the twenty guests in attendance brought him back to reality, and he was once again in the loft, hiding behind the half wall and spying on his former fiancée.

As the newly married couple walked back down the aisle, they were surrounded by their guests; each enthusiastically wishing them well and pulling them into hugs. Someone collected the portrait of Melanie's grandmother and carried it under their arm.

Phoebe was there, materializing from the back corner where she always stood. Cash hadn't noticed her earlier. His attention had been entirely focused on Melanie. Now it remained on Phoebe, and his heart swelled again with feelings for her, both old and new. They liked each other and got along. He found comfort in the familiar and expected. Except for when she went off in an unexpected direction that infuriated him. She wasn't boring, he'd give her that.

The wedding party gathered near the barn entrance. He'd learned from looking at the file notes that Melanie and her husband were having a dinner at Phoebe's parents' inn for all the guests. They'd spend the night at the inn and embark on a honeymoon trip in the morning. He waited several minutes after the group had left, with Phoebe leading the way, before creeping back down the stairs.

With each step, his emotions continued to ebb and flow. He did his best to return them to the murky recesses where they'd been hiding and to close his old wounds.

He might have accomplished that if Melanie hadn't appeared from the shadows at the bottom of the stairs, tears in her eyes and a lace handkerchief pressed to her lips.

He froze in place. She did, too.

"My God. Cash, is that you?"

It seemed she'd recognize him anywhere, too. Even at her wedding.

"Hi, Melanie." He shifted uncomfortably. "I'm sorry if I disturbed you."

"No, I..." She faltered.

"Is everything all right?" Dumb question. Clearly not. She was alone and crying mere moments after her wedding.

"What are you doing here?" she asked.

"Nothing. Checking on... Sorry," he repeated lamely. "I had no business whatsoever intruding. But when I heard you were getting married here, I was curious. It's been a long time."

"Are you getting married, too?"

Okay, she didn't know. "Laurel and I own Wishing Well Springs."

"Seriously?" She gaped at him with confusion and incredulity.

"We inherited what was left of the ranch from our grandfather. His attempt at making things right for us, I suppose, after what we went through. We turned the property into Wishing Well Springs."

"This was your family's horse ranch?"

"At one time."

"And Phoebe works for you?"

"She's our partner in the wedding business. She and Laurel mostly run the day-to-day business. I work for an architectural outfit in Phoenix and come up on weekends."

"Good for you." A wobbly smile replaced her confusion. "I always knew you'd go far."

"What about you? Molding all those young minds?"

"I took a different path. I'm a director for a child welfare nonprofit. It's challenging work but very rewarding."

"You're lucky."

"I am. Truly. Don't let my earlier tears fool you. Emotions have been running high today, and I needed a minute alone."

"I understand."

"Ron's an incredible guy. Really good to me and my family. It's been a rough year for us. Chemo. Radiation."

"I can imagine." Cash remembered what his family had gone through with his grandmother's heart condition.

"He's in remission," Melanie said, sniffling a little. "Cancer-free."

"I'm glad." Cash probably should leave her alone, given the circumstances, but he couldn't bring himself to leave. "I know this is not the right question to ask you on your wedding day, but do you ever think about us?"

"Of course. You were my first love and a big part of my life for a long time. Other than how things ended, I have nothing but fond memories."

He hadn't had those same fond memories. Watching her get married changed that, however. "We were happy together," he agreed. "Until my injury when you…left me."

Her demeanor abruptly changed. "Is that what you think? That your injury caused our breakup?"

"I had to quit school and rodeoing. I postponed our marriage. You were tired of waiting."

"I was upset about you constantly delaying the wedding—that part is true. I didn't understand why we couldn't go ahead with it."

"I wasn't able to work, and I was drowning in medical bills."

"That didn't matter to me."

He had trouble believing her. "We would have had to live on your wages."

"Temporarily."

"Which wouldn't have been fair. You'd have resented me."

"You really believe that?"

"You don't?"

She shook her head. "Not in the least."

"I guess we had a miscommunication."

"That's the thing, Cash. We never communicated at all. You wouldn't. You clammed up after your surgery and cut me off completely."

He remembered differently. She'd turned away from him. Unless her turning away was a response to him.

"I could see you were hurting and wanted to help you," she continued. "You refused to let me. After a while, I couldn't take any more and left."

"I was going through a lot."

"The thing is, you didn't have to go through it alone. You chose to build a giant wall around yourself." Her voice cracked. "When I got that job offer, I felt like the universe was showing me a new path. I really hoped you'd come after me. I waited and waited. When you didn't, I moved on."

"Melanie. If I had known—"

"We were young."

"I messed up."

"We both did." Her wobbly smile returned. "Things have a way of working out, though. I just married the love of my life, and you turned your inheritance into this amazing venture. It was Ron's idea to get married here. He saw an article." She looked around. "Speaking of which, he's probably wondering where I disappeared to."

Cash still had more questions. He couldn't ask Melanie to stay and neither would he suggest they keep in touch.

"Congratulations on your wedding," he said. "I really wish you the best."

"Thank you." She hesitated a moment before giving him a quick hug. "I wish you all the best, too."

With a little wave, she turned and walked away, hurrying toward her new husband and new life.

"Wait," Cash called out.

She paused. Smiled.

"I like your hair."

"You do?" Laughing softly, she brushed aside a long purple lock and then disappeared around the corner.

Cash doubted he'd see her again, but that was all right. They were both in better places and where they should be. And she, at least, had found her someone special.

He left the barn through the rear door and drove to the main house. After a half hour of pacing in the attic room—he was too agitated to think about sleep—he headed downstairs to the kitchen for a snack. Seeing the lights on in the business offices, he found Phoebe sitting at her desk and staring at the computer screen.

She glanced up at his arrival. "Hey. What's up?"

Cash went still, utterly captivated.

The light from her desk lamp struck her face at such an angle, her hazel eyes sparkled as if lit from within and her flawless complexion glowed. Phoebe wasn't just pretty, she was gorgeous, and his pulse began to hammer. That had been happening a lot this past week.

"You're staring. Do I have food in my teeth?"

"No." He chuckled, only to stop short.

She did that, got to him in ways no one else did. Even when they were at each other's throats, Cash enjoyed himself. She stirred feelings in him. Got a rise out of him. Knew exactly which buttons to push and liked pushing them.

Wasn't that better than boring and bland?

"You're not still upset about Melanie?" she asked.

"I actually spoke to her. After the wedding," he added at her startled look. "I accidentally ran into her."

"What happened? Do I need to worry about refunding their fee or us facing a potential lawsuit?"

"Nothing. I swear." Unless he counted seeing his former relationship from an entirely new perspective. "We wished each other well, hugged and parted friends."

"All…right."

"You going to be here awhile? I can stay. Keep you company. Protect you from potential danger."

"Oh!" She batted her eyes and clasped her hands in front of her. "My hero."

"You joke, but bad things happen."

"I'm finished anyway." She closed her computer and rose from her desk. "Thanks for the offer, though."

"I'll walk you to your car."

"Seriously, Cash. That's not necessary. I'm parked in the garage."

"I insist."

She rolled her eyes. "Whatever."

As they left the office he caught sight of her smile. Ha! She wasn't irritated with him despite pretending otherwise. Just the opposite, apparently.

They locked the front door, made a last-minute sweep of the house before setting the security alarm, and then went through the kitchen to the garage.

"See you in the morning," Phoebe said over the rumble of the overhead garage door opening, tossing her purse onto the front passenger seat of her car.

"Drive careful."

He had no reason to dawdle. He should have already bid her goodbye and returned to the kitchen for that snack. But who knew a dull overhead light could cast such an appealing glow? Phoebe's hair shone like strands of spun gold.

With one arm halfway into her coat sleeve, she paused, her brow furrowing. "What now?"

"Just seeing you safely off." He moved to stand beside her. Taking hold of her coat, he held it while she slipped her other arm into the sleeve. When she was done, he grabbed the lapels and pulled the coat snug around her, fastening the top button.

"I'm not a child, Cash. You don't have to dress me."

"There's a storm front headed our way. You need to stay warm."

"I have a ten-minute drive."

"Your heater will have barely kicked in by then."

"Are you sure nothing happened earlier with Melanie?" Concern tinged her voice.

He let his hands drop but remained rooted in place. "Not with *her*."

"Then who?"

His gaze fell to her mouth, where it remained riveted. The gloss she'd recently applied emphasized the soft peach color of her lips. "Have you ever wanted to kiss me, Phoebe?"

She jerked slightly. "What kind of question is that?"

"Because I've been thinking about kissing you a lot lately." He dipped his mouth several inches.

"Is this little encounter between us because you saw your ex-fiancée tonight and want to erase her memory?"

"Don't underestimate yourself, Phoebe." He traced his thumb along her coat lapel. "You're the only woman I'm thinking of right now. The only woman I want to think about."

"I have my doubts," she said, her tone edging on playful.

No, she didn't. Why else would she angle her head so that they were two tiny inches from satisfying their mutual curiosity?

"Try me," he coaxed. "You won't be disappointed." As tempting as it was to make the first move, she had to be the one.

Their gazes locked, their breaths stilled, and then it happened. Her arms lifted to loop around his neck.

"Are you bragging?" she asked in a voice that had gone low and sultry.

"I'm stating a fact." A fact he'd prove if he ever got to taste those peach-colored lips.

"I guess I'll just have to see for myself," she said and drew his mouth to hers.

Her kiss was soft and sweet at first. Then a little demanding. Altogether irresistible. Turned out *he* was the one not disappointed.

Circling her waist, he drew her tight against him. They took their time, the two of them relishing these previously undiscovered sides to each other. She sighed with contentment. He whispered endearments against her lips.

Unfortunately, all things must come to an end. Phoebe slowly disengaged herself from his embrace, and he reluctantly loosened his hold on her.

"You're right." She flashed him a coy smile. "I wasn't disappointed. And I have thought about kissing you." She didn't add that she'd been having those thoughts since they were teenagers.

"Wish I'd known. I might not have waited so long."

"Yeah, me too." Imagine how different their lives might have been. "Not to spoil the mood or anything, but what really just happened? Are we starting something?"

"Honestly, I'm not sure."

She promptly sobered. "I see. This was a lark. A fun distraction. An experiment."

"It was none of those, Phoebe, I swear. I won't tell you I'm ready for a committed relationship, because I'm not. That would be wrong and unfair to you."

"Yes, it would."

"I know I like you. I always have. You're not easy a lot of the time, but nothing worthwhile ever is."

"I need a better answer than that. I have a heart to protect."

He nodded. "Can I think on this for a day or two? I don't want to say the wrong thing."

Except he had, something immediately evidenced by her chilly tone.

"You definitely don't. Trust me." Sliding in behind the wheel, she fastened her seat belt.

"Phoebe, I'm sorry." He was apologizing a lot tonight. "It wasn't my intention to mislead you."

She put out a hand, a silent warning for him

to keep his distance. "Until you know what you want and where we stand, don't kiss me again. I'm not interested in starting something you have no desire to finish."

"Fair enough." He retreated a step.

She shut the car door and started the engine.

A minute later, Cash was standing alone in the garage, contemplating just how badly he'd screwed up not only his friendship with Phoebe but possibly their working relationship.

If he didn't fix this blunder right away, his sister would have his hide when she got home…and justifiably so.

CHAPTER SEVEN

"READY, BOYS?" Cash clucked to the horses and jiggled the reins. "Walk out."

Otis and Elvis obediently followed the command, triggering a cacophony of sounds. Wheels groaned as they labored to pull the wagon, the harness chains clinked and clanked, side boards creaked in harmony along with the seat springs, and dirt and stone crunched beneath the heavy weight.

"Let's pick up the pace."

At his encouragement, the horses plodded along from the carriage house to the main house. Watching their heads bobbing and tails swishing, it was easy to forget their advanced age and that they hadn't been driven in months.

"Whoa, there."

Cash reined them to a stop in front of the house and waited. A moment later, the front door flew open and Phoebe emerged, squeezing her middle and distorting the green face of Dr. Seuss's Grinch.

Bingo. His plan had worked.

"Where are you going?" she called.

"Get your coat. You don't want to freeze."

"There's a problem with the menu for tonight's wedding. We may have to consult the bride and groom."

"These guys need a workout."

"Hello. Catering problem. Menu item not available."

"We'll talk to Trudy in person at the inn."

Phoebe heaved a huge sigh. "That'll take hours. And we can't just close down the office."

Cash refused to give up. She'd been mad at him for three days now, since he'd bungled answering her questions after their kiss. As of yet, despite several attempts, he'd failed to regain lost ground. Left with no other option, he'd stooped to using a tried-and-true tactic.

"Your calendar's clear this morning. I looked."

"There's plenty of work to do."

"The wedding isn't for another ten hours." He tightened his grip on the reins when Otis started pawing the ground. "Forward the office phone to your cell and put a sign on the front door."

Her face telegraphed the war waging internally. She used to love riding in the wagon. Hopefully, she still did.

"Give me a minute," she finally said and vanished inside.

Cash grinned. "Well done, boys."

Five minutes later, Phoebe reappeared, bundled in the same coat she'd been wearing the other night and carrying a blanket for her lap. She locked the door and hung a sign that read Be Back Shortly along with the office number.

Jogging down the porch steps, she slowed to a fast walk as she neared the wagon.

Transferring the reins to one gloved hand, Cash reached out his other hand to help her up. She batted it away, struggling on her own to scale the side of the wagon while grappling with the blanket.

"There's nothing gained from being stubborn."

"Says you." She glowered at him and plopped down in the seat, rocking them both.

"Ready?" he asked, trying not to let his disappointment show when she arranged the blanket over her legs. There went his chance to gawk.

"I am now."

The wagon lurched noisily when they took off, causing Cash and Phoebe to bump shoulders. She tried to scoot away, but the seat was only so big, and she had nowhere to go.

"What changed your mind?" Cash asked when they were halfway down the long driveway.

She straightened her spine and sniffed. "I was wondering if you'd finally figured out the right thing to say."

Direct and to the point. Something else he liked about her.

"I had no business kissing you when I wasn't serious about pursuing a relationship. We work together. And as much as I like you, as attractive as I find you, I think crossing boundaries could lead to problems if our personal relationship soured."

"We're both professionals, Cash."

"Absolutely. But there's your friendship with Laurel and our mutual relationship with your parents' inn to consider. I'd hate to negatively affect those. Lastly—"

"There's more? My, my. You've been busy."

He smiled. "Long-distance relationships aren't easy to sustain and fail more often than they succeed."

She considered a moment. "I don't disagree."

"I was wrong, Phoebe. And I regret hurting you."

"I wasn't hurt."

"Make you angry, then. Disappoint you."

She ignored him and watched a flock of starlings flying overhead.

"It won't happen again," he said.

"Okay."

He nudged her arm with his elbow until she reluctantly turned to face him. "Can we be friends again? I've missed you these past few days. Missed sparring with you."

"Isn't that what we've been doing? I've done nothing but snap and argue. I'd think you'd be weary by now."

"Not the same thing. Sparring is entertaining."

The corners of her Cupid's-bow mouth tilted up.

Progress, he thought. And better than the cold shoulder he'd been getting.

"I also miss you bossing me around."

She snorted with disgust.

Much, much better. The rest of the ride to the inn passed in amiable silence, the rift between them closing with each rhythmic clip-clop of the horses' hooves. Before long, he swung the wagon onto the drive leading to Joshua Tree Inn. Realizing the familiar destination was near, Otis and Elvis increased the pace to a trot.

Midmornings were always busy at the inn, especially on weekends. They passed guests loading and unloading their vehicles, workers busily tending the immaculate grounds and pushing housekeeping carts, and patrons streaming in and out of the restaurant entrance, brunch diners replacing breakfast diners. The horses and wagon drew a lot of attention in the form of open stares and friendly waves.

Cash reined Otis and Elvis to a stop in front of the inn. The next instant, the big red door opened, releasing a small pack of very young humans. They scurried and scampered down the walkway, yelling and squealing with excitement.

Phoebe's nieces and nephews, Cash garnered from the shouts of "Auntie Phoebe!"

"Stay back, kids," she warned while climbing down from the wagon. This time, she didn't refuse Cash's offer of assistance. "You could scare the horses and get hurt."

Her words went completely unheeded. The four—make that five—kids mobbed Otis and Elvis. They wrapped their little arms around the horses' legs and grabbed their big heads. The pair simply stood there, tolerating the attention with their customary patience.

"Children, children." Phoebe's mother speed-walked down the walkway. "Behave, please." She clapped her hands to get their attention. It didn't work. "No, Ian. Don't hang on the harness. Millie, take that disgusting thing out of your mouth this instant." She reached Phoebe and enveloped her in a warm embrace. Releasing her, she said, "Cash, how are you?"

"Couldn't be better, Agnes. And you?"

"We're running ourselves ragged." She brushed at the square of short blond bangs framing her face. "I love the holidays, I swear I do, but they're tiring." She marched forward in a way that reminded Cash of Phoebe. "Johnny, don't pull your cousin's pants down. That's rude."

"Where's Trudy?" Phoebe asked.

"Resting on the couch in your dad's office," Agnes answered carefully.

"Is she all right?"

Cash heard the concern in Phoebe's voice and saw it flash in her eyes.

"She's fine. For now." Agnes's glance cut to the children and then back to Phoebe.

Cash saw the unspoken plea. *Let's not talk in front of the kids.*

"Mom?" Phoebe grabbed Agnes's arm. "What's going on?"

"Don't panic. Trudy will tell you everything. I'll stay here and keep an eye on the ruffians. Their parents are doing some you-know-what shopping at the *m-a-l-l*. I volunteered to babysit." She glanced at her watch. With luck, I'll be relieved in an hour. Better be an hour. We're hosting a big private party tonight in addition to catering your wedding."

Phoebe fidgeted, anxiety radiating off her. "Maybe you should head back to Wishing Well Springs," she told Cash. "I may be a while. I'll get someone to give me a lift."

"That's one possibility," Cash agreed. "Or I could take these kids for a ride in the wagon for the next hour. Give you all a chance to talk." He knew Phoebe would be a wreck until she learned the nature of her sister's apparent crisis and was actively involved in the resolution. "As far as work goes, stay here as long as you need."

"The wedding tonight…" She let the sentence drop.

"We have time. I'll call Georgia Ann when I get back to see if she can come in early. Now, round up these kids."

"Are you sure?" Agnes asked, grimacing. "Because they're a lot to handle all at once. Maybe I should go with you and supervise."

"What about Trudy?" Phoebe protested.

"You can fill me in later."

"I guess." Phoebe's fidgeting intensified.

Cash had the feeling something serious must be going on with her sister. Why else would her mother be so willing to let the kids go on a wagon ride?

"Let's load up," he said.

"Children." Agnes clapped her hands again. "Pay attention. I have some exciting news."

"What, Grandma?"

"Tell us, tell us!"

"Only when everyone is listening." She put a finger to her lips and waited until all eyes were on her and talking had ceased. A big smile spread across her face. "You're going to go on a wagon ride with me and Mr. Montgomery."

The kids went wild, cheering and piling onto each other.

"But only if you're good. *Very good.* Like, Santa-is-watching-you good." She waited for the ruckus to settle. When it did, she continued. "Now, I'm going inside for our jackets and will be right back. Wait quietly until then."

Phoebe stayed behind, wringing her hands and shooting anxious glances toward the inn.

"Remember, children. Behave," Agnes called from the porch.

Within twenty seconds of the front door closing, the kids' composure deteriorated. Phoebe's warnings went unheeded, drowned out by giggles, crying, burping, squabbling and fussing.

"Hey, mister, can we gallop the horses?"

"I want to sit with you."

Agnes returned a few minutes later, her

arms laden with jackets and sweaters, to confront complete chaos.

"Oh my goodness. You are hopeless." She pretended to pull her hair out. The kids all laughed as she and Phoebe dressed them for the wagon ride.

Cash was starting to see where Phoebe had inherited her quirkier traits. Her dad must have the patience of a saint. He had not only a wife but five daughters and a litter of grandkids with abundant energy and big personalities.

"See you later, Cash." Phoebe raced toward the inn the second the last button was fastened and without a backward glance.

Agnes lifted the kids and deposited them in the wagon bed one by one. They were joined by a young woman who was apparently best buds with the kids. They greeted her with, "Tina, Tina, bo-bina" and "Do you have any gum?"

"I hope you don't mind," Agnes said to Cash. "I invited our part-time hostess along to help with crowd control."

"The more the merrier."

Between an old wooden crate, a toolbox, a bucket and one bale of straw, there were almost enough seats to go around. The two oldest kids stood and held on to the sides. The entire time, Otis and Elvis were champs and stood unmoving.

Agnes dropped down beside Cash on the seat while Tina sat in the back with the kids, keeping arms and small bodies inside and breaking up squabbles. When everyone was settled, Cash clucked to the horses and they set off. He decided to avoid the main road and instead circle the barren fields belonging to the organic farm east of the inn.

"Thank you, Cash." Agnes patted his leg. "You're a good man."

"Is Trudy going to be all right?"

"I'll let Phoebe fill you in. And don't worry about the wedding reception tonight. We'll find an acceptable substitute and make sure the couple is happy."

They conversed over the din of the wagon in motion and five excited kids.

"I'm not worried about that," he assured Agnes.

"Phoebe is. And I suspect that if she's worried, you are, too. I can see you care about her."

Something in her voice put Cash on alert. Did she sense that his feelings toward Phoebe had recently changed from those of a coworker to a man interested in a woman? Had Phoebe mentioned their kiss?

He rethreaded the reins through his gloved

fingers. It was a ploy to buy time—Otis and Elvis walked peacefully along the dirt road circumventing a large field as if on automatic pilot.

"She's important to Wishing Well Springs," Cash said. "She's responsible for much of our success. You're our lifelong neighbors. Naturally, I care."

"Sure. Whatever you say." Agnes grinned knowingly and then swiveled in her seat. Pointing a finger, she reprimanded two of her grandkids who were intent on besting each other in a shoving contest. "Knock it off, you two. And, Tina, bless your heart. I'm giving you first choice of hours next week."

"Really? Cool."

"Wait until the wagon ride is over. You might think differently after dealing with this crew." Agnes returned her attention to Cash. "I'm most likely speaking out of turn, and Phoebe would be mortified if she ever found out, but I'm a mother and I'll protect my daughters no matter what."

Where, Cash wondered, was this going? "Okay."

"Phoebe likes you. She always has. I would hate more than anything to see her hurt."

"Understood."

"I know she appears strong and capable and

bulletproof on the outside. But on the inside, she's fragile. Sam did a real number on her. I don't want that to happen again."

"Neither do I."

Agnes smiled and nodded. "Good talk."

The rest of the wagon ride progressed without incident. Nothing more serious was discussed than the holiday events in town. When they returned to the inn, Agnes and Tina unloaded the kids, who, at their grandmother's prodding, chorused their thanks.

"I'll fetch Phoebe for you," Agnes said before heading inside.

But rather than Phoebe coming outside, Tina did.

"Phoebe says to go home without her. Her dad'll give her a ride to the ranch later."

"Everything okay?"

"She said you'd ask that and to tell you it's fine."

"All right."

Cash turned the team of horses around. If his conversation with Agnes wasn't cause for alarm, Phoebe staying on at the inn assuredly was. What, he wondered, was happening with her sister?

PHOEBE PRACTICALLY jettisoned into the barn. To her enormous relief, everything appeared in place and ready for the wedding in… She checked the time on her phone. Two hours! Had she really been gone all day?

Good grief. Losing track of time was so unlike her.

"Sorry I'm late," she blurted, apologizing to Georgia Ann and the crew.

"Did Danielle and Marcus approve the menu change?" Georgia Ann asked.

Phoebe had to think for a second. Right. The shipment of crab had been unavoidably delayed. The bride and groom had chosen to go with shrimp rolls instead. She'd been so involved with Trudy and the situation there, she'd forgotten about their phone call.

"Yeah. We got the green light." She looked around. "Where's Cash?" He hadn't been at the main house; she'd stopped there first. And her calls to him had gone directly to voice mail.

"He's in the hayloft, setting up the party machine."

Oh my gosh. Something else Phoebe had forgotten. A quick inspection of the rear storage area assured her that the floating cranberry candles were stacked and ready to be placed on the gold linen sheathed tables. Despite Cash's diligent efforts, they hadn't been able to locate nutcracker couple centerpieces. Still, the wedding and reception would be lovely. The fake crystal icicles hanging from the ceiling, lighted tree and red ribbons on the backs of chairs added just the right Christmassy touch.

"Cash was a real help today," Georgia Ann continued. "He really stepped up. He repaired the broken leg on the table behind the altar and picked up Marcus's former army buddy at the bus stop. Oh…and he mended a hole in the runner."

"Wow." Phoebe was impressed. "He can sew?"

"Must have learned from Laurel."

"I suppose." What other hidden talents did Cash possess?

"You want me to get him?" Georgia Ann started for the hayloft.

"No. You stay and supervise."

Phoebe owed him an explanation. And they'd need to talk, though now wasn't the best time.

She climbed the narrow steps to the hayloft. Her boots thudding on the wooden steps must have alerted him that he had company, for he was looking up expectantly when she reached the top.

"Hey, you. Welcome back." He stopped fiddling with the party machine and sent her a smile.

Good. He wasn't angry with her.

"I apologize. I didn't mean to abandon you."

"How's Trudy?"

"She's…" Tears pricked Phoebe's eyes. There went her resolve to keep her emotions in check. "She has preeclampsia."

"Not sure what that is."

"It's serious. High blood pressure, for one. Dangerously high. Her liver and kidneys could be affected."

"Ah, shoot, hon." He took a step toward her. "Is there a cure?"

"Having the baby. Except she's not far enough along. If the doctor induces labor, the baby might have life-threatening complications or…not survive."

"Is there any other treatment?"

"Keeping her blood pressure under control. The doctor wants her to quit work and go on complete bed rest. He'll monitor her closely."

There was more to her sister's treatment plan, but Phoebe would wait to tell Cash that part.

"What can I do?" he asked. "You need some time off?"

He had no idea how much time off from Wishing Well Springs her family wanted her to take.

"I might. Yeah. Let's talk more after the wedding. Or tomorrow."

"You sure Trudy's okay? You look upset."

Fresh tears threatened to fall. She blinked them away. "For the moment, both she and the baby are fine. And we have a crazy-in-love couple wanting to get married."

Cash had set the party machine on top of a small portable table and aimed the nozzle over the half wall of the hayloft. The snowlike particles would rain down on Danielle and Marcus right when the minister announced them man and wife, just like they wanted.

All because of Cash. Even though he'd considered the party machine silly and a waste of money, he'd found one, rented it and set it up. For the couple, yes. But also for Phoebe.

If kissing him wasn't such a bad idea, if she hadn't warned him off unless he was serious, she'd throw her arms around him and lock lips.

"I have to say, Cash, I'm impressed. This wedding wouldn't be happening without you."

"That's what assistants are for."

"And thanks for giving me time with my family today. You didn't have to, and it means a lot."

"You work your tail off. It's the least I could do."

They stared at each other for a long moment. She thought, maybe, there was something more in those chestnut eyes than just appreciation for a business partner. But that was probably wishful thinking.

"I've underestimated you," she said. "No, that's not right. I haven't been giving you enough credit. You're proving to be a lot more than the mostly silent partner in Phoenix who just handles the finances and watches the expenses."

"Is that a compliment, Phoebe Kellerman?"

"Don't make more of it than it is."

"Trust me, I am. And I'm going to remind you of this conversation the next time we disagree about money."

She laughed at that. He, in turn, flipped a switch on the party machine, and a burst of white particles exploded from the nozzle. Shutting off the machine, they both looked over the half wall at the cloud drifting down to the altar where Danielle and Marcus would be soon standing.

"Nice," Phoebe said.

"You think Danielle and Marcus will be happy?"

She imagined the delight on their faces and felt the best she had all day. Her sister and the baby were both going to be okay. She had to believe that. She wouldn't *not* believe that.

"I think they'll be thrilled."

Cash conducted a final inspection of the

party machine, unplugging it for good measure. "You ready to head down?"

Phoebe's phone pinged as they descended the stairs. "I just got a text. The food's on the way."

"Without Trudy I take it?"

"Our kitchen supervisor is filling in."

At the bottom of the stairs, Cash turned and held out a hand. Phoebe considered waving him off; she didn't need his assistance. Neither should she encourage any physical contact between them, not after what had happened the other night.

Her insides tingled at the reminder of their kiss, which had greatly exceeded anything she'd imagined—and she'd done plenty of imagining over the course of the last fifteen years. For a few minutes, her long-held dream of being with Cash had come true. Then promptly evaporated.

She meant to decline his offer of help but instead reached for his hand. The steps were narrow and the lighting dim. No sooner did her foot touch the floor than he drew her into his arms.

"Cash! Wait!"

This wasn't what they'd agreed on. He'd said he wasn't ready for a commitment. Plus, she was still a little mad at him.

"Shh. Quit squirming." He tightened his hold on her. "It's just a hug. You look like you need one."

She did. And the sensation of his arms enveloping her acted like a balm. Instantly, her frazzled nerves calmed and her troubles eased. If only she could bottle his magic fix and take it home with her.

Later, tonight maybe, she'd examine this moment in minute detail. Replay it in her mind over and over. Cash had triggered all sorts of emotions in her over the years. Comfort had never been one of them.

It was, without a doubt, disconcerting and worrisome. But it was also intriguing and compelling. She could resist unattainable Cash, the one who had his defenses in place and who paid her little notice. But this kind, considerate, compassionate and attentive version of him was much too appealing. She'd be a goner if she wasn't careful.

A few more seconds, she told herself, inhaling the spicy scent of his shaving cream—he must have showered after the wagon ride. Then a few more seconds after that while her fingers pressed into the firm muscles of his shoulders.

Apparently, he possessed stronger willpower than her, or perhaps sounder judgment, for he gently withdrew.

"Better," he said.

Was that a question directed to her or an expression of how he felt? She couldn't be sure.

Tugging on the hem of her Grinch sweater, she collected herself. "It's showtime," she announced, as she did before every wedding.

DANIELLE AND MARCUS'S wedding went off without a single hitch. When Cash turned on the party machine at the end of the ceremony, the guests cheered. Danielle cried tears of joy. So did Phoebe, watching from her usual corner.

Tall propane heaters kept the outside area warm. While guests filed through the reception line and photographs were taken, Phoebe, Cash and the crew transformed the barn's setup from wedding to dining with impressive efficiency. The kitchen supervisor's hard work paid off—the dinner was both delicious and impeccably served. Everyone loved the shrimp rolls. Danielle and Marcus thanked Phoebe profusely before heading off to their honeymoon destination in a rented town car.

For the ninth night in a row, Phoebe and Cash were up late, helping with the cleanup and readying for tomorrow's wedding.

"These Christmas weddings are going to be the death of us," Georgia Ann complained good-naturedly. Like Phoebe, she loved both weddings and the holidays, and couldn't be happier when the two were combined.

"At least we get to sleep in tomorrow morning," Phoebe said, stifling a yawn.

"Hooray for that. We don't have a single break until January first."

Tomorrow's wedding was another small, intimate affair. None of the weddings this coming week were particularly large or complex. The two weeks following that, however, would be an endurance test. Besides the family reunion, they had a wedding on Saturday with more than one hundred and fifty guests. There was also the secret-couple wedding, and the Christmas Day vow renewal ceremony that was growing bigger by the day.

It was past eleven o'clock when they finally finished and wheeled shut the barn door. Cash slid the padlock in place, closing it with a firm click. Goodbyes were called out as the crew ambled toward their vehicles parked behind the barn, their feet dragging.

Phoebe couldn't remember ever being so tired. It had been a long, grueling day, both emotionally and physically. Even so, she wasn't sure she could fall asleep. Not until she and Cash talked.

"I know it's late," she said, "but do you have a few minutes?"

He hopped into the golf cart and patted the seat beside him. "Come on. We can chat on the way."

She climbed in, and he started the engine. The air went from cold to frigid as they tooled along the dirt road, and Phoebe hugged herself. The feeble attempt to stay warm didn't stop her teeth from chattering. Why hadn't she brought a coat?

Well, duh! She'd come straight from the inn and her mind had been elsewhere.

"What's up?" Cash asked over the golf cart's quiet hum.

She tried to suppress her shivering. Even so, her words came out choppy. "Trudy won't be returning to work until after the baby's born."

"I kind of figured as much from what you said earlier."

"She was already planning on going part-time in order to stay home more with the baby. Now she's thinking of not returning at all, for a few years anyway. She and Dennis are hoping for a second baby, and she's worried she'll have the same health problems. Her doctor said the stress from being on her feet all day contributed to her preeclampsia."

"That puts a real hardship on your parents. Trudy's great at her job. Replacing her won't be easy."

Phoebe stared at the headlight beams slicing the inky blackness and mustered her courage. "Joshua Tree Inn has always been a family-run business."

"Yeah. No employee is ever as invested in the business as family."

"My parents said the very same thing earlier today." When they were pleading their case to Phoebe.

"Except for you." Cash took his gaze off the road long enough to send her a grin. "You're completely invested in Wishing Well Springs."

"Yeah. About that…"

They pulled up in front of the garage and into the glaring white glow cast from a security light. Cash activated the fob on his key ring and the garage door shook and rattled on its upward journey. Cash's truck and Phoebe's car sat side by side, just like their owners.

Phoebe didn't immediately get out of the golf cart despite the cold and her constant shivering.

Cash studied her questioningly. "Something wrong?"

"My folks want me to…to…" Out with it, she told herself. "To take Trudy's place."

The question in his eyes turned to surprise and then panic. "Are you quitting us?"

"No, no. I'm saying that's what my parents want."

"What did you tell them?" He spoke slowly. Carefully.

"I didn't refuse. But only because they're worried sick about Trudy and I hated adding to that."

"So…you're not quitting us?"

"This is my family, Cash."

"I understand. But you also have an obligation to Laurel and me. You're our partner. We started this business in large part because of you."

She closed her eyes and rubbed her temple, where a headache had lodged. "This is a brutal decision for me. I love being a wedding coordinator. It's all I've ever wanted to do with my life. And here I'm my own boss, not working for Mom and Dad. I'm part of a growing company where I get to make a real difference. I wouldn't have those things at the inn."

"All good reasons to stay."

"Except I can't turn my back on my family."

"I'm sure they could hire someone to replace Trudy. The kitchen supervisor did a pretty good job covering for her today."

"He did. But like you said, will he or whoever is hired be as invested in the company as I would be? And with my parents worrying about Trudy, the added pressure of replacing her is a lot for them to handle right now."

"What do *you* want to do, Phoebe?" He took her hand in his and squeezed her fingers.

She stared into his eyes, now black in the glare of the bright security light. "I need some time to process and talk again with my family when we're less shell-shocked from the news about Trudy's condition."

"You want to get Laurel's input? We can video chat with her."

Phoebe shook her head. Concentrating was hard with Cash's thumb drawing little circles on her skin. "Let's not bother her with this right now. She's running herself ragged in Palm Springs."

Laurel had sounded harried and over-wrought during their latest phone call with her this morning. The bride's crash diet and determination to drop weight before the wedding was causing numerous fittings and alterations.

"If you're sure," Cash said.

"Even if I decide to stay on here, I'll need some time off after the holidays to help my parents until they hire Trudy's replacement."

"That we can do."

"You may have to continue handling some of my work. Come to Payson more often."

He smiled. "I was already planning on

being here every weekend through the end of March."

"You were?"

"I have plans."

The tingle from earlier returned. Was he reconsidering their status?

"What plans?" she asked.

"Overseeing construction on the expansion."

"Right."

The mock Western town. Not her. How stupid could she be?

She withdrew her hand from his and hopped out of the golf cart. "See you in the morning."

"Good night. Drive careful."

Walking toward her car in the garage, she hid her face from him, certain he'd see her disappointment. The decision whether to stay on at Wishing Well Springs or to leave to work for her parents would be so much easier if Cash had changed his mind about them dating. But he hadn't.

CHAPTER EIGHT

"WHAT DID THE rep from Affordable Storage Solutions say?" Laurel asked. "Is she okay with rescheduling?"

Even from the distance of the coffee table where Cash had propped his tablet, he could discern her drawn features and the dark circles beneath her eyes. Her voice, normally bubbly, droned on tiredly. He half expected her to nod off during the video call from lack of sleep.

They were all tired, their schedules hectic, but Laurel carried a tremendous weight on her shoulders.

"She's fine with rescheduling for January seventh," Phoebe answered. She sat beside Cash on the couch in the client waiting area. "But it'll have to be in the afternoon. I sent you an email."

"And the package from Fabric Fusion?" Laurel flipped through her notepad.

"It'll be here tomorrow." Cash leaned in close to Phoebe so that they appeared side by side in the little box tucked in the screen's lower corner. "According to the delivery service's tracking app."

Laurel's shoulders sagged with relief and she made a note on her pad. "Good."

"Cash and I also met with Mrs. Gillroy."

"For what?" Laurel's head snapped up.

"She showed up unexpectedly wanting to see her future daughter-in-law's dress."

"Tell me you sent her away!"

"Eventually. She was ready to run me over until Cash intervened. He sweet-talked her into waiting until you returned and the bride was here. I have to hand it to him, the woman went from saber-toothed tiger to meek kitten in less than five minutes."

Laurel's eyes widened with interest, her fatigue apparently forgotten. "Sounds like you two are playing nice while I'm gone."

Cash felt Phoebe tense and heard her soft intake of breath. They had been getting along these past four days. Ever since she'd told him about her sister's health emergency and that she might leave Wishing Well Springs, he'd been trying his darnedest to make her job, her life, easier. Yes, so that she'd stay.

"We're managing," Phoebe admitted. "He's no longer breaking out in hives every time we talk about flowers or wedding cakes or decorations, which is an improvement. And he's stopped criticizing the couples' choices."

Cash turned to face Phoebe and gave her an apprizing once-over. "Is that another compliment?"

She glowered at him. "Shut up."

Laurel didn't scold them for bickering. "Thank you, both of you. Without the two of you cooperating and you, Cash, giving up your vacation, I couldn't have taken this job."

"No problem. My bill's in the mail."

Phoebe gave him a small jab in the side.

He chuckled. "All kidding aside, how's it going?"

Laurel sighed wistfully. "Endless problems aside, this dress is one of my finest creations. The mother-in-law's and flower girl's aren't half bad, either."

"As if there was ever a doubt," Phoebe said. "You're amazing. And while we're on the subject of good news, I got a call a little while ago from a Suzanne Levy. She's the executive assistant for the mayor of Palm Springs. Seems the mayor's daughter is getting married in October of next year and scouting destination wedding locations. The *mayor's* daughter. They're planning on visiting us in January and, if we knock their socks off, we'll book the wedding—the assistant's exact words, by the way. The daughter is particularly interested in having the wedding outdoors in the Western town. I assured the assistant that construction would be completed by late summer."

"You didn't mention the part about her being *particularly interested.*" Cash gloated just a little. The expansion had been his idea.

"Don't make this about you."

"Stop it, you two," Laurel said, "and tell me everything about the call."

Phoebe obliged her for the next few minutes. "I also spoke to another of your client's acquaintances yesterday. Head of the town's Fine Arts committee. She's getting back to me after the holidays."

"I'm proud of you, sis," Cash told Laurel. "This trip of yours is going to pay off."

"Thanks, big brother. Which reminds me, how is trimming the expenses coming along? Are we going to save enough to reupholster the furniture? With so many important visitors, the office could really use a refresh."

"Too soon to tell," Cash answered. At Phoebe's crestfallen expression, he added, "But we're trying, and I'm optimistic."

Her smile returned. He probably would have said anything to see that, even lied if necessary. She'd been preoccupied for days, Trudy's health concerns always on her mind.

"I should get going." Laurel glanced over her shoulder. "I need to finish the lining today so I can start on the beadwork."

"One thing before you go," Phoebe quickly added. "I have something to tell you. Well, both of you." Her glance cut briefly to Cash.

He sat up, instantly all ears. Was she giving her notice? He'd probably blown it again by not telling her how much she mattered to him—er...Wishing Well Springs.

What if she was leaving because of their kiss? He'd sworn there'd be no repeat and had kept his promise even when they hugged. Not easy, by the way.

Nah, if anything, she was leaving because of his inability to commit. Make that *unwillingness* to commit. Phoebe wanted and deserved more. A man who'd let nothing stand in the way of them being together.

"Sounds important," Laurel said, her tone cautious.

"It is. There's a complication with Trudy's pregnancy." Phoebe went on to explain preeclampsia, the treatment and the likely outcome. "She's on complete bed rest per doctor's orders and won't be returning to work after the baby's born."

"Aw, sweetie, I'm so sorry to hear that. How can we help?"

Don't quit, Cash silently mouthed and then reprimanded himself for being selfish. Trudy's health and that of the baby was what mattered most.

"I'm going to need some time off in January to cover for Trudy at the inn until my parents decide on her replacement," Phoebe said. "A week, at least. Maybe longer. I'll try not to let it affect my job here too much."

Cash didn't hear what was said next, his thundering heart blocking out all sound.

She wasn't quitting! She was staying on at Wishing Well Springs. He wasn't losing her. He and Laurel weren't losing her. Nothing else mattered.

The conversation continued with Cash finally able to relax. They all agreed Phoebe should take off from January fourth through the eleventh, their slowest week of the month. After that, they'd be diving into the Valentine's Day wedding rush, and she'd be indispensable.

Cash reiterated that he'd be returning every weekend and Georgia Ann could increase her hours. The call ended on a positive note. Laurel's VIP job was going well and generating potential new business. Everything was under control at Wishing Well Springs. Phoebe wasn't quitting. Cash's world had righted and was spinning nicely on its axis. He could concentrate on work and gearing up for the start of construction.

He and Phoebe retreated to their respective desks. She took the phone off automatic answering and listened to the voice mail messages that had been left while they were on the video chat with Laurel. Cash tackled the payables and moved money from savings to checking via the bank's website. He heard Phoebe talking in the background but didn't pay much attention.

"Cash, you busy?" she asked a short time later.

He paused in the middle of entering expenses into a spreadsheet. "What do you need?"

"Not me. The Brooks-Diaz bride. I have her on hold."

He thought a moment. That was the couple getting married tonight in the small, no-frills ceremony. He gave them credit for not spending a fortune. Phoebe had said the bride and groom had both been previously married and wanted something different. Whatever the reason, Cash approved of keeping costs at a minimum.

"Yeah?"

"She knows it's late notice but wondered if they could use one of the horses in their photos. Apparently, her little boy just loves horses and is going through a cowboy phase. Do you have time to get either Elvis or Otis ready and to the barn by five thirty?"

Cash glanced at his watch and mentally reviewed his tasks for the day. If he didn't run into a problem, he'd be able to quit by four, leaving him plenty of time.

"Tell her sure thing."

"She said she'd pay extra."

"Charge her the regular rate." The goodwill would no doubt result in a referral or two.

"Thank you, Cash." Phoebe returned to her call.

He liked the warm quality of her voice when she said his name. That had been missing these last four days.

When she ended her call with the Brooks-Diaz bride, he said, "Just so you know, I'm glad you're staying on. Though I would have understood if you'd left."

"I'm glad I'm staying, too."

He stared at the partition separating his desk from hers, wishing he could see her face. Her warm tone hadn't revealed enough. Maybe her expression would. He considered concocting an excuse to get up, only to change his mind. They were on an even keel again. Better to not take any chances.

Work passed quickly for the next three

hours. Twice Phoebe had to leave and meet one of Laurel's clients in Bellissima. One had brought in photos of her grandmother's wedding dress for Laurel to look at, and the other had dropped off a pair of shoes needing to be dyed.

Cash answered the phones while Phoebe was occupied. He also snuck in a few of his own calls—to Lexi about the reclaimed material at Mountainside Building Supply, another to Burle about his cabin, and the last to the feed store. He also returned a call from Marguerite, his boss at Strategic Design, regarding the Horizon Bank Tower project. When he was done, he reclined in his chair, stretched out his legs and clasped his hands behind his neck. These periodic breaks from wedding stuff lifted his spirits.

He stopped at Phoebe's desk on his way out and waited for her to remove her earbuds. "I'm heading to the paddock. You okay holding down the fort while I'm gone?"

"Nothing I haven't done before."

He noticed her computer browser was open to the website of their favorite party supplier. "New tablecloths?"

"I'm not buying anything. Just checking prices."

"Kind of like you were checking prices on reupholstering the furniture?"

"Our tablecloths are getting dingy. We have the big vow renewal ceremony and secret-couple wedding coming up. Two important events. And the mayor's daughter from Palm Springs is visiting."

"The mayor's daughter isn't getting married until October. And you don't know that the bride and groom are A-listers. They could be D-listers or nobodies."

"Would nobodies have us sign nondisclosure agreements?"

Phoebe had been gushing about this wedding for over a month, ever since the secret couple's personal assistant had booked Wishing Well Springs for their wedding. Every precaution was being taken to ensure there were no paparazzi there to spoil the nuptials. Cash, Phoebe and Laurel had even been required to sign NDAs. After the brief ceremony, the newlyweds would be whisked away with minimal fanfare.

Because Phoebe was acting like a starstruck teenager, Cash liked giving her a hard time. He was increasingly convinced the couple were complete unknowns or, at the most, minor celebrities. It wasn't like Brad Pitt or Taylor Swift was going to emerge from the limo. They'd be getting hitched on some private tropical island or at a château in France. Not a wedding ranch in Payson, Arizona.

He opened his mouth to warn her about keeping costs down and changed his mind. Why spoil what had so far been a good day? Let her have her fun looking at new table-cloths.

At the paddock, he readied both Otis and Elvis for the photo shoot. The old pair did everything together and hated being separated. The bride could choose whichever horse she wanted for the pictures, or both. Cash didn't care.

While he was grooming them, Georgia Ann came by to confirm the time and ask if he needed help. She offered to weave red and green ribbons into the horses' manes and tails, something she accomplished while Cash polished hooves.

Georgia Ann stood back to inspect their combined efforts when they were done. "Pretty handsome for a couple of old men."

"Not bad."

"I told Phoebe I'd pick her up at the house and drive her to the barn." Georgia Ann had been using the golf cart to transport supplies between the house and barn.

"Go on. I'll see you there."

Otis and Elvis might have been big, but walking them was akin to a leisurely stroll with a pair of well-trained dogs. Cash changed into his warmer jacket before heading up the road with them, a lead rope in each hand.

It was dark by the time they reached the barn. He tied the horses to a hitching rail built in his great-grandfather's days. He was securing the last knot when a small caravan of vehicles appeared. The wedding party had arrived.

Someone inside the barn flipped on the exterior lights, momentarily blinding Cash. For that reason, he couldn't quite make out the face of the woman approaching. She must be the bride, given her long gown and the little boy accompanying her.

When she got close enough and his eyes had adjusted, he started to speak—only to have the words shrivel on his tongue. Shock rendered him motionless. He could only stand there and stare.

"Hannah?" he finally managed to croak. "Is that you?"

"Cash? I…didn't… Oh my God!" All color drained from her face.

A normal reaction for someone who'd just come face-to-face with their former fiancé.

"Look, Mommy." The little boy stared up

at Hannah and then pointed a finger at Cash. "Cowboy."

"Yes, a cowboy," she said, and then started to sway.

PHOEBE MADE A visual sweep of the barn's interior. Not a chair out of place. Not a brown poinsettia leaf in sight. Granted, the Christmas tree had passed its point of peak freshness—another trip to the nursery was in her near future—but it wasn't so dried out anyone would notice in the dim candlelight. Twenty guests would be attending tonight's wedding. Each one of them would be carrying a candle, the only illumination other than the candles on the altar table.

Very romantic. Phoebe couldn't wait to see the effect. And so appropriate for an intimate holiday wedding. She'd heard the groom would be wearing a dark green suit and the bride a red dress. Wasn't the color red considered good luck in some cultures? She'd also be carrying a small bouquet made from evergreens. A lovely added detail, and Phoebe approved.

Satisfied all was in order, she started across the room. As she passed the open door, she spotted Cash with the horses by the hitching post. He'd brought both Elvis and Otis—she should have seen that coming. The old horses were connected at the hip; one didn't go anywhere without the other.

Phoebe smiled. Her worries had eased a little during the phone call with Laurel earlier. She'd hated postponing telling her best friend about her pregnant sister's serious health condition. Under any other circumstances, Laurel would have been Phoebe's go-to confidante and sounding board.

Staying on at Wishing Well Springs was the best decision, though she'd debated the pros and cons for days—Cash being one of the cons. Even though they'd agreed their first kiss would also be their last, it still wasn't easy working alongside him. Knowing what it was like to be held in his strong arms and have his lips take possession of hers had only increased her feelings for him.

In the end, though, she'd chosen to stay. She'd made a commitment to both Cash and Laurel. If she left, she wouldn't be just an employee quitting, she'd be severing a successful partnership. A move that could put Wishing Well Springs in jeopardy. Not to toot her own horn, but replacing her would be no minor task.

Perhaps most important, she loved her job. She'd grown up at the inn and wouldn't loathe replacing Trudy. But neither would she experience the satisfaction and pure happiness she got from being a wedding coordinator. Every morning Phoebe walked into the office excited about the day ahead. Giving that up wouldn't have been easy. Trudy understood, and had encouraged Phoebe to follow her heart.

She was searching for the butane torch to light the candles when she once more passed by the open barn door. Oh good, she thought, the wedding party had arrived. The bride and her son were with Cash and the horses, the two adults talking.

Phoebe peered past them. Where was the photographer and why weren't they taking pictures? That was the whole purpose of having the horses there.

Maybe they hadn't started yet. Except... She halted. Was Cash frowning? Yes, and the bride looked poised to flee.

Marching forward, Phoebe stopped short when Cash spotted her and shook his head. Really? What the heck? She considered disregarding his warning only to think better of it. He wouldn't indicate for her to stay away without good reason. They were probably discussing photos of the horses. What other explanation could there be?

The crew had already left, save Georgia Ann, who was in the storage area prepping for tomorrow's wedding. No one from Wishing Well Springs, other than Phoebe, was a witness to this peculiar drama between Cash and the bride unfolding.

None of the guests was around, either. They and the groom lingered by the vehicles. Were they giving Cash and the bride some privacy? If so, why?

Phoebe ducked behind the door, continuing to discreetly watch. She was good at interpreting body language and the subtle dynamics between couples, if she did say so herself. It was a skill she'd honed and one that helped her excel at her job. She didn't have to be an expert to see something was off between Cash and the bride. *Way* off. This was no thanks-for-bringing-the-horses conversation.

He gripped the hitching post with such force, his entire arm bowed. His shoulders hunched forward, not in interest but defense. For her part, the bride had plastered her son close to her side, almost like a buffer. Her glance darted nervously around.

What in the world was going on? If Phoebe didn't know better, she'd say the bride and Cash were previously acquainted and having a disagreement.

The bride. Whose name was... Hannah!

Phoebe shoved her fingers into her hair, her

mind a sudden whirl. It couldn't be. Hannah, as in Cash's former fiancée? No. Impossible! Cash had checked all the upcoming weddings through March, half seriously, half in jest, after running into Melanie. None of the brides had the last names of his other two fiancées.

Realization dawned, shocking Phoebe to her core. This was the *second* wedding for both the bride and groom! They'd mentioned as much several times, and it had factored heavily into their plans.

My God! The bride *was* Cash's former fiancée. There could be no other explanation for their strained and highly charged conversation.

Phoebe gnawed her lower lip. Should she interrupt them with a fake problem? Leave them alone to talk it out? Call Cash on his cell, giving him an excuse to escape if he wanted one? Call Hannah?

He appeared upset, yes. On closer inspection, however, he wasn't anxious to bolt. Whatever they were discussing, while difficult, might also be necessary. Maybe they were finally clearing the air. Or maybe Phoebe was entirely wrong about the woman being Cash's former fiancée.

Nope. This was Hannah. *His* Hannah. Who else could she be?

Phoebe made a mental note to check the

brides' names for all their upcoming weddings, searching for Cash's third fiancée. Except she'd personally booked every wedding herself. There was no bride named Silver.

Was that her real name or a stage name? She should ask Cash. Silly as it sounded, they couldn't be too careful. Not after tonight.

The boy must have grown restless, for he suddenly started tugging on his mother's hand and shouting, "Horsies, horsies. Want up, Mommy."

After a brief back-and-forth, Cash lifted the boy onto Otis's back and instructed him how to hold on. A middle-aged man emerged from the wedding party and wandered over. The photographer, given the camera bag slung over his shoulder. A discussion then ensued, presumably about the pictures.

All at once the groom strode forward. Frankly, Phoebe was stunned he'd waited this long. She was even more stunned when the bride—Hannah—gestured in a direction away from the barn and indicated for them to go.

Cash brought Otis, the boy still on the horse's back, his mom walking along beside her son, and followed in the direction Hannah had pointed, leaving Elvis tied to the hitching rail. Phoebe gawked at them, openmouthed, as the photographer went along. Just them. Not the groom or anyone else.

She heard Hannah say to her fiancé, "We won't be long," and saw her offer him a wobbly smile.

The man frowned, clearly not liking what was happening but choosing to avoid a scene.

Phoebe would give anything to follow them. She couldn't; she had no reason. And in Cash's current mood, he would doubtless not take kindly to her interference.

But, oh, she wanted to hear what was being said between them. Like the groom and the rest of the wedding party, she was simply going to have to wait.

CHAPTER NINE

THE CHILLY NIGHT air seeped through Cash's jacket as if it were made of gauze rather than heavy cotton. Then again, it might not be the weather affecting him but rather his companion and her less than enthusiastic response to seeing him.

Why orchestrate this semiprivate meeting with him, then?

"Are you cold?" he asked Hannah as they walked.

There'd been a time he would have put his arm around her and drawn her close. But not now, not when she was about to say "I do" to another man. In Cash's wedding barn of all places.

He still couldn't believe it. Two of his former fiancées getting married in the same month right here! What were the odds?

"I'm fine." Hannah answered in a tone that conveyed, like him, she was anything but fine. "I hope you don't mind. I just had to get away from there. Give myself a minute to recover."

"Sure. No problem."

"Look, Mommy. I riding a horsie!"

"Yes, sweetums. You're a real cowboy."

The little boy grabbed Otis's mane between his chubby little fingers and grinned with excitement. The old horse didn't so much as blink, and he dropped his head when they at last reached the tree Hannah had picked out.

Standing several feet away, the photographer starting snapping pictures from various angles. Farther off, the rest of the wedding party waited, their eyes glued to Hannah and Cash. They had to be wondering what the heck was going on and why she'd insisted the groom remain behind.

Cash shifted uncomfortably. "Does he know who I am?" he asked in a low voice.

She shook her head, maintaining a forced all-is-well smile that she flashed the wedding party and photographer.

Cash didn't inquire about whether or not she planned on telling her fiancé about this *Twilight Zone* experience of theirs. How to explain that the man holding the horse in the wedding pictures with your son was your ex? Well, there was always photoshopping.

"I told Eddie I was engaged to someone briefly before my first husband." Hannah swallowed. "But I didn't tell him that the someone is you."

They kept their voices low so as not to be heard by either her son or the photographer.

"Did you know I co-own Wishing Well Springs?"

She hesitated before responding. "Yes."

"Then why get married here? It's a fair question," he said in response to her sharp glance.

"Eddie attended a friend's wedding here last spring. He really liked the place. I didn't have the heart to tell him no."

"You weren't worried about running into me?"

"I researched you. Dropped a few innocent questions to Phoebe when we met and reserved the barn. She mentioned you only come to Payson on weekends. I figured you wouldn't be here and that we'd be safe."

And, normally, she'd have been right. Still, Cash thought, she should have told her fiancé the truth. He might not like getting married at a venue belonging to his wife's ex. Cash wouldn't. And if the guy ever found out, Hannah would be caught in a lie. Not that Cash had any reason to care.

A thought hit him. Had Hannah wanted to run into him? Requested the horse and arranged the whole thing to spite him or to rub her new husband in his face? No, he decided. She wasn't like that.

Of his three fiancées, she'd been the most fun. The most adventurous and free-spirited. Had the best sense of humor and the biggest heart. While she'd wanted to go exploring and try new things, especially on the weekends, he'd had his nose perpetually pressed to the Strategic Design grindstone, chasing the elusive promotion that came too late for them.

She'd complained regularly about his fifty-to sixty-hour workweeks. Cash had to admit, whenever she'd managed to drag him away from the office, they'd had a blast. A trail ride in the Bradshaw Mountains. A trip to Vegas for the National Finals Rodeo. She'd once convinced him to take line dancing lessons.

Seeing Hannah tonight reminded him of those great times. Cash didn't think he'd relaxed and recreated once since then. Rather than strive for a promotion, these days he pressed his nose to the grindstone to grow Wishing Well Springs. His reasons were the same now as then: ensure a future free from financial worry and strife.

Come to think of it, Phoebe reminded him a little of Hannah in that regard. She also liked having fun and frequently accused him of not stopping to enjoy life's small moments. Was he really that bad?

"Let's get a few pictures with you, too," the photographer said, motioning to Hannah.

"Um…"

"Please, Mommy," her son cajoled.

"Go on." Cash unclipped Otis's lead rope and stepped back.

Hannah must have understood he was removing himself from the shot. She nodded her thanks.

"How about a few with the groom?" the photographer asked.

"We'd better get back." Hannah's eyes darted to and fro nervously. "We're late starting the wedding."

Cash reattached the lead rope to Otis's halter and walked slowly ahead. They had only a few minutes remaining to talk. He had so many questions, so much he wanted to say, but he wasn't sure where to begin.

"Giddy up!" the boy hollered and kicked Otis's side with his feet, which was no more annoying to the big horse than a large fly landing on him.

"Your son," Cash said. "He's cute."

"The only good and worthwhile thing my first husband ever did was give me Tyler. He left us six weeks after I gave birth."

"I'm sorry."

"It's okay. I'm happier now than I've ever been."

"Sounds like Eddie is a nice guy," Cash commented.

"He's wonderful. Not many men would be willing to take on a child who isn't theirs. He treats Tyler like his own, and Tyler adores him."

"I'm glad for you, Hannah." They were almost to the barn. Cash said what was weighing most heavily on his mind. "I sometimes wondered what might have happened with us if you'd been willing to hang in there until I got that promotion and saved enough money."

She stopped and stared at him. "That's not why I left."

"You said you were tired of waiting."

"No, I didn't. Maybe that's what you heard, but it's not what I said."

He shook his head. He'd been so sure.

"I was frustrated that you kept postponing the wedding—that much is true. And with your insistence that we needed more money for a house and a new car and a retirement account. Me? I'd have been happy with our little apartment and my old Honda."

"You should have told me."

"I did. More than once I accused you of worshiping the almighty dollar to the point of endangering our relationship. But I might as well have been talking to a brick wall."

Hadn't Melanie said something similar? She'd accused him of shutting down and closing her off. He'd apparently done the same with Melanie.

"Eventually," she said, "I realized we were too different and would never, ever, make a go of it. Not with you worshiping the almighty dollar like you did."

"Wow. I must have been awful."

"You treated having fun like it was a crime."

Her assessment of him stung. "I can't believe you didn't leave sooner."

"I needed more in my life than work and money, Cash. I told you that when I left."

Had she? He tried to remember.

"I'm sorry, Hannah. I messed up."

"Water under the bridge." She beamed a smile at her groom, this one genuine.

Cash reached for her son and lifted him down to the ground. The boy wasn't happy about his ride being over. Hannah took hold of his hand and started toward the wedding party waiting at the entrance to the barn.

"Good luck to you, Cash," she said over her shoulder. "I wish you the best."

"Congratulations, Hannah."

Cash doubted she'd heard him. She and her son were being welcomed into the fold of her fiancé, family and friends.

He noticed Phoebe standing over to the side and caught her worried look.

He had no intention of waiting around and watching any part of this wedding. His mind and heart were too full of conflicting emotions and jumbled memories he couldn't untangle. He hadn't been wrong to want to move up at Strategic Design. With the promotion, they wouldn't have found themselves in the same boat as his parents.

That wasn't what Hannah had implied. In her version of their shared history, he'd been razor-focused on getting ahead and blind to what she'd needed: a man able to strike a balance between work and play and willing to compromise on priorities.

Collecting Elvis from where he'd left him tied to the hitching rail, Cash started down the hill, a horse on each side. They didn't press him for information, which, in Cash's opinion, made them good company. He was in no mood to talk.

"Cash, slow down."

He turned his head to see Phoebe hurrying after him and groaned. What did she want?

Short of an earthquake, he wasn't returning to Hannah's wedding.

"Cash. Cash. Stop, will you?"

He did.

Phoebe reached him, huffing and puffing. "These boots are hard to run in."

He looked down. No one with a lick of sense wore boots with three-inch stiletto heels, much less completed a hundred-meter dash in them. She was a broken ankle waiting to happen.

"It's cold," he told her. "You should go back to the barn."

"Seen one wedding, seen them all."

Any other day, he'd have laughed at her joke. Tonight, his sense of humor had deserted him.

"This isn't a good time, Phoebe."

"The bride isn't by chance your former fiancée Hannah?"

"We're not having this discussion." He started walking. The horses, too.

"I'll take that as a yes."

"Leave me alone."

She hurried along beside him, hugging herself. No coat again. What was with her?

"That must have been strange, seeing her right before her wedding to someone else."

He said nothing.

"She has a son, huh? Bet that was even stranger."

If he wasn't wearing a cowboy hat, he'd have pulled out his hair. "I repeat, we're not discussing this."

"Okay. Sure. I understand." She was silent for six whole seconds. "You want me to lead one of the horses?"

Cash passed her Otis's lead rope. "What about the wedding? Don't you need to be there overseeing?"

"I put Georgia Ann in charge."

Cash considered that. "Does she know about me and Hannah?"

"No. I certainly didn't tell her. I don't think Hannah would. She's getting married. She's not about to start yapping with one of the venue crew about her former fiancé."

"Probably not." He felt some reassurance.

Phoebe patted Otis's nose when the horse nudged her arm. "Hannah being previously married would explain why her last name didn't ring a bell with you."

He nodded. "It would."

"I never met her before she and the groom toured the barn. That's why I didn't recognize her."

"No reason you would."

In the days when he and Hannah were dating, Cash had rarely come to Payson. He and Laurel had both worked in Phoenix, his mom had moved to Globe and his grandfather had been living with his aunt. And, as Hannah had pointed out, he'd been slaving away at Strategic Design.

"Do you think she knew you and Laurel own Wishing Well Springs?" Phoebe asked.

"She did. She told me."

"And she still chose to get married here?"

"The way she explained it, her husband attended a friend's wedding here and he really liked the place." *Husband* seemed like the right word. If Eddie and Hannah weren't married yet, they would be in a few minutes.

"Okay, but didn't she think she might run into you? Or, ooh…" Phoebe made a pained face. "Did she not tell her husband about you?"

Cash shrugged. "She admitted to researching me and asking you some questions. Apparently, she figured I'd be in Phoenix on a Wednesday."

"Whoops!"

"Yep, you can say that again."

His and Phoebe's breath came out in short frozen gusts, the horses' in long white streams. She must be freezing. What was with her and not wearing a coat?

Elvis crowded Cash, knocking him into Phoebe. He tried to move out of the way but couldn't. Elvis refused to budge. Was the horse some sort of matchmaker?

"Did you and Hannah hash things out by chance?" Phoebe asked. "Not that it's any of my business."

"Kind of." He turned to her. "Do you think I'm like Scrooge?"

"Scrooge? What gave you that idea? You're not miserly."

"Hannah said I worship the almighty dollar. I'm starting to think she's right." Admitting it out loud made the idea a little less scary.

Phoebe snorted. "Honestly, Cash, that's the silliest thing I've heard in a long time. You are conservative when it comes to spending, that's true. Not Scrooge, however."

"You called me a penny pincher."

"Did I?" She waved off his remark. "If I did, I'm sorry."

"You might be right."

"Does this mean I get to reupholster the furniture without having to cut costs?"

"Not a chance."

She laughed, the sound like music filling the space surrounding them. He wished he could be more carefree, find that balance between work and play, and stop worrying about repeating the same mistakes his grandfather and father had made.

Change was possible, he supposed. If he tried. If he worked at it. If he quit defining himself by his past failed relationships.

"Do you need help putting Elvis and Otis away?"

"Nah." He took in Phoebe's shivering form. "You should get back to the wedding."

"Georgia Ann will call me if there's a problem."

"Go inside, at least." They stopped in front of the main house. "Get warm. You're shivering."

"Are you going to be all right? You just ran into Hannah. Two former fiancées, actually, a week apart. That doesn't happen every day."

"It's been…different."

"Enlightening? Educating?"

"More like thought-provoking."

"Will we be seeing a new and improved Cash 2.0?"

"Don't count on it."

"Wouldn't it be something if your last fiancée showed up?"

"As luck would have it, she's in New York."

"You keep tabs on her?"

"Sometimes her face mocks me from the front of a tabloid at the grocery store checkout line."

"You ever buy a copy?"

He chuckled. "I really like you, Phoebe." The remark slipped out before he realized it.

"I really like you, too, Cash."

"Come on." He dropped the horses' lead ropes and took hold of her arm. "Let's get you in the house before you lose a few fingers to frostbite."

"What about Elvis and Otis?"

"If they go anywhere, it'll be back to the paddock."

Proving him right, the two old horses turned and ambled down the drive in the direction of the carriage house.

"See?" Cash led her up the porch steps to the door.

"You coming in?"

"I'm heading upstairs as soon as I put the horses away. I have an early morning and a taskmaster for a partner."

At the door, she pivoted to face him. "Do you think you'd get back together with any of your former fiancées, assuming they were single?"

"Trust me, those ships have sailed. And, as far as Melanie and Hannah are concerned, for the better. They're both newly married to great guys, by all appearances."

"Hannah's husband did seem nice. Really sweet with her little boy."

"I'm glad for her. It's hard to explain, but seeing her and Melanie doing well, it's helped me let go of the past a little."

"Just a little?"

"I feel better. More optimistic. Aware of my faults."

"Those are big steps forward."

"Let's not celebrate yet. I have a habit of regressing."

She scrunched in closer. He didn't back away. "Does this mean you might start dating again?"

"I might. If I met the right woman."

"What if the right woman is someone you've already met?"

An innocent inquiry? Or was she putting herself out there? Cash suddenly realized how much he wanted it to be the latter. His feelings for Phoebe had been gradually changing, and he was curious to see where this was leading.

"Do you have someone in mind?" he asked, forcing his tone to remain neutral.

"I'm cold," she murmured and leaned into him.

The contact triggered an electric shock. The addictive kind. "Phoebe."

"Are you going to put your arms around me or what?"

All right. That was a clear enough message. Even so, he hesitated.

"You told me to stay away, specifically not to kiss you again until I knew what I wanted and where we stood."

"Don't you? Know, I mean. I was listening to you on the walk here, and I heard someone who's open to possibilities. Am I wrong?" she asked when he took too long to answer.

"I'm thinking."

"Think faster before I freeze to death." She unwrapped her arms from her own waist and wound them around his.

"I'm not sure I can think at all with you holding me."

She sighed, hugging him tighter. The moment of truth had arrived. They either went no further or he committed.

"Casual," he said, folding her into his embrace. "One step at a time. There's a lot to consider. A lot of potential pitfalls."

"I've never known you to go slow."

"I don't want to screw up. I care about you too much." There, he'd said it.

"Thank you for not giving business and our partnership as the reason."

"You matter more."

She lifted her face to his, her lips slightly parted in what could only be described as an invitation. "Quit dillydallying, Cash, and kiss me. As long as you're in, we can work out the details later."

"I'm in." Who was he to argue? Besides, there wasn't anything he wanted more.

Cash soon forgot about putting the horses away, heading upstairs and that his former fiancée was a quarter mile away. Phoebe could do that to him. She had a way of communicating with soft caresses and tender kisses that demanded his full attention, which he gladly gave her.

CHAPTER TEN

PHOEBE EYED THE gaily wrapped Christmas present. She then bounced it in her hand, pondering the potential contents.

"Just open it, for crying out loud," one of the women servers complained.

Was she Phoebe's Secret Santa in the annual gift exchange? Possibly.

Every December, Phoebe's parents hosted a holiday breakfast party for all the employees. It was the only time all year the public dining room was closed and not serving guests.

Phoebe hadn't worked at the inn in well over two years, since becoming Cash and Laurel's business partner. She was still invited to the party, however, and participated in the Secret Santa gift exchange. Her parents insisted and, frankly, she loved the party. One of the dishwashers was her Secret Santa recipient, and she'd gotten him a pair of Rudolf socks and a battery-operated tie with flashing lights. Everyone had immediately guessed the gift was from her. Go figure.

Sensing a multitude of eyes on her, she picked at a corner of the wrapping paper. They weren't watching her in anticipation of opening her gift. Rather, they were curious about her plus-one. Two days after their kiss in front of the house, Phoebe and Cash were officially stepping out as a couple.

Her sisters had gone berserk at hearing the news. Trudy especially. Her parents had been more reserved, expressing reservations about Phoebe and Cash mixing business with pleasure, as her dad put it. She'd stressed that their relationship was very new and proceeding slowly. Trudy had declared that to be unromantic and said as much with a disdainful snort.

"Your audience is growing restless." Cash nodded at the present in her hands and flashed his boyish grin. The one that caused her to feel giddy and silly and go all gooey on the inside.

She could hardly believe they were dating. Not boyfriend and girlfriend. Too soon for that. Still, she'd been walking around in a dreamy haze the last two days, breaking into a huge, silly grin every time she saw him. At the nursery yesterday while buying a fresh tree and more poinsettia plants, he'd spontaneously kissed her beneath mistletoe. She'd almost burst into song.

"All right, all right. Cool your jets." Grinning at him, she tore open the wrapping paper and revealed a wallet phone charger. "This is so cool! Thank you, whoever gave this to me." She scanned the room with its nearly forty occupants, searching for a telltale expression. "I can really use this."

"Did it come with a lanyard?" her dad asked. "That way you can wear it around your neck alongside your phone."

The room erupted in laughter.

"I know you all think my phone obsession is hilarious, but I don't care. I love this." She held the charger to her cheek.

The next person took their turn, and the party continued. When the last gift was finally revealed, Phoebe's dad made his annual speech. He thanked the employees for their service and offered optimistic predictions for the coming year. Cash and Phoebe held hands beneath the table. A small tingle traveled up her arm when he stroked her fingers.

At the end of her dad's speech, Phoebe stood. "I'm going to talk to Trudy for a bit before we leave. You mind?"

"Go on. Have fun."

Her pregnant sister sat a few tables over, feet elevated and resting on the empty chair beside her. Phoebe would have preferred she'd stayed home this year, as her doctor had advised, but Trudy had insisted a short reprieve wouldn't hurt.

Phoebe's dad appeared beside her and grabbed the back of her chair. "I'll keep him company while you're gone."

She stared at him, suspicion brewing. "Do I have reason to worry?"

"Nonsense." Her dad gestured for her to move along.

"Hmm." Phoebe wavered, uncertainty eating at her.

"I'm not going to interrogate him. I swear." Her dad dropped down into the empty seat and scooted closer to Cash.

Phoebe placed a hand on his shoulder. "I apologize in advance for anything my dad says that's out of line or rude or intrusive."

He gave her hand a pat and winked. "It's okay. I can handle myself."

"Be nice, Dad," Phoebe warned before weaving through the tables to where Trudy sat.

"Can I drive you home?" Phoebe asked. She lifted Trudy's feet, sat in the chair, and then arranged them in her lap.

"Mom already volunteered. We're leaving in ten."

"Good. Promise me you'll go straight to bed."

Trudy leaned as close to Phoebe as her pregnant belly would allow. "You and Cash are so cute together. I'm glad you brought him."

"I can't believe he agreed." Phoebe frowned. "You don't think Dad's grilling him, do you?"

They stared at the two men, who seemed to be hitting it off.

"No." Trudy shook her head. "They're probably talking sports or the economy."

"Let's hope."

"What are you really worried about?"

"It's just that he and I…we're new. Really new. We don't have anything figured out yet. If Dad starts needling Cash, insisting he declare his intentions or whatever, I'll be mortified."

"He won't. He's not that bad." Trudy reached out and grabbed Phoebe's hand. "What about you? How are *you* feeling about the two of you?"

Phoebe couldn't help herself and went soft and gooey inside again. "Fantastic. Wonderful. Still in a state of shock."

"Where are you going on your first date?"

"We, um… He hasn't asked me yet."

"No? Oh dear."

Phoebe hurried to Cash's defense. "In all fairness, we have weddings every single day and most of those are in the evening. When would we go out?"

"Mmm." Trudy knit her brow disapprovingly. "He needs to get off the stick."

"Don't say anything to him." Phoebe pulled her hand away and leveled a finger at her sister. "Under any circumstances. I won't have you scaring him off."

"If he scares off that easily, he's not the right guy for you."

"I mean it, Trudy."

"Fine." She crossed her heart. "I promise not to ruin your newfound happiness. You're radiant, by the way."

Phoebe placed a palm to her warm cheek. "It seems unreal. All these years I've waited, hoping he would notice me."

"I'm really happy for you, sis. I bet Laurel is, too. What did she say when you told her? Did she squeal? Scream? Wish I'd been there to see it."

The heat instantly left Phoebe's cheeks and her radiance dimmed. Laurel's reaction had been the one negative so far. "Actually, she wasn't all that thrilled."

"What?" Trudy drew back in surprise. "How come?"

"She has concerns. She doesn't want to see either of us hurt if things don't work out."

"I understand. Mom and Dad have the same

concerns. But she's your best friend and Cash is her brother. She should be more supportive."

"She's under a lot of stress right now. This VIP client in Palm Springs is very demanding, and we have a lot riding on the outcome." Phoebe shrugged. "And she's not wrong to be concerned. Cash and I mixing business and a personal relationship could affect Wishing Well Springs for the worse if things don't work out."

"And for the better if they do!"

Her sister, ever the optimist. "We'll see. We're still in the early stages."

The room had nearly emptied while Phoebe and her sister were chatting. She glanced at the time on her phone and gave a small gasp. "We'd better hurry. The office was supposed to open fifteen minutes ago." She jumped out of the chair and bent to give her sister a peck on the cheek. "I'll call you later."

To her vast relief, Cash and her dad were discussing business and apparently agreeing, given their amiable tones.

"Sorry, Dad, but I need to steal him from you."

"Yeah, I suppose it's that time. Duty calls."

Cash rose and shook her dad's hand. "Nice talking with you, Kent."

"Will we see you over the holidays? Our

New Year's Eve party is legendary in these parts."

Cash shot Phoebe a glance. "Count on it."

"Well, then." Her dad appeared to be mulling over his next remark.

Phoebe gritted her teeth in dread. He'd once told her ex, Sam, that he'd better take good care of his daughter.

"The wife and I are looking forward to it."

Whew! That was close.

After returning to the ranch, Cash gave her a swift, warm kiss before they went inside. Phoebe made fresh coffee while he retrieved the packages sitting outside the front door.

"What do we have?" he asked when she examined the labels.

"Supplies Laurel ordered and candles for the barn. I bought them in bulk."

"I approve."

He got right on his latest task the moment they sat at their desks, having taken the lead on the big, upcoming family reunion. Phoebe checked the voice mail messages, returned calls and replied to emails.

One happened to be from the personal assistant to the secret couple. She was inquiring about a back entrance to the barn.

Phoebe read the email out loud to Cash. "Isn't this a bit overboard?"

"I've thought that from the beginning."

"I think the bride is Senator Michaels's daughter," she said, naming one of Arizona's most prominent politicians.

"Isn't he the one making a lot of enemies in Washington because of his stance on government spending?"

"Yes, but that wouldn't be the reason for all the secrecy. His daughter's engaged to that European royal. The guy's only eighth in line to the throne, but it's a big deal nonetheless."

"Only eighth?" Cash said teasingly.

Phoebe stared at the cubical wall separating them as if she could see through it. "You're missing the point. Imagine what it'll mean for Wishing Well Springs if we can say we hosted a royal wedding."

"But we can't."

"Six months from now we can, when the nondisclosure agreement expires."

She spent the next hour prepping for tonight's wedding. A little before noon, she heard Cash rise from his desk. His arms appeared over the top of the cubicle as he stretched and, from the sound of it, yawned.

"I'm heading out for lunch."

"Oh. You are?" she said flatly.

He came out from behind the cubical wall. "What's wrong?"

"I was hoping to leave for a while. I need a break." She rolled her stiff shoulders.

"Come with me. You don't have any appointments."

He was right. While her calendar had been filled the first half of the month and she'd be busy again starting in mid January, most couples, it seemed, were too busy with holiday activities to view venues and book weddings.

"Are you asking me to lunch?" She couldn't keep the note of expectation from her voice.

"I'd like nothing more than to take you to lunch. Today I'm just grabbing some fast food on the way."

"To where?"

"I'm meeting Channing and his dad at their cabin. We're conducting a walk-through."

Not a lunch date. And Phoebe detested most fast food. But the alternative was staying here all by her lonesome and feeling sorry for herself.

"Let me grab my purse and shawl."

"We're not eating in the truck, are we?" Phoebe made a face.

That was precisely what Cash had been planning. At her expression of sheer horror, he changed direction, heading away from the drive-through lane at the fast-food restaurant and toward the parking area.

Climbing out, he went around to open the truck door for her, but she was already on the ground and straightening the enormous wrap thing she'd called a shawl. Thick and fluffy, it practically swallowed her.

He hoped she'd continue wearing it inside the restaurant. If not, he and all the other customers would be forced to stare at Rudolf's flashing red nose. No wonder everyone at the holiday party this morning had correctly guessed she was the dishwasher's Secret Santa. Her sweater matched his socks and battery-operated tie.

To his surprise, he'd enjoyed himself. Her family, which he usually found loud and boisterous and exhausting, was actually a lot of fun. He'd always liked her dad, and the two of them had gotten along well. If the older man had any reservations about Cash and his youngest daughter dating, he'd refrained from expressing them.

At the food counter, Phoebe ordered a salad, the only item on the menu she deemed edible.

"No french fries?" he asked.

"Please."

"You don't know what you're missing."

They ate quickly, Cash explaining that he'd

agreed to meet Channing and his dad at twelve thirty. She gawked as he polished off a double cheeseburger in six bites and demolished a side of fries.

"I work hard," he mumbled while chewing.

She speared one of those little tomatoes with her fork. "It's a wonder your arteries haven't completely clogged and your heart hasn't stopped."

"My heart's too cold and hardened to clog."

"You act all tough, Cash." She dabbed at the corner of his mouth with a napkin. "But in truth you have a soft spot."

"Says who?"

"I've seen you with the horses and that stray cat."

"Stubby isn't a stray."

"I rest my case." She took another small bite. "For the record, I think it's cute."

"*A soft spot* and *cute*. You do realize you're killing my reputation."

"I promise not to tell. Your secret's safe with me."

He reached across the table for her hand and brought it to his lips. "Sharing secrets. I like it. Our first big step as a couple."

She laughed. "I thought that was us going together to the holiday party."

"Nah." He turned her hand over and kissed the inside of her wrist. "Secrets bind us."

"Cash." Phoebe inhaled softly. "That's the most romantic thing any man has ever said to me."

His phone pinged. He let go of her hand and almost missed the look of disappointment in Phoebe's eyes. Too late now.

"Sorry. It's from Channing." He read the text. "He and his dad are at the cabin. We should probably get going."

Conversation passed pleasantly enough on the drive to the cabin but lacked the intimacy from the restaurant. Just as well. Cash felt more comfortable being back in the safe zone. Yet a part of him had liked that brief foray into the dangerous territory of connecting with another person on a deep level. The last time he'd let a woman in, the last *three* times, he'd wound up hurt.

Channing and Burle were standing in the cabin's side yard when Cash and Phoebe pulled into the driveway. They'd been inspecting the brick chimney, which, even from a distance, appeared to be crumbling in places.

They greeted Phoebe as if they'd been expecting her all along, which Cash found interesting. He hadn't mentioned bringing her. Did the two of them give off a couple vibe?

Then again, Channing and Burle might have assumed Phoebe had tagged along simply because she and Cash worked together.

Once inside the cabin, he opened the folder he'd brought along and distributed the drawings and notes he'd made.

"In my opinion," he said while Channing and Burle read, "the structure is basically sound and the floor plan is functional with a few basic modifications."

He went on to explain how he'd increase the size of the kitchen and cramped bathroom, which were both sorely in need of updating and modernizing, by moving two walls.

"I've always liked the big living room," Burle commented. "Plenty of space to move around."

"If you look at the second drawing—" Cash pointed "—you'll see I'm suggesting you also tear down the wall separating the kitchen from the living room and build a breakfast bar. That'll open up the kitchen and give the illusion of space."

"I like it," Channing said.

They walked the cabin's interior, discussing each room and the changes Cash recommended. When possible, he'd included a less expensive option, though maybe not as nice or functional. Phoebe trailed along behind them, offering her opinion when asked for it.

The walk-through continued outside. Cash agreed that the chimney was indeed crumbling and required significant repair.

"It won't last another winter," he said. "And your well house isn't much more than a pile of rotted timber. Same for the porch."

"How much is all this going to cost us?" Burle asked.

"A better question might be how much are you willing to spend?" Cash countered. "Some work is necessary, like the chimney repair and porch. New flooring. Painting. Patching roof leaks. But you don't have to tear down the wall or enlarge the kitchen and bathroom."

"We have to make the cabin more appealing in order to attract renters."

They returned inside and resumed their conversation. There, on an old rickety table, Cash sketched out a few more drawings; less costly options for their consideration.

"I like this idea," Burle said when Cash suggested they use the discarded wooden planks from the well shed to construct planters in front of the cabin. "That'll really spruce up the place."

"Do you have any old material at the rodeo arena we can repurpose?"

"Possibly. Can you meet us there one day and have a look around?"

"Sure." At Phoebe's glance, Cash said, "Not till after the first of the year."

"No rush. We're all busy."

At their trucks, the men talked for a few more minutes, mostly about getting together for another calf roping session before the first pro rodeo of the new year in mid January. Phoebe checked her emails and called the office's voice mail system. There were no emergencies.

Burle shook Cash's hand. "You're mighty good at what you do."

"Appreciate you saying so."

"You could make a living at this if you wanted."

"I am making a living."

"Not them fancy, highfalutin office buildings. I'm talking about right here in Payson. Plenty of old houses and cabins and barns people are looking to remodel or convert into luxury homes."

"Appealing as that sounds, I've got more than enough keeping me busy with starting construction on the mock Western town."

"Just saying, if you're ever looking for a career change."

Did the older man have any idea how much

Cash had been considering that very subject lately? But if he quit his well-paying job at Strategic Design, he'd have no money for the expansion.

"Maybe one of these days."

This time he beat Phoebe to the passenger door and opened it for her.

"Thanks." She smiled when he helped her up onto the running board and into her seat.

"You had some good input back there."

"It was interesting."

"I figured you'd be bored." He swung the truck onto the road.

"Not in the least."

Cash decided he was getting used to having her in the passenger seat beside him. No, more than that—he liked it. She looked good sitting there, as if she belonged.

"I enjoyed seeing you in action."

He chuckled. "You see me in action every day."

"At Wishing Well Springs and rodeoing back in the day. Your other life… Cash the architect? That's new to me. Your drawings, your expertise, it's impressive."

"You were around—" He stopped himself. He'd been about to say she'd been around when he'd renovated the barn and the main house. Except she hadn't been. She'd dropped by occasionally to check on the progress, as Laurel's friend and an observer. They hadn't started talking partnership until construction was nearing completion. "There you go again," he joked. "Feeding my ego."

"You are good, Cash. And Burle was right. You could make a living here if you wanted."

"I'm not ready to leave Strategic Design."

"I get that. Starting a new business, it's a little scary."

"It is. Been there, done that."

But with Wishing Well Springs, he'd had his sister and then Phoebe. The burden hadn't been his alone to bear. Plus, he and Laurel already owned the property. Starting an architectural practice was entirely different. He'd be responsible for funding start-up costs and building a clientele base from scratch. No one else. If he failed, he'd suffer the same shame as when his family had filed for bankruptcy. Cash didn't think he could go through that again.

At the house, he parked next to Phoebe's car in the garage. "I'll be right in," he told her. "I want to see how Otis is doing. His eye wasn't looking good this morning. I'm worried he might have another infection." Last year, they'd spent months dealing with a recurring bout of equine conjunctivitis. "I may need to call the vet."

"I'll come with you," Phoebe said.

"What about work and the wedding later?"

"We'll need to hit the ground running when we get back."

"How unlike you," he teased as they walked hand in hand to the paddock. "Playing hooky again? Am I being a bad influence?"

"You're being an influence." She grinned up at him. "Not sure it's all bad."

At the paddock, Cash squeezed in through the gate while Phoebe waited on the other side of the fence. The old horses meandered over in search of a handout.

"Sorry, boys." Cash gave each of them a friendly pat. "Nothing until dinner."

Otis's eye wasn't any worse. Neither was it any better. Cash took out his phone and called the vet, who said he could stop by at six if that wasn't too late. Cash readily agreed.

"Mind if I'm a little late helping with the wedding tonight?" he asked Phoebe.

"Of course not."

Near the gate, he spotted the end of a horse-shoe sticking out of the dirt. Where had that come from? He bent, picking up the heavy weathered object.

"What's that?" Phoebe asked when he exited the gate.

Cash brushed off the horseshoe. Flecks of

dirt and particles of rust fell like rain. "I found it on the ground. I'm thinking I might clean it up and keep it."

"Why?"

"For luck."

She slipped an arm through his and snuggled up against him. "We don't need luck. We found each other."

Using his free hand, he cradled her cheek and kissed her. All these years, Phoebe had been right under his nose. What an idiot he'd been not to have noticed. Then again, timing was everything.

CHAPTER ELEVEN

"GOOD GRIEF, GIRL. Are you okay?" Phoebe held up her phone and stared at the screen.

In the last week, Laurel's appearance had drastically worsened. Phoebe couldn't recall the last time she'd seen her best friend's usually meticulously styled hair bound with a ratty scrunchie. Wrinkles crisscrossed her blouse. Wrinkles! And was that a food stain on her collar? As a fashion designer, Laurel endeavored to always look put together, a walking advertisement for her bridal shop.

"Are you coming down with a cold?" Phoebe asked.

"Just tired. And not sleeping well."

"You need a break. If you drop from exhaustion, you won't do anyone any good."

Laurel rubbed her eyes. "Five more days and I'll be done with the dresses. For better or worse—no wedding pun intended."

"We miss you and can't wait to have you home. And the dresses are gorgeous."

Laurel had been sending Phoebe photos on

a regular basis, chronicling her progress on the wedding gown and dresses.

"I have to run soon." Laurel's glance darted to the side, probably at a clock or the doorway. "But I need a favor from you first."

"Name it."

Phoebe sat at her desk, nursing her morning coffee. Cash had yet to wander into the office. He was probably tending Otis's infected eye and conversing with the cat. She smiled at the thought of that. Big, tough guy and his little kitty.

"Go to Bellissima and grab the Simmons dress for me," Laurel said. "It's hanging on the ready rack."

"I *love* that one." The pale yellow creation, an unusual color for weddings, was to die for. "What's going on?" Phoebe held the phone as she walked.

"The four graduating tiers in the back are similar to the ones on this dress. But I'm having trouble getting these tiers to lay correctly. I'm sure I'm missing something. I need you to model the dress for me. You and the bride are the same size."

"She's a lot taller than me."

"Use the mini platform in the alteration area. Change into the dress and call me back when you're ready. Lean the phone on the notions shelf so I can see you head to toe."

"Will do."

In Bellissima, Phoebe found the gown exactly where Laurel had said it would be. Ducking into the dressing room, she slipped out of her clothes and into the dress. Other than the train dragging on the floor, the gown fit like it was made for her. Phoebe couldn't help admiring herself in the mirror. She'd tried on wedding dresses before. Her sisters' when they'd gotten married, at their insistence and just for fun. And she occasionally helped Laurel when fittings were needed and the bride wasn't available. Like today.

Imagining herself at her own wedding wasn't hard. All Phoebe had to do was to close her eyes and she could see herself walking down the aisle, rows of poinsettias on each side, music filling the barn at Wishing Well Springs—because where else would she exchange vows? With each measured step, she drew closer and closer to the altar where…

Cash waited.

His face and form materialized as if she'd summoned him. Even though they weren't at that place yet in their relationship, there wasn't anyone else she wanted to marry except him.

He'd finally asked her out on a real date. Another dream of hers coming true. Last night, during one of their breaks from kissing, he'd shyly and very charmingly invited her to dinner tomorrow. The wedding would be over by three and the last guests gone by four at the latest. Phoebe had accepted his invitation on the spot and now couldn't wait.

If not for the increasing cold and impending snow, they might have stood outside for hours, kissing and canoodling. But eventually she'd gotten into her car and he'd climbed the stairs to the attic room. Phoebe had grinned foolishly the entire drive home.

Propping her phone on the notions shelf as Laurel had instructed, she clicked on the video call icon. As the phone rang, she gathered the long train in both hands and hopped onto the mini platform.

"Hi. Can you see me?" she asked loudly when Laurel answered.

"You're too close."

It required several attempts, adjusting the phone and moving the stool, before Laurel was satisfied.

"Now," she told Phoebe, "turn slowly around in a full circle. Be careful. Don't trip."

The word *stool* was misleading. Custom built, it was more of a small platform than a stool and easily three feet across.

When Phoebe had finished, Laurel said, "Again. And this time end with your back to me."

Phoebe took tiny steps, glad she'd thought to remove her clunky boots first.

Laurel made several more requests of Phoebe. Raise her arms over her head. Lift the sides of the gown to her knees. Sweep the train sideways. Get down off the stool and twirl as if dancing. She then requested Phoebe hold the phone behind her so that she could get a close-up of the tiers. That proved awkward and caused Phoebe's muscles to cramp.

"I think we're done," Laurel said in a weary voice.

"You sure you got everything you need?"

"I hope so."

"If not, call back." Phoebe was about to say goodbye when Laurel knocked her for a loop.

"I heard you and Cash are going out to dinner tomorrow."

"He told you?"

"He did."

The idea that Cash had shared the news of their impending date pleased Phoebe and relieved some of her anxieties.

"I was going to say something, I really was, but you've been busy and stressed."

"And you figured because I didn't exactly

throw a party when you broke the news, I'd be upset. I regret that, sweetie. I should have been excited for you and Cash. I am excited."

"You're also worried about us. With good reason." Rather than return to the dressing room, Phoebe took the phone with her to the viewing-slash-fitting area. Gathering the dress's long folds, she perched on the velvet love seat. "For the record, we're going really, really slow."

She thought of her and Cash's kissing session last night. That hadn't felt slow. The exact opposite of slow, in fact.

"There's nothing I want more for either of you than to be deliriously happy. I just wonder…is he ready? There's no denying Silver was a rebound."

"You think I'm a rebound from her? It's been a few years now."

"I don't. Absolutely not." Laurel hesitated and started again. "He hates admitting it, but he's had his share of heartache."

"Did he tell you about running into Melanie and Hannah?"

"Yeah." Laurel shook her head. "What are the odds?"

"I think he was able to get a new perspective of what led to their breakups and lot of closure. He seems in a better place now."

"I hope you're right."

Phoebe wished she heard more confidence in her friend's tone, but she pushed aside her disappointment. She reminded herself that Laurel's intentions were good and her worry came from a place of love.

The pep talk didn't have quite the desired effect, unfortunately. A small seed of doubt that hadn't been there before suddenly appeared and took root.

Were she and Cash rushing things? What if neither of them was in the best place right now for a relationship? His financial worries had contributed to all three of his broken engagements, and they were getting ready to start the expansion. He constantly fretted about funds and about whether they'd run out before the construction was complete.

On the other hand, she did want to marry and start a family in the not too distant future. He knew that. She refused to pretend otherwise because he might be scared off.

Putting the brakes on might be prudent, given his history. It wouldn't be easy, though. One look at Cash, and she tended to throw caution to the wind.

"Shoot," Laurel said and grabbed her phone, causing the picture of her to shake. "I'm late. Thanks again, sweetie."

"Me, too. I should be opening the office as we speak." Phoebe rose from the love seat, adjusting the train as she did.

"You're not mad at me?" Laurel asked.

"Never."

"You have the worst poker face."

"I'm not mad," Phoebe repeated. Later, when Laurel got home, they'd have a heart-to-heart. "I agree Cash and I have some challenges facing us, which is why we're not rushing."

"Frankly, I don't know what you see in him. He can be a pain in the butt."

"You say the same thing about me."

"You're right! Maybe you two *are* perfect for each other. Life won't be boring, that's for sure."

They said their goodbyes and disconnected. Phoebe headed for the dressing room where her clothes waited. Today's Christmas sweater was one of her favorites, an Advent calendar with little toys behind each door.

She didn't quite make it there, however. Wanting one last look at herself in the dress, she dragged the stool over to the three-way mirror. Climbing on, she rearranged the train so that it stretched out to the side like a shimmering yellow river.

Personally, she'd prefer a white gown. While the color of this one was gorgeous, Phoebe was a traditionalist when it came to weddings. She did adore the style, however. Tiny cap sleeves that fell slightly off the shoulder flattered her neck and décolletage. The snug-fitting bodice flared out into a voluminous bell-shaped skirt that emphasized her trim waist. With all the tiers in the back and the beading in the front, she felt like a princess.

Capturing her long, straight hair in her hands, she piled it into a haphazard bun on the top of her head. Should she wear her hair like that or down? She released the bun, and her hair tumbled down to cover her bare shoulders. Too straight, she mused. She'd need a body wave. That, or corkscrew tendrils framing her face.

She then swiveled her head side to side and examined her ears. Would Grandma Kellerman let her wear the pearl earrings and matching necklace Grandpa Kellerman had given her? That could be Phoebe's something borrowed. Or her something old. Then she could wear Trudy's lace petticoat as her something borrowed.

On another whim, Phoebe stepped off the stool, removed a short veil hanging on a nearby hook that Laurel often used to give brides an idea, and placed it on her head, adjusting the clips that held it in place. When she was done, she studied her reflection, her breath catching.

Even more than when she was modeling the dress for Laurel, Phoebe could picture herself walking down the aisle, a bouquet of white lilies in her hand, her stomach all aflutter. Joy—real, not imagined—bubbled up inside her and broke free. A huge smile spread across her face and her cheeks bloomed pink.

It could happen. It *would* happen. With Cash. She need only believe. Her time of waiting and longing was finally at an end. He wouldn't be like Sam, stringing her along for years only to disappoint her.

She angled her upper body and arched her back, posing for an imaginary photo.

"What are you doing?"

Phoebe jerked at the sound of Cash's voice behind her. Releasing a small gasp, her hands fluttered nervously. A charm from her holiday bracelet snagged the end of the veil, inadvertently pulling it askew.

"I, uh…" This was stupid. She'd done nothing wrong. Her fantasies were just that—fantasies. If he didn't like that she'd tried on a wedding dress…well, he'd have to get over it. "Laurel phoned. She's having trouble with the tiers on the gown she's making. She asked me to model this one for her. We had a video call so she could see the dress—we just finished."

"I see."

"I was having a little fun is all."

"Okay."

Phoebe collected the train and stepped down from the platform. She lifted the train and draped the bulk of it over her arm, then started back toward the dressing room. Her route took her right by Cash, but it couldn't be helped.

As she neared, he put out a hand to stop her. His fingers closed over her elbow, sending a mild tremor shooting through her. "Wait. You're going to lose this." He plucked the veil from her head and returned it to her.

"Right. Thanks." She pressed it close against her middle. "Honestly, Cash. Laurel needed my help. You can ask her if you don't believe me."

"I believe you." His dark eyes didn't dispute her. Neither did they reveal anything.

"Girls will be girls. Even adult ones like to play dress-up and pretend." Why did she feel such a need to defend herself?

His expression softened the tiniest degree. "You make a beautiful bride, Phoebe."

"Um, thanks." Flummoxed by his remark— what did he mean by it exactly?—she escaped to the dressing room and stayed there longer than was necessary to change clothes. When she eventually reappeared, Cash was gone.

Crossing the entryway separating Bellissima from the business office, she realized he was on the phone and, from the sounds of it, ordering building material for the expansion. Nothing out of the ordinary there.

Settling in her desk chair, she willed herself to relax and powered up her computer. Sensing a shadow fall over her, she looked up and her heart leaped. Cash stood there staring down at her.

"Phoebe."

"The dress. It was no big deal. I promise."

"Not that."

"Oh."

"I'm glad we're giving us a try," he said. "I do want to see where we go. But, to be clear, I'm not ready for marriage. I'm not ready to get serious yet, either."

"I get it. You've said as much. But let me be clear, too. I want us to go somewhere. That's important to me. It's necessary. Slow is fine, as long as we're moving forward in the direction of a commitment."

He nodded. "All right. I just wanted to be sure you're fine with being patient awhile."

"I am."

She watched him return to his desk. What she'd wanted to ask was, what was his definition of a little while? A few weeks? A few months? Her ex, Sam, hadn't been ready to get married after three years. Phoebe couldn't—wouldn't—wait that long again. Not even for Cash.

PAYSON MAY HAVE A population nearing sixteen thousand people, a number that was growing every day, but many still considered it a small town. Proof of that: the selection of upscale restaurants open on a Sunday evening was limited.

Cash had spent considerable time debating where to take Phoebe for dinner. Her parents' inn had great food and service, but that wasn't his first choice. He happened to know she liked Chinese food. A table at the busy all-you-can-eat buffet didn't appeal to him, either.

He'd finally settled on the Longhorn Steak House. No, she probably wouldn't order a steak. But he'd gone online and read the menu. There were some fish and seafood and salad options that should, hopefully, satisfy her non-beef palate. And the quiet, cozy booths offered a comfortable setting where they could converse without her family hovering nearby or be forced to talk loud to be heard over the noisy commotion of hungry buffet diners.

Their first date. The thought caused his stomach to constrict with excitement and, he had to admit, unease. Until yesterday morning, he'd been eagerly anticipating their outing.

Then he'd caught Phoebe trying on the wedding dress. Yeah, she'd had an excuse—she'd been helping Laurel. But then, by her own admission, she'd been imagining herself as a bride. Marrying him? Possibly.

Cash knew what that glittering smile and those star-spangled eyes meant. His three former fiancées had all worn the same expression when they'd tried on dresses or pored over bridal magazines or perused wedding websites. Of course, they'd been engaged to Cash at the time. He and Phoebe hadn't yet gone out. Running errands together and grabbing a quick bite at a fast-food restaurant didn't count.

Holding his disposable razor beneath the bathroom faucet's thin stream—the water pressure in the attic room was next to nonexistent— he tapped the razor on the side of the sink and finished shaving. Toweling his face dry, he evaluated his reflection in the small mirror.

No nicks. No cuts. No red rashes. He supposed he'd do in a pinch.

Opening the tiny closet door, he selected the best Western dress shirt from the clothes he'd brought with him from Phoenix and slipped it on over his T-shirt. Next, he sat on the bed and tugged on his cowboy boots. On his way out the door, he plucked his Stetson off the dresser.

It occurred to him on the drive to Phoebe's

that he'd never been to her place before. He knew her address; it was listed on their business paperwork and her payroll records. And he had a general idea of the location. But it wasn't until his phone's GPS system announced he'd arrived at his destination that Cash realized this was his first visit to Payson's newest town-house community.

He suffered an attack of first-date nerves on his stroll up the neatly appointed walkway, which wasn't like him. The knock on her door echoed inside his hollow stomach. That wasn't like him, either.

Was he making too much of her modeling the wedding dress? Jumping to the wrong conclusions? Phoebe had assured him she was willing to go at a slower pace. That should be good enough for him.

The door suddenly swung open. Cash's train of thought completely derailed and the nerves he'd been struggling to control started short-circuiting.

"You, ah…" He drank in the sight of her. "Wow!"

She glanced down at her dress. Fiery red and clingy, it emphasized her lovely figure. "Too much? I could change."

Too much? Heck no. Cash wanted more. Lots more. "You look nice." Heck, she was a knockout. Funny how seeing her in a wedding dress triggered one reaction and seeing her in a red cocktail dress triggered an entirely different one. "I've never seen you..."

"In something other than work clothes?"

"Without a phone dangling from your neck."

She laughed, vanishing the tension from the last day. "Come on in while I grab my coat and purse."

Cash removed his Stetson and stepped over the threshold. She shut the door behind him. While she disappeared down the hall, he surveyed the living room.

Phoebe's good eye when it came to decorating and designing for weddings was equally apparent in her home. The large, bold, colorful prints on the walls complemented the comfortable furniture and fieldstone fireplace. From what he could see of the kitchen through the entryway, her tastes ran to the modern and eloquent.

"You like to cook?" he asked when she joined him. There seemed to be a plethora of pots and utensils hanging from hooks in the kitchen.

"I do!"

"Are you any good?"

"Are you wheedling an invitation?"

"I'm a guy who lives alone. I'm always wheedling invitations. Speaking of which..."

"Yes?" She locked the front door behind them.

"My mom called today about Christmas dinner."

"How is she?"

"Fine. She mentioned I could bring a plus-one."

"She did?" Phoebe's eyes shone. "You have anyone in mind?"

"I talked to Georgia Ann, but she's busy."

"Cash!"

He grinned, loving their easy banter. "Phoebe Kellerman, will you come to my mom's Christmas dinner with me?"

She kissed him on the lips. "Yes, I will."

They walked to where he'd parked his truck, and Cash opened her door.

"My family always meets early at the folks' house on Christmas," she said, settling into the passenger seat. "Mom makes a big breakfast, and we exchange gifts. Then it's off to work. No holidays off for people in the restaurant and wedding businesses."

She crossed her legs and the ankle-length coat opened to reveal her spectacular gams. Cash glanced away from the road, momentarily distracted. Defying the cold and the light snow earlier today, she'd ditched her heavy tights and worn some sort of sheer hose. On her feet were a pair of red shoes that made him picture her kicking them off as they sat snuggled together on her couch in front of her fireplace.

"Christmas Day dinner is a big deal at the inn," she continued. "There aren't many restaurants open and serving a traditional holiday meal. Reservations are booked weeks in advance, and there's always a long wait list."

"But you *are* free later in the day?"

"You sure you want me to be there?" Her tone had changed, becoming cautious. "Christmas dinner is a big step."

He reached across the console for her hand and pressed it to his lips. "Please come to my mom's Christmas dinner. It would mean a lot to me."

"We have the vow renewal in the afternoon that day. We won't be free until early evening."

"Mom'll postpone serving dinner till then. She understands."

"All right." She smiled.

He did, too. A family dinner was a big step, one he was willing to take.

Their evening at the Longhorn went better than Cash had expected. He and Phoebe steered clear of hot-button topics like work expenses and past relationships. He told her about his latest reclaimed-material find—Lexi had located iron bars from an old property outside of Green Valley that they could use for the mock jail. Phoebe updated him on her sister's health. While Trudy was going stir-crazy from constant bed rest, the doctor was cautiously optimistic with her progress.

They split a dessert at the end of the meal, caramel cheesecake, and fed each other bites. Phoebe kissed away a stray crumb on the corner of his mouth. He tucked a strand of hair behind her ear and then nuzzled her neck. Whatever floral scent she wore was fast becoming his new favorite scent.

When they were done eating and the tab was settled, Cash helped her into her coat. On the walk to his truck, they linked fingers.

"You in the mood for a drive?" he asked when they were sitting at the parking lot exit.

During dinner, his mind had traveled more than once to that image of him and Phoebe snuggling on her couch. He wasn't going to suggest it, however. But if she did, he'd agree in a heartbeat.

"A drive?" Her eyes widened with interest and she leaned in. "That sounds romantic."

"Could be. I hope so."

"Where to?" she asked.

He leaned over and stole a quick peck. "You'll see."

CHAPTER TWELVE

"THE BARN? SERIOUSLY?" Phoebe affected a playful pout when she and Cash pulled into the driveway to Wishing Well Springs and took the right fork. She was thrilled to be anywhere with Cash. That said, when he'd suggested a drive, she'd been thinking more along the lines of up the mountain to Scout Pass or to Christopher Creek and back. Both offered spectacular night views. "That's not very romantic."

"I thought we could walk up the hill behind the barn."

"Ooh. Now we're talking."

They parked in front of the barn in the spot usually reserved for the golf cart. When Cash reached for her hand, she took the initiative and slipped her arm around his waist. He, in turn, slung an arm around her shoulders and pulled her close. Yes. Much better.

The hill separated Wishing Well Springs from Phoebe's parents' inn and could be reached from either side by well-traveled foot trails. Couples often used the setting for wedding and, on occasion, engagement photos. Not so much in winter because the trees were bare. Though, after this morning's light storm, the snow-covered ground would provide a lovely background.

"You okay in those shoes?" Cash asked when they started up the trail.

"It's not far."

"I'd hate for you to break a heel and for me to have to carry you."

"Is that so?" She flashed him a mischievous smile. "Because I wouldn't hate that at all." And any scuffs her shoes sustained would be so worth it.

As they continued, they listened to the hoots of owls, the soft hum of distant traffic and the crunch of stones beneath their feet. Phoebe sighed to herself, glad the tension from yesterday had dissipated. It had been as she'd said—trying on wedding gowns was something women did. She hadn't necessarily been picturing Cash as her groom.

Except, well, she had been picturing him, and he'd probably surmised as much.

A small dark shape appeared from between the branches overhead and swooped past them, close enough that Phoebe felt a breeze on her cheek. Startled, she let out a high-pitched squawk.

"What kind of bird was that?"

Cash peered at the night sky in the direction the creature had flown. "Not a bird, a bat."

She drew up short and grabbed his arm, using it as a protective barrier. "Tell me you're kidding."

"You're afraid of bats?"

"Not afraid. I'm wary. They carry diseases, like rabies."

"Some. Less than one percent. Out here, you're more likely to contract rabies from an infected raccoon."

Hearing a rustling in the brush, she jumped. "Thanks. I feel much safer now."

"Bats are beneficial animals. They keep the insect population under control and pollinate plants."

"They're icky."

"I disagree." He stopped and pulled her into his arms. "In my opinion, they provide one very good benefit."

She nestled into him. "What's that?"

"They give me a reason to do this."

Cash brought his mouth down to hers. Phoebe had anticipated his move and was ready, her lips slightly parted in invitation and her arms raised.

The kiss was sweet at first and then escalated in intensity. Phoebe's grip around his neck tightened. Cash responded by lifting her off the ground and swinging her in a circle. Or was it her soaring emotions that made her feel like she was flying?

"I care about you, Phoebe," he said, setting set her down. "A lot."

"I care about you, too."

"And I'm glad you're coming to my mom's Christmas dinner."

That meant as much to her as him admitting he cared. "I wouldn't miss it for the world."

Smiling, he grabbed her hand, helping her along the uneven ground. Near the top of the hill, they were met by an unexpected sight. Coming to a halt, they looked at each other with surprise and, in Phoebe's case, a tingle of alarm.

They weren't alone. A couple stood beside a cluster of the hill's many Joshua trees. Phoebe stared, and her racing pulse slowed. The couple didn't appear dangerous. Nor did they seem aware of Phoebe and Cash, having eyes only for each other.

"I think someone had the same idea as us," she said in a low voice.

"Great minds think alike."

"Should we go?"

"I suppose. They were here first."

The couple stood facing each other, their heads bent, their foreheads touching and engrossed in conversation. Not kissing as Phoebe had initially assumed. She could hear the murmur of their voices.

A niggling sensation tickled the fringes of her mind. She'd watched this scene before. No, not that. Something else. But the familiarity couldn't be denied.

"Come on." Cash gave her arm a gentle tug.

"Right." She knew they should go. Before she walked two steps, recognition lit her memory like a light switched on. "Wait! I know them. Him. Her, too. Kind of." She spun around and squinted, attempting to bring the couple's features into focus. "That's Enrico. He works at the inn."

"The dishwasher? Your Secret Santa person?"

"Yes! And she's his girlfriend. I saw her dropping him off when I was at the inn last week with Trudy. They kissed in the car before he jumped out."

"Enrico. Okay." Cash started forward, his gaze focused on the trail ahead. "We could drive up to Scout Pass. Or call it a night and head back to your place."

"Sure. If you want—" She sucked in a gasp. "Oh my God. Look!" She jiggled Cash's arm. "Enrico is proposing."

"He… Are you sure?"

"He's getting down on one knee." Tears filled her eyes. "Unless she's lost a contact, he's definitely popping the question."

Enrico took his girlfriend's left hand in his. She clapped her right one over her mouth.

"We really should go," Cash said. "We're intruding on their privacy."

"You're right. We are."

Phoebe wanted to move. She did. Her feet had other ideas and insisted she stay. She'd never witnessed a proposal in real life and didn't want to miss this one. Not until she knew for certain Enrico's girlfriend accepted. At the moment, he was still down on one knee, talking.

The closest she'd come before tonight was at a baseball game when a proposal had flashed across the Jumbotron. Shouts had erupted on the other side of the stadium and then the couple appeared on the screen just as the man withdrew a ring box from his pocket. After that, the crowd cheered and applauded.

"Phoebe." Cash shifted uncomfortably. He was apparently less sentimental than her.

"Two more seconds."

Enrico must have slipped the ring on his girlfriend's finger, for he stood. She held her hand at arm's length as if to see the ring's stone catch the moonlight and then threw herself into his arms.

Yes! She'd accepted.

"Okay," Phoebe said, beside herself with glee. "Let's get out of here."

Together they descended the hill. With each step, the joy filling Phoebe expanded until she felt like she was walking on a cushion of air.

Not Cash. He'd gone silent. Why was that? Did inadvertently stumbling upon someone's private moment cause him discomfort? If so, she understood. Or did proposals in general make him want to turn tail and run? After three broken engagements, that was a possibility.

Rather than ask him outright, she approached the subject indirectly. "No lie, that's the sweetest thing I've ever seen. Like an early Christmas present. I bet she was shocked."

"It was…nice."

"Nice?" Phoebe tsked. "Honestly, Cash. They were adorable. Stop being a guy for one second."

"I heard him talking at the holiday party."

"About proposing?" She twisted sideways and stared him down. "And you didn't say anything to me? Argh! Men."

"Not about proposing. He was telling one of the other dishwashers that his car's been out of commission the last few weeks. It needs a new fuel pump, and he doesn't have the money."

"That's a shame." And it explained why his girlfriend—his new fiancée—had been giving him rides to and from work. "But he'll be getting a holiday bonus along with everyone else."

"He's going to need every cent to cover his car repairs and the deposit on that ring."

She gave Cash's arm another shove. "You're hopeless! He just proposed to the woman he loves. And you're worried about his personal finances?"

"He's the one who should be worried about his finances."

"Maybe he didn't spend any money and gave her his mother's ring." That would have been romantic, too, she decided.

"I hope you're right. Then he can use his entire bonus for the car repairs."

She sighed with exasperation. "What am I going to do with you?"

He didn't answer. And while Phoebe had been poking fun at him, a small part of her did worry that he was too fixated with money and had little or no appreciation for life's special moments.

They reached the bottom of the hill. Cash cautioned Phoebe to watch her step in the dark, and they went around the side of the barn to the front.

"This was one of the highlights of their lives," she said, not yet ready to abandon the subject. "Can't you be a little happy for them?"

"The guy obviously doesn't have two nickels to rub together. He spent money on a ring that he should have spent on his car."

"You don't know that for sure."

"It's a reasonable guess."

"Apparently marrying the woman of his dreams is more important than getting his car fixed. Besides, for all we know, they could be planning on a long engagement. Or he gave her a promise ring. You know, some couples prefer to shop together for their wedding rings."

"Is that what you want? To pick out your own ring?"

"Perish the thought." Phoebe wanted the first time she saw her engagement ring to be when her future husband proposed.

"Look," Cash said. "He's young. Twenty? Twenty-one? Just starting out. He's not ready to get married."

"Who are we to say when a person is or isn't ready to get married?"

"He's a dishwasher. He can't earn much money."

"He's a good worker. He could get promoted."

"Promotions don't always happen when you want them to. Take it from me."

"I think he's living at home. Maybe he's working part-time while going to school."

"I rest my case. Not ready to get married."

She groaned again. "This is like talking to a brick wall."

They reached the truck. Cash helped her into the passenger seat, pausing before closing the door.

"You're right, Phoebe. Enrico getting engaged while in debt and without a running vehicle is his decision to make and his problem to deal with, not mine. But I have been in his shoes before. Engaged at a young age, with a substantial college loan and medical bills to repay. I'm just saying, getting married then would have been a mistake and unfair to my fiancée."

"That was you and Melanie," Phoebe continued once Cash was behind the wheel. "Circumstances might be very different for Enrico and his girlfriend. She could have a good job. Or they could be content living with less."

"There's nothing wrong with wanting a decent home and to be earning decent wages," Cash insisted.

"Absolutely not. For you. Not necessarily for everyone else."

"Once more, you're right. I stand corrected."

His marginally condescending tone irritated Phoebe. She suspected he was saying what he thought she wanted to hear and not what he truly believed.

"I choose to be happy for them and wish them all the best, regardless of their circumstances."

"You wouldn't be you if you didn't," he said.

Was that a compliment or an insult?

They talked little on the drive home, though Cash did hold her hand across the console. Phoebe tried convincing herself this was just another difference of opinion, not an argument.

"Are you mad at me?" she asked when they pulled onto her street.

"Why would I be mad?"

"You were quiet the entire drive."

"I'm fine."

She didn't believe him. "You want to talk? We can go inside."

"I do want to go inside. I also want to talk. Just not about Enrico and his girlfriend."

"I'm good with that."

Enrico proposing to his girlfriend wouldn't come up again tonight. But it was clear to Phoebe that her and Cash's difference of opinion on the subject couldn't be ignored forever. She'd spent too long waiting on a man whose readiness for marriage hadn't matched hers. She wasn't willing to do that a second time, not even for Cash.

PHOEBE DIDN'T OFFER to light a fire and snuggle with Cash on the couch. He figured that particular fantasy of his would have to wait for their second date. The mood had lightened considerably but only because they'd dropped the subject of Enrico and his girlfriend.

In hindsight, Cash should have kept his mouth shut. Phoebe was a hard-core romantic. When they'd crested the hill and come upon a couple in the midst of a proposal, pulsating hearts had appeared in her eyes like some cartoon character. Rather than let her enjoy watching the proposal, which to him had felt like an invasion of privacy, he'd tried his best to talk some sense into her.

In his opinion, he wasn't wrong. Enrico doubtless lived paycheck to paycheck on a dishwasher's wages, and had blown his bonus on a ring instead of getting his car repaired. Surely, Phoebe would see the lack of logic in that decision once she came down from the clouds.

Had they continued their debate, their first

date would have quickly circled the drain. Cash was determined not to waste this second chance. There'd be no discussing Enrico's proposal, money or business. They'd avoided hot topics at the restaurant, and look how well that turned out.

"You want anything?" she asked, peeling off her coat and draping it over the back of a dining chair. She had one of those popular floor plans that featured a living room-dining room combo. "Coffee? Water? A beer?"

"Coffee would be great."

She inclined her head toward the arched doorway. "Come into the kitchen with me."

He stopped along the way. Following her lead, he hung his jacket and cowboy hat on the dining chair next to hers.

If Cash gave a lick about cooking, every pot, pan, tool and utensil he'd ever need could be found in Phoebe's kitchen. While not large, the design utilized the available space to its best advantage, giving the impression of size. Kudos to the architect, he thought, making a few mental notes for future reference.

"I'm impressed."

She smiled at his compliment. "Do you have a preference?" She pointed to a tree-shaped object on the counter that held a selection of coffee pods. "I have French roast, Colombian,

Donut Shop, Kona, French vanilla, mocha, decaf..." She spun the tree as she spoke.

"Any of those plain old coffee?"

"Breakfast blend?"

"Sounds good."

She plucked a pod from the tree and dropped it into the coffee maker. Depressing the handle, she selected a cup size and gestured toward the breakfast bar.

"Okay if we sit here?"

Any last shred of hope Cash had for a cuddle session on the couch evaporated. "Sure."

She brought him a steaming mug and then joined him a few minutes later with one of her own. "Have you finished your Christmas shopping?"

A safe topic. Good. He sipped his coffee. The hot liquid felt good going down and warmed his insides. "I had. Until recently. Seems I have someone new to buy for."

"Oh?" Her eyes twinkled.

"Any suggestions?"

"She loves surprises."

He chuckled. "You're no help."

"Sorry. You're on your own, buddy."

"Mom and Laurel are pretty much the only people I shop for, and they're easy." He took another sip of coffee. "They like gift cards. I stock up on wine and gourmet nuts at the box store in case I'm invited to a party and need to bring a gift for the host."

"My, my. You really get into the spirit of giving. Not."

"I haven't had any complaints."

She snorted with disgust.

"I suppose you put a lot of effort into shopping."

"As it so happens, I do." She lifted her chin and sniffed. "I shop for people all year round. Whenever I see something I think someone might like, I buy it and put it away."

"Of course you do."

"I also keep a list. That way, if you happen to fancy a certain item and mention it in passing, I won't forget when Christmas rolls around."

"Is this the part where I say I fancy Tesla cars and Rolex watches?"

"Ha, ha, ha."

"Worth a try."

She grinned and bumped shoulders with him, only to sober the next instant. "Laurel will be home Thursday. Can you believe it? Doesn't feel like she's been gone two weeks already."

"I, for one, can't wait."

"Ah. Ready to return to Phoenix and the daily grind at Strategic Design?"

"Not that. I miss her, and I worry she's been working herself to the bone."

"She has been working hard." Phoebe gave him a shy look. "You haven't hated helping me, then?"

"*Hate*'s a strong word."

"You're impossible."

He did like teasing her. "To be honest, I've had more fun than I thought I would. And don't let this go to your head or anything, but I've actually learned a few things from you."

"What?" She held a cupped hand to her ear. "Did I hear correctly? You learned a few things from me?"

"You were right about the Christmas tree and poinsettias, for one thing. The clients love them."

"Mmm. Keep talking."

"I've fielded quite a few phone calls from wedding guests who raved about the decorations and set appointments to tour the barn. There's been one or two positive reviews recently posted online."

"One or two? More like ten or twelve."

Phoebe checked daily and had an app on her phone.

"You've also been able to cut expenses," he said. "But not by ten percent."

"Ye of little faith." She smiled smugly. "I have two weeks left before the thirty-first."

"You might need those fabric books, after all."

"I'll call Calico Cover Up tomorrow."

He traced his knuckle along her jawline, marveling at the silky texture of her skin. "Bringing you into the business was the best decision Laurel and I ever made. You are exceptional at your job, Phoebe. And you're good at riding roughshod on me, which... I need. I can get a little too stingy with the purse strings."

Her demeanor softened even as the air between them crackled with electricity. "I was thinking..." She leaned closer.

Tiny slivers of awareness arrowed through him. "About what?"

"If we're not too busy, I could drive down to Phoenix midweek for the afternoon sometime. It's not that far. An hour and a half, if traffic's not bad. It just can't be the week I'm filling in for Trudy at the inn—I promised my parents."

"I like that idea." Cash watched, mesmerized, as the color of her eyes shifted from hazel to dark jade.

"We can have a late lunch."

"A late and long lunch." Very long, to make her drive worthwhile.

"I can catch you up on all the happenings here."

"That, too." He'd had other ideas. All kinds.

"Any chance you'll miss being here when you go?"

"What's to miss? I'll be here every weekend starting in January."

"Miss being here full-time, I mean."

Her voice held a note that let Cash know there was more to her question. What she really wanted to know was the likelihood of him eventually moving permanently to Payson and the potential for a future together.

He tugged on his shirt collar, which had grown tight and uncomfortable.

"Cash, did I say something wrong?"

"No."

"What are you thinking?"

He had some news he hesitated sharing with her. In light of their post "proposal on the hill" discussion and her less than subtle hints at his relocating, he worried she'd get carried away. Phoebe often heard what she wanted to hear.

On the other hand, it was clear they differed greatly on some very key issues. Their relationship was doomed from the start if they couldn't reach a compromise. His news might be a good launching point for a meaningful discussion.

"Burle wants to hire me."

"To design his cabin remodel?"

"That, and to oversee the construction."

Phoebe sat straighter. "Are you taking the job?"

"I'll complete the drawings, for sure. I haven't decided about the rest. The extra income would give a nice boost to our remodeling budget. But once I start back at Strategic Design and construction on the expansion begins in January, my free time will be limited."

"Can Lexi run the job under your supervision?"

"I'd have to think about that and run it by Burle." Cash polished off his coffee. "He also gave my name to a friend. She owns the Beeline Highway Motel and is looking at remodeling the entire property."

"That sounds like a big job."

"Pretty big."

"You considering it?"

"I haven't spoken to her yet."

"You will, though?"

"I'm torn. I feel like I should as a courtesy to her and Burle. But I don't want to overcommit. Wishing Well Springs and the mock Western town are my priorities. She wants to start construction late fall, which means I'd have to begin work now. That's not possible with my schedule."

"Sounds like a great opportunity, though."

"It would be if I was looking to leave Strategic Design and open my own practice."

"What if you did? You've talked about opening your own practice before."

Cash tugged on his too tight collar again. "Someday, yeah. But I'm not ready yet."

"Why not?" Phoebe's voice rose with excitement. "With two projects, you'd have a great start. Plus all the work at Wishing Well Springs. And before you say it's all about the money—"

"It is all about the money, Phoebe. I'm personally funding half the expansion from my salary. If I quit, that funding will come to a screeching halt and so might the project. We can't allow that. We have potential clients wanting to book weddings because of the mock Western town. I have to keeping working at Strategic Design. I don't have a choice."

At his sharp tone, she drew back.

"Sorry. That came out stronger than I intended."

She slid off the stool, gathered their empty coffee mugs and carried them to the sink. "I know we agreed to go slow and I said I wouldn't pressure you, but the fact is there's only so far we can take this relationship with the two of us living in separate cities."

"We haven't discussed me moving. We're not there yet." He began to say she shouldn't have assumed, then thought better of it.

"When will we be there?"

Before he could answer, Phoebe's phone pinged. She glanced at her screen and then turned it to face him. The text was from Laurel.

How did the date go?

"What do I tell her?" Phoebe asked, her gaze drilling into him.

CHAPTER THIRTEEN

CASH GOT HIMSELF a glass of water while Phoebe replied to Laurel's text. He wouldn't lie to himself. He was glad for the chance to organize his thoughts. And, no, he wasn't going to answer the separate text Laurel had sent him. She could wait until the morning.

His phone pinged again and a second text appeared from Laurel.

I'll call you later ☹

Mad face emoji? Great. He'd be getting an earful from Laurel. As if in response to his thoughts, his phone pinged again. He shut it off without reading the message and guzzled his water.

Setting his glass down, he turned to find Phoebe staring at him.

"You were saying?"

He glanced at her phone.

"On silent," she said. Then, to remind him,

added, "You were about to tell me where we're headed."

"Did you ask Sam where you were headed on your first date with him?"

She scowled. "That's not fair. The circumstances were different."

"This line of questioning isn't fair, either. We agreed to go slow. You agreed. Has that changed?"

"Like I said, slow is fine with me as long as we're moving steadily forward. I'm not into casual dating with no specific goal in sight."

"Nor am I. But neither am I rushing toward that goal at breakneck speed." He paused for a moment to regroup. "I've made mistakes in the past, ones I don't intend to repeat."

"I've had a crush on you since high school, Cash. A bad crush."

Not what he'd expected her to say. "Since high school?" he repeated.

"You didn't realize?"

"I was young. My life was falling apart."

She nodded, her expression still showing hurt. "The only reason I dated Sam and needled him to marry me was to get over you. You were who I wanted to marry. Every time you got engaged, my heart shattered. Every time you broke up, my hopes soared."

Cash considered her admission for a moment. This perhaps accounted for some of Phoebe's need to have a firm commitment from him. "Why didn't you tell me this before?"

She looked at him as if he'd lost his mind. "Seriously? In high school, you barely knew I was alive. Then you got engaged. Again and again. After that, we started working together."

"All right. I agree the timing's been off for us. But that's no reason to rush now that we've started dating."

"I want this." She gestured to the two of them. "Us. Together. A storybook ending. I always have. It's what I've dreamed of for the last fifteen years." She bit back a sob. "Sam strung me along and along and along. I can't do that again. I need reassurances."

Cash worked his jaw. This wasn't new to him; his three former fiancées had insisted on similar assurances.

"I understand."

"Do you?"

"I'm interested in you. More than a little. I have strong feelings for you. I won't mislead you, however, like Sam did."

She waited for him to continue.

"Marriage isn't anything I'll consider until the expansion is done, Wishing Well Springs has recouped the investment and we're on solid financial ground. If that requires I remain in Phoenix working at Strategic Design, then it does."

She nodded. "I'm not trying to make things harder on you, Cash. Or to be high-maintenance. I swear."

He wasn't sure about that. By her own admission, she could be demanding and difficult. Traits she often attributed to being the youngest child of five.

"As much as I want to be the guy who loses his head and throws caution to the wind, I can't. It's not in me. But if you're willing to wait, I think we have a shot at this."

"Wait how long?"

"I just told you, when Wishing Well Springs is operating in the black."

"Six months?" she asked.

"Probably longer."

"Can you be more specific?"

She was attempting to pin him down. His defenses kicked in. "Fine. How's this for specific? We date for three months and then decide if we have potential. If yes, we date for another year. Then, if finances are in good shape, we get serious."

"Engaged?"

"Possibly. Eventually."

"Will you be moving to Payson then? Opening your own architectural practice?"

He was growing weary of this. They were on their first date. They should be cuddling and learning each other's funny quirks. Not sparring about when they might marry.

"I ask because opening your own practice will require a financial investment and give you another excuse to postpone marriage."

"Wow. Really, Phoebe? We're going to fight about something that hasn't happened and may never? What's got into you?"

Her gaze turned inward. "Seeing Enrico propose to his girlfriend got me thinking. Even though they have no money, they love each other and are willing...no, they *want* to face the challenges life throws at them together. Because there's more to being happy and successful at marriage than financial security."

"You're right."

"Am I? Because the way you talk, you don't believe one can exist without the other."

"For me, I guess they don't. I've told you over and over I won't make the same mistakes my parents did. And you'll never convince me going broke didn't cause my parents' divorce."

"There are no guarantees in life, Cash. Even people who take every precaution can be blindsided. Like your grandmother. Her illness was unexpected."

"Granddad didn't take every precaution." Cash clenched and unclenched his fist. "If he had, he wouldn't have lost almost the entire ranch."

Phoebe forced out a breath through gritted teeth. "How much of this has to do with you being engaged three times before?"

"I'd be lying if I said nothing. Three strikes, you're out. I have reason to be cautious. In fact, I'd think *you'd* be cautious. I don't have a good track record."

"That sounds like an excuse. Do you want me to break up with you?"

She wasn't hearing him. "Maybe we're just too different to make this work."

"Couples don't have to agree on everything."

"They have to agree on the important things. Like when to get married." He reached across the breakfast bar to take her hand.

She moved it before he could. "You've been engaged three times. And three times you put on the brakes."

"I had good reasons." At least, he'd thought he had. But talking with Melanie and Hannah recently had given him a different perspective.

"If everyone in the world waited until circumstances were ideal," Phoebe said, "there'd be no weddings. We'd be out of business."

"It's easy for people who haven't lost everything to dismiss a lack of money as unimportant."

Her spine stiffened. "That's unkind and untrue. At least where I'm concerned."

"Relax. It's not an insult. You've been lucky. You haven't once wondered if you'll lose the roof over your head or have enough money for groceries after you pay your bills."

Some of the starch left her. "I don't share the same experiences as you. That doesn't mean I'm unsympathetic. I am." She sighed.

"I've been honest with you from the start. You know my history. You know where I stand."

Tears filled her eyes. "I do. Clearly. I just stupidly thought things would be different with me. That I'd be the one to break down your barriers."

"You can be. If you're patient. Anything worthwhile is worth waiting for."

"I have waited for you, Cash, for half my life."

He considered before he spoke, leery of hurting her. "My feelings for you are new. I need to get used to them, explore them, without being constantly pressured."

"Do you say that to all the girls?"

Her joke fell flat. Unless it wasn't a joke.

He made another stab at reasoning with her. "There's not just us to consider. We're partners. Our personal relationship is bound to spill over into the business. That could be risky."

"Heaven forbid we endanger the business."

"You're ignoring a very important point," he said. "Laurel and I have our jobs and the security that comes with them. If Wishing Well Springs fails, you lose your share of the business *and* your salary. That's a big deal."

"I hate that you reduce every personal and serious conversation we have to money."

"I didn't start this." He disliked the sharp edge in his voice that came out when he felt attacked.

"Well, we can stop right now. No problem."

"I don't want to end the evening on a bad note."

"Too late," she snapped.

His anger escalated. She was being intentionally flippant. "I should go before either of us says something we regret."

"I agree."

He pushed off the stool. In the dining room, he grabbed his jacket and cowboy hat. "We can talk tomorrow."

"Not about this."

"A break isn't a bad idea."

She accompanied him to the door. "At last we agree on something."

He reached for her. A kiss was out of the question. One on the lips, anyway. Cash aimed for her cheek…and missed when she stepped away.

"Fair enough," he said.

She crossed her arms over her middle and glared at him.

"You're hurt and mad," he said. "I've disappointed you. You were hoping for a declaration. A grand gesture like Enrico proposing to his girlfriend. You didn't get one."

"You make me sound shallow and silly."

"I don't think that. I am concerned you have certain expectations. Sam didn't meet them and apparently neither am I. You refuse to wait for me like you did him, only to be dumped. Am I close?"

"You've hit the nail on the head. Good on you, Cash. I'm not willing to stay in a relationship where there's no chance of a ring in my future, and you have a commitment phobia. That, by the way, is really strange for a guy who's been engaged three times. Why'd you ask them, anyway, if you had no intention of going through with the wedding?"

She was taking shots at him. It required all his willpower not to retaliate.

"You're giving me grief when all I'm doing is keeping things real."

"You need to go home. Now."

He plopped his hat onto his head and shoved it down hard. "See you in the morning."

"No, you won't. I'm taking a half day off to help Trudy. I just decided."

Okay, she was punishing him for disappointing her. So be it.

"Give her my regards." He stopped on the stoop and pivoted to face her. "Good night, Phoebe."

"Good night." Her lips barely moved when she spoke.

The next instant, he was staring at a closed door.

Cash stood there, overwhelmed by a sense of déjà vu. He'd experienced this very scene before. Three times to be exact. It didn't get easier. In fact, this was the hardest one yet.

Why? He and Phoebe had hardly dated. He didn't have years or even months or weeks invested in the two of them. Yet, it was as if his heart had been ripped from his chest.

Was it possible he cared for her more than he was willing to admit?

He started down the walkway toward his

truck, ignoring the voice inside his head screaming at him to turn around and go back, to fight for her.

Instead, as always, he kept going. Better they learned now they weren't right for each other than later when they had far more on the line to lose.

"You want another pillow? More juice?" Phoebe stood over Trudy, who lay on the couch with her feet elevated. "I'll grab the heating pad from the bathroom cabinet."

"Good grief! Quit hovering and park it. If I wasn't restricted to bed rest, I'd throw your scrawny behind out of here."

Phoebe pouted but did as she was told and flopped down on the padded ottoman. "Just trying to help."

"I have everything I need within reach. My darling hubby made sure before he left for work." Trudy pointed as she rattled off the list. "Phone and portable charger. Earbuds. TV remote. Book. Magazines. Healthy snacks. H2O. Sleep mask." She dug in between the couch cushions and extracted a small cardboard box. "Caramel candies he doesn't know about."

"Isn't there some laundry needing folding or dishes to wash?"

"Are we perhaps avoiding Cash?"

"Like the plague."

"You ready to talk about what happened last night?"

"I wasn't wrong."

"I didn't say you were." Trudy popped a caramel in her mouth and offered the box to Phoebe.

She declined, not in the mood for sweets. "I may have pushed him a little too hard. Made one or two tiny demands."

"May have? Tiny?"

"I wanted, needed, some reassurances. Is that so terrible?"

Trudy thrust her head backward onto the pillow and grimaced. "On your first date! Honestly, Phoebe, that's not pushing. It's steamrolling. I'm assuming he balked."

"He did."

"What were you thinking? Wait, I'll tell you. You were thinking that you wasted three precious years on Sam the loser, and you're not about to make the same mistake with Cash."

Phoebe grumbled to herself about know-it-all sisters.

"Cash isn't the kind of person who can be hurried along. He's proved that repeatedly."

"I hoped things would be different with me."

"Aww, honey. I know you're hurt. But you can't lay the entire blame on him. You've loved him since high school. You were ecstatic when he finally asked you out. You assumed that because you were ready for a big commitment, he was, too."

"He reduced every one of our discussions to money."

"What else did you expect? That's who he is. You can't change him. And if you can't accept him as he is, with all his imperfections, then you're probably better off without him."

Phoebe bit her lower lip to hold back the sobs threatening to erupt. Her efforts were in vain, and she burst into tears.

"Don't cry." Trudy struggled to a half sitting position and then swung her legs over the side of the couch.

"You're s-supposed to b-be lying d-down," Phoebe blubbered.

"One minor breaking of the rules won't hurt. Besides, seeing you like this is sending my blood pressure skyrocketing far more than sitting up will." She grabbed Phoebe's hand and tugged her over onto the couch with her. "Maybe you and Cash aren't meant to be."

Phoebe cried harder. Trudy pulled her into her arms, patted her back and cooed soothingly. Eventually, Phoebe's sobs eased.

"Better?" Trudy drew back and inspected Phoebe's face. Using the cuff of her bulky sweatshirt sleeve, she wiped away the streaks on Phoebe's cheeks. "That darn husband of mine forgot to leave me a box of tissues."

"I've wanted to be with Cash for so long and then what do I do? Screw things up on our first date."

"Talk to him. Reach a compromise."

"He won't consider a serious commitment until Wishing Well Springs is on solid financial ground." She explained Cash's position in more detail. "That could be years."

"Sounds to me like the ball's in your court. You either wait or not."

"I'll be thirty-one next summer."

"You have plenty of time. Look at me—I got married at thirty-three."

"You were happy being single. I'm not. I've wanted to get married since I was fourteen and a flower girl in Cora's wedding."

"Amazing how meeting the right man can change everything." Trudy smiled and rubbed her belly.

"What if I wait and wait and Cash gets cold feet again?"

"He may not be the marrying kind."

"Okay, but why keep proposing if he's not?"

"A very good question. My guess is he'll get married when he's really and truly ready. Not before."

"What do I do?"

Trudy stroked her hair. "Follow your heart."

"I think I need to follow my head. My heart isn't reliable."

"What does Laurel say?"

"I haven't told her. She's coming down to the wire on her VIP job and doesn't need me and my problems distracting her."

"She might have some valuable insight."

Phoebe shook her head. "I doubt that. She cautioned me against getting involved with Cash. Now I understand why. He and I really are different. She saw that. Mom and Dad did, too. Why didn't I listen? Why did I push him?"

"In order to see what he'd do?"

"No!" Had she?

"Intentionally sabotage the relationship?"

That was worse. "I'm not the kind of person who plays games." She massaged her forehead. "Work is going to totally suck. I skipped out this morning. I couldn't bring myself to face Cash after last night."

"You can't hide forever."

"Unfortunately not. We have a wedding this evening and one or two every day until January first. On top of that, there's the secret-couple wedding and the Christmas Day vow renewal. Is a holiday wedding really that romantic?"

"Yes," Trudy answered without hesitation. It was. Phoebe loved the idea of a Christmas wedding.

"You think you and Cash can work together without problems?"

"What other choice do we have?"

"You could always quit," Trudy suggested. "Take over my job at the inn. Mom and Dad would be thrilled."

"That's not fair to Cash and Laurel. They depend on me."

"Give them ample notice."

"The business will fold without me."

"You're amazing, I'll give you that. But no one is irreplaceable. The wedding coordination side of the business may take a temporary hit. But they'd continue to rent out the barn and grounds. Probably promote Georgia Ann or one of their other employees to handle reservations and coordinating."

Phoebe imagined Georgia Ann taking over the job she'd created, and a sour taste filled her mouth. She disliked the idea of anyone replacing her; even someone competent and capable and whom she liked.

"We have a partnership contract," she said.

"Contracts can be broken. See an attorney."

An attorney! That was a huge step. A scary step. "I'm not ready."

"Fine. Forget quitting for now. If you find that working with Cash is too hard, then you can reconsider."

Phoebe had to admit, as much as she adored her job at Wishing Well Springs, leaving to work at the inn held a certain appeal. She'd be surrounded by family and coworkers who loved her and had her best interests at heart. She wouldn't have to deal with Cash. She'd heal faster with distance between them and maybe, finally, get over him once and for all.

Oh but Laurel would be devastated. She counted on Phoebe. The initial idea to bring Phoebe into the business had been Laurel's. What if she viewed Phoebe's leaving as a betrayal? Their friendship would suffer. Hadn't Cash warned her that could happen?

Hearing a noise, she turned to see Trudy stifling a loud yawn. "You tired?"

"How could I be tired? I do nothing but rest all day." She yawned again.

"I should get going. I have a ton of stuff waiting for me at the office. And Cash is probably coming unglued right about now. He's not the best at answering phones and dealing with clients."

Trudy waved her off. "It'll do him good. Teach him to appreciate you more."

"He does appreciate me. Work-wise."

If only getting him to appreciate her personally could be accomplished by disappearing for a few hours.

"I love you, sis." Trudy pulled Phoebe into a bone-crunching hug.

"Call me if you need anything." She patted Trudy's protruding belly. "And take care of Junior for me."

Phoebe saw herself out, insisting Trudy remain on the couch. On the fifteen-minute drive to Wishing Well Springs, she braced herself for seeing Cash. Halfway there, her phone rang and Laurel's picture appeared on her car's info-display.

Her stomach clenched. Phoebe had sent Laurel a few vague texts late last night saying she'd call today when they were both free. Laurel must have grown impatient.

She pressed the answer button. "Hi. How's it going?"

"Phoebe, my God. Why didn't you call me? I'm so sorry, hon. I did warn you, however. Cash can be an obtuse jerk. Are you all right? He said you took the morning off."

He'd obviously told her about their disagreement.

"I'm fine. Just checking on Trudy."

"How is she?"

"Good as can be expected. The doctor's keeping close watch on her."

"I'm glad. Now, about you and Cash…"

There went Phoebe's attempt to sidetrack her friend.

"How can I help?" Laurel asked.

"You can focus on your job. That's what's important."

"What happened?"

"We went out to dinner and decided a relationship isn't a good idea at the moment. End of story."

"That's not what Cash said."

What had he said? Phoebe pictured the conversation in her head—him blaming Phoebe and claiming she'd pressured him. "He has his version of the story, and I have mine."

"He told me it was all his fault. That he misled you and shouldn't have suggested you start dating."

Ouch. While true, that cut Phoebe to the quick. She'd rather Laurel had told her Cash believed he'd made a terrible mistake and wanted Phoebe back.

She covered her mouth, trapping a sob behind her hand.

"What's that?" Laurel asked.

"Nothing. Taking a sip of coffee." *Liar, liar, pants on fire.*

"You aren't going to quit us, are you?"

Funny that Trudy had also mentioned quitting. "No…"

"You are! I swear I'll strangle my brother."

"It has crossed my mind, but that's all."

"Please don't leave us, Phoebe. Yes, Cash is the biggest fool on the face of the earth. But he's going back to Phoenix soon, and things will return to normal."

Normal? Was that what Phoebe wanted? She'd gotten used to this new arrangement. Not Laurel being gone but Cash being around all the time.

"I'm not leaving." Not now, anyway. A lot depended on Cash.

"Gosh darn it!" Laurel exclaimed. "I have to go. Let's talk tonight."

"Yes. Let's." With luck, Phoebe would be in better emotional and mental shape.

"I love you, hon. Hugs and kisses."

"Love you, too. 'Bye."

At the ranch, she drove straight to the garage. Activating the automatic opener, she waited while the door rumbled open.

To her surprise, Cash's truck was missing. Hurrying inside, she found the office deserted and the phone on Call Forward—apparently to his cell as she hadn't received any calls.

Taking the phone off forwarding, she immediately punched in his number. The call rang once and went to voice mail.

Where was he? They couldn't both take off and leave the office unattended. He should have texted her at the very least.

Irritated, she went to the front door and removed the Be Back Shortly sign. Instead of tackling her many tasks, however, she stared endlessly at her computer screen. A half hour later Cash pulled into the ranch. She watched through the window as he took the road leading to the barn.

She saw it then. The back of his truck was loaded with a Christmas tree and several dozen poinsettia plants.

Her throat constricted and her eyes stung. He'd said he didn't want to spend money on a second tree and fresh plants. That it would blow their budget. And yet he'd gone to the nursery.

For her? What, if anything, did that mean?

CHAPTER FOURTEEN

"You're home." Cash greeted Laurel with open arms.

She shoved her carry-on bag at him and, without waiting to see if he caught it, spun on her heels and charged toward the open rear of her SUV.

He followed after her, the carry-on bag in his hand. "Need help with the rest of your stuff?"

"How could you?"

"Offer to help you?"

"Quit pretending to be an idiot. You know what I'm talking about."

He did. He was just waiting for a question he could answer.

Laurel tugged on a huge suitcase filled to capacity, brushing aside Cash's hand when he tried to help. The suitcase toppled onto the concrete garage floor with a noisy thud. While she was freeing a second suitcase from between boxes and bins and sewing machines, he secured the carry-on bag to the top of the first suitcase.

"Phoebe," she snapped when he didn't respond. "She's going to quit."

He remained calm. Laurel had a habit of overreacting. "Is that what she said?"

"Not precisely. But it's crossed her mind."

"Okay."

"That's all you have to say?" Laurel fired a round of invisible daggers at him.

He grabbed the second suitcase and waited while she hoisted a case containing one of her prized sewing machines. Together they hauled their load into the house. Dusk had recently fallen, which it did early this time of year. He'd been relieved she'd arrived home before dark— he'd worried about her on those winding and dimly lit mountain roads.

"Her parents want her to take over for Trudy," Laurel said, huffing and puffing on her way to the foot of the stairs, where they deposited their loads.

Cash figured they'd bring everything inside first before carrying whatever needed to go upstairs to Laurel's workroom and bedroom.

"Them wanting her to take Trudy's place has nothing to do with Phoebe and me," he said on their second trip to the car. "She's family."

"And you've given her extra motivation." Laurel's voice cracked. "What if she goes?"

"My guess is she won't. She loves her job

and being part of Wishing Well Springs. She doesn't love being a catering manager."

"She doesn't love working with you, either."

"She's mad and hurt and having a knee-jerk reaction."

"Thanks for mansplaining that to me." Laurel extracted a crate from the back of her car and jammed it into Cash's gut. "Have you even tried to fix this mess?"

"I've stayed out of her way as much as possible."

When he wasn't helping with weddings and events or burying himself in ranch financials, he immersed himself in the Western town expansion. Tracking down the best prices on lumber, pricing out subcontractors, conferring with Lexi and obtaining the necessary permits from the city.

Yesterday morning he'd met with Burle's friend, the owner of the Beeline Highway Motel. What had started out as a courtesy for a friend hadn't ended that way. Cash liked the motel owner and had been excited and energized during the meeting. Her vision for the renovation was both on-trend and made sense with the current layout.

She'd wanted to hire him on the spot. Instead of telling her no, he'd asked for a week to consider and review his schedule. A mistake, for sure; he'd only disappoint her and delay her hiring an available architect. Yet, in his spare time, Cash found himself sketching rough drawings for the motel and liking them.

"Where is Phoebe, by the way?" Laurel asked, the upper half of her body disappearing into the cargo area of her SUV. "At the wedding?"

"Yeah." Last he'd seen her, she'd been driving the golf cart toward the barn.

"Why aren't you there helping her?"

"I'm helping you," Cash said, groaning when Laurel dumped another heavy crate on top of the stack he was already holding. "She said she had everything under control."

"More likely she's avoiding you."

"That, too."

Conversation stalled while they finished bringing in the rest of Laurel's things and hauling them either upstairs or to Bellissima. If he thought he was getting away scot-free after that, he was sorely mistaken.

"Where are you going?" Laurel demanded when he started in the direction of the office.

There went his plan of finalizing Burle's drawings for the cabin remodel and packing his own suitcase.

"Apparently nowhere," he said.

"You got that right." She hitched a thumb toward the kitchen.

"Aren't you tired after your long drive? You should rest."

"We're not done here."

"Yes, ma'am." He readied himself for the verbal lambasting she was no doubt planning to give him and went with her to the kitchen. "How'd the dresses come out? Your bride happy?"

"She's happy, her mother-in-law-to-be is happy, the mother of the flower girl is happy, and I have the names of four new potential clients. Now, quit changing the subject." Laurel sat and kicked out the chair next to her.

"Am I safe?" He held up a hand like a shield. "Or do I need protection?"

"You shouldn't have gone out with Phoebe in the first place if you weren't ready to commit. You know her—all she's ever wanted is to get married."

"I lost my head."

It had been easy to do, especially when kissing Phoebe. But there'd been much more to his attraction than that. She was fun and interesting even when she was irritating him. She kept him on his toes. Didn't cut him any slack. Challenged him. Amused him. Impressed him with her intelligence, resourcefulness and in-genuity. Made him smile.

"That's no excuse," Laurel continued. "Phoebe's had a crush on you since she and I were freshmen in high school."

"Hey, I didn't know that until she told me. And, trust me, no one was more surprised than me to realize I have feelings for her."

"You have to do something, Cash." She stabbed the tabletop with her finger. "We can't afford to lose her. She's half—no, three quar-ters of the reason Wishing Well Springs is a success."

"You're not telling me anything I don't al-ready know."

"We need a plan. Have you apologized?"

"Multiple times. I also handled all the grunt work for the secret-couple wedding on Satur-day night and the vow renewal on Christmas Day. I've told her repeatedly what a great job she's doing. Brought her favorite drink from Coffee Calamity every day."

"I can't believe she hasn't fallen at your feet, begging your forgiveness and swearing to wait for you till the end of time."

He propped his forearms on the table. "Tell me, oh wise one, what should I have done?"

"You can start by admitting you're wrong."

He mulled that over for a moment.

"Oh good grief!" Laurel nearly came apart at the seams. "You can't honestly believe you *weren't* wrong?"

"I shouldn't have asked her out when I wasn't ready to get serious. But she was wrong, too. I told her from the beginning that I wanted to go slow, and she agreed. Then she changed her mind."

"Men." Laurel's tone sharpened. "Let me spell out for you the many mistakes you made. You didn't handle her heart with care. You were disrespectful of her feelings. You thought you could call all the shots and set all the rules without considering her. You got immediately defensive and didn't reassure her when she was feeling insecure."

"Please. Don't hold back on my account."

"Being flippant isn't helping. This is very serious, Cash. We could lose Wishing Well Springs if Phoebe quits."

He had thought of that. But only now did the full impact hit him.

History could very well repeat itself. Without intending to, he'd put himself and Laurel in the same position his grandfather and parents had been in—at risk of losing their business because of a poor decision. All his hard work, his sacrifices, could be for nothing.

How could he have let that happen? And, on top of that, he'd hurt someone he cared about.

"Make things right with Phoebe," Laurel said.

"Maybe after a few days of not seeing me she'll be more receptive."

"Where are you going?"

"Phoenix. I'm leaving tomorrow morning at six. I promised Marguerite I'd be in the office by nine."

"Cash, no!" Laurel's eyes widened. "What about Phoebe? What about Christmas dinner with Mom?"

"I'll be back."

"That makes no sense. Just stay through until after Christmas."

"There are projects that have been put on hold until my return. I can't expect Travis and Marguerite to keep picking up my slack."

"You can't go."

"We agreed. I'd help out here while you were gone. You're back."

"We're in a state of emergency!"

"I have no more paid vacation."

"You're running away, just like with every other relationship you've had," she accused.

"My former fiancées dumped *me*, and I'm big enough of a man to admit it."

"You ran away emotionally, which is just as bad."

Melanie and Hannah had said essentially the same thing. "I may have," he admitted.

"It's almost like there's something inside you that drives you to recreate what happened to us as kids."

"Grandma dying? The family going broke? Losing the ranch? Why would I recreate any of that?"

"Dad. Him abandoning us." Laurel's features lost some of their hard edges. "It messed with us. Screwed with our heads. He's the reason we can't have lasting relationships. Why we retreat into our work. Why you're fixated on having enough money. Why I obsess over every dress, never satisfied. He made us think we're not worthy of being loved."

"I'm not a teenager anymore. I'm past that."

"Are you? Because I think you subconsciously orchestrate events. You push people away, emotionally abandoning them before they abandon you. What do they call that? A self-fulfilling prophecy?"

Cash rubbed his throat, which had gone dry. "That's...um..." He'd wanted to deny it. To tell Laurel she was off her rocker. He couldn't do either. "You've been thinking a lot."

She lifted one shoulder. "I've been alone for

almost three weeks, two days of which I spent on the road."

Recognizing the truth in what she said didn't make it easier to accept.

"Don't return to Phoenix." She reached for his hand. "Stay through until Christmas. Make up with Phoebe. Convince her not to quit. Break the pattern. You two deserve a second chance."

He shook his head. "She wants more than I can give her."

"Or more than you're willing to give her."

She had him there.

Returning to his desk in the office, he considered the pros and cons of calling his boss, Marguerite, and asking for an extension. Laurel was right—he couldn't leave. Not until he and Phoebe were on better terms. He had treated her badly, stringing her along not unlike Sam had.

He decided he'd offer to take the time off unpaid. It would cut into the portion of his pay he'd designated for the mock Western town, but that was the price he paid for screwing up.

While he waited on hold for Marguerite to pick up, he spun the old horseshoe in his hands. Cleaned and polished, it had found a place on his desk. He'd planned it to be a continual reminder of the good luck he and Phoebe would surely enjoy. He couldn't have been more wrong.

To his relief, Marguerite gave him the extension without any fuss. Seemed his projects had slowed over the holidays.

"Thank you," he said.

"Merry Christmas, Cash."

"Same to you. And see you on the twenty-sixth."

He hung up. The next second, Laurel popped around the partition. She threw herself at him, giving him a huge hug.

"I'm so glad."

"You were eavesdropping?"

"Naturally. I'm your sister." She squeezed him tight. "Everything's going to be okay."

Was it? Cash wished he had her confidence.

PHOEBE SWUNG INTO the employee parking area behind her parents' inn and shut off her car's engine. She'd come here several times this week to avoid Cash. But that was no longer necessary as he'd left for Phoenix this morning.

At last, she could stop ducking around corners when she heard his footsteps and finding reasons to be gone when he was in the office. She'd eaten her last lunch in the barn rather than the kitchen. No more smiling politely and speaking civilly if their paths did happen to cross.

Her efforts to avert conflict had worked in large part because of Cash. It seemed he was equally proficient at ducking around corners and speaking civilly. And now that he was gone for the next few days, she should be able to breathe easy again.

And yet, here she was once more at the inn, this time avoiding the other Montgomery sibling.

Laurel had gotten home last night. Phoebe had been too busy with the wedding and Laurel too tired from her long drive for them to connect. Today would be different. Laurel would want to commiserate with Phoebe over morning coffee. Rake Cash over the coals. Offer her undying support. Phoebe wasn't ready for the sympathy and platitudes her best friend would heap on her.

As she walked toward the inn's back door, she spied one of the maids pushing a cart laden with linens and cleaning supplies. The woman wore a lopsided Santa hat along with a holiday sweater over her uniform. Stopping in front of a room, she saw Phoebe and waved.

"Morning, Gillie." Phoebe mustered a smile and waved back. She knew the names of most of the staff, even the ones who'd been hired after she'd left to work at Wishing Well Springs.

"Merry Christmas, Phoebe."

The inn's rear entrance opened into a hallway lined with doors to the various offices. At 7:30 a.m., neither Phoebe's sister Cora nor her other sister Lilly was at their desks. They wouldn't arrive until eight.

Phoebe counted her blessings. Her sisters were all astute and would instantly notice her sullen expression and the lines of fatigue, which she'd tried to camouflage with concealer. Phoebe could turn on the charm and cheeriness for Wishing Well Springs' clients. Faking it with her family was much harder.

Her destination appeared ahead of her—the beverage counter in the nook outside her dad's office. She released a long sigh. Someone, her dad most likely, had made coffee. He wasn't anywhere in sight, either—he'd probably been called away on a maintenance emergency. Her mother had been fighting off a mild stomach bug, so she was probably at home.

Looking around, Phoebe smiled with contentment. Her plan to hide out for a while was falling into place. She had coffee and solitude. Exactly what she needed. Mug in hand, she went into her father's office and plopped down in the visitor chair.

On impulse, she snuck a peek at the time on her phone. Cash must be on the outskirts of Phoenix by now and hitting rush-hour traffic on his way downtown.

They'd had a quick, unmemorable good-bye yesterday before she'd hopped in the golf cart and headed to the barn for the evening's wedding. Neither of them had mentioned his mom's Christmas dinner. Phoebe had texted her the day before, saying she wouldn't be there and to thank her for the invitation. Yes, she should have called, but she'd chickened out, unsure how much Cash's mother knew.

A cold fist of pain pressed against her chest—she'd hoped the hot coffee would melt it away. Where would she spend Christmas evening now? Her parents would be busy at the inn, as usual. After a long day that started early with the family breakfast and gift exchange, they'd hit the sack early, utterly exhausted. Her other sisters would be at their in-laws' homes, splitting the day between sets of grandparents. Phoebe supposed she could hang out with Trudy and her brother-in-law. Not the same as having dinner with Cash, his mother and Laurel.

The fist pressed harder against her sternum.

What was the big deal? This was hardly the first time she'd been hurt by, and frustrated with, Cash. Though, to be fair, most of those times hadn't been his fault. Heck, he'd not even been aware of them. She'd been the one pining while he'd remained oblivious.

One might think by now she'd face facts. She and Cash weren't meant to be together despite their incredible attraction. They were complete opposites, and whoever had romanticized the idea that opposites attract should have their head examined.

"Hey, you. How's my favorite girl?"

She started at the sound of her dad's voice, nearly spilling her coffee. Pulling herself together, she blinked back the tears that had gathered in her eyes. Just in time. He shuffled into the office, filling every available inch of space with his larger-than-life presence.

"Hi there." She glanced up and produced a smile.

He kissed the top of her head before going around his desk and dropping into the chair. He left behind the lingering scent of his familiar aftershave.

Cash had a distinctive scent all his own, too. More woodsy than spicy, which she assumed came from the time he spent outdoors and with the horses. She'd become quite used to it these last three weeks, often detecting it the moment she entered the main house. Would she start missing the scent now that he was back in Phoenix?

A few days, she told herself, and she'd be over him. Yeah, right. Like that would happen. Fifteen years, three of those as the girlfriend of another man, and she hadn't gotten over him. Why would this time be different?

What would it be like for them when he returned? To start with, there'd be no more spontaneous moments. No kisses in the moonlight. No heated glances from across the room. No private jokes just between the two of them. No brushing of fingers and knuckles skimming cheeks.

Her eyes pricked with fresh tears. Pretending to brush a stray lock of hair from her face, she snuck a subtle wipe with the back of her hand.

"To what do I owe the pleasure of your company this fine day?" her dad asked.

"I was in the neighborhood."

"You're always in the neighborhood. You work next door."

"How's Mom?" Phoebe asked. "Any better?"

"Fit as a fiddle this morning. She'll be in shortly."

"Glad to hear. I know she dreaded being sick over the holidays."

Phoebe was truly lucky to have both her parents and no doubt took it for granted. How hard it must be for Cash, completely estranged from his dad and not that close to his mother. He had no support system to fall back on, other than Laurel. He'd had her, too, she supposed, before they'd made their ill-fated attempt at dating.

She should be more understanding of him and more compassionate. She definitely shouldn't have pushed him for a commitment.

"Speaking of our neighbor," her father said, "shouldn't you be at work?" He talked while skimming through a stack of papers on the desk.

"A girl can't visit her dad?"

He set the papers down. "Your mother told me you and Cash had a falling-out."

"Darn Trudy and her big mouth."

"They're worried about you."

"I'm fine."

"People who are fine don't hide out in their dad's office."

Phoebe's shoulders drooped. "I'm not hiding from Cash. He left for Phoenix this morning."

"Who or what, then?"

"Laurel."

"She's not mad at you over this, is she?"

"No, no. She's just going to smother me with best-friend compassion. I'm not ready."

"This isn't like you, little girl. You don't run from people and problems. You face them head-on. Trample over them and stomp them into the ground. That's the Kellerman way."

She sniffed. "He hurt me, Dad."

"Bad enough for you to quit Wishing Well Springs and take Trudy's place? Because nothing would please your mother and me more."

"Um…"

He chuckled. "I figured as much."

"You're not disappointed?"

"'Course not. You love Wishing Well Springs. And as far as Cash goes, he was being Cash. Acting like he always has. If you were hoping for a different version of him, you needed to give him more than a couple of days."

"I know."

"What happened?"

"I got scared," she admitted. "We accidentally interrupted Enrico proposing to his girlfriend."

"I heard he got engaged."

Phoebe shook her head. "Cash's reaction and mine couldn't have been more different. I thought it was wonderful—he thought they were making a huge mistake. Then he started talking about money and being financially secure and blah, blah, blah."

"That's what he does."

"Yes." She sniffed. "When he hemmed and

hawed about us, I started thinking he was going to string me along just like Sam did."

"I see. And that's when you got scared."

"I figured if I pressured him to commit, he'd settle into the idea. And I would be less worried about him leaving me down the road."

"You know, that's not very logical."

"I do now."

Her dad's voice gentled. "You made a mistake, little girl. But the world didn't come to an end. It's still turning."

"A little bumpy."

"That'll improve. Give it time." He clapped his hands together. "Now for the hundred-dollar question. Do you want another shot with Cash? It's clear to me you still have feelings for him."

"I do have feelings. But he refuses to consider marriage until he's financially secure, and I won't date for two or three years without a firm commitment from him. I just won't."

"Then you have your answer. You move on and figure out how to work together."

Did fathers always know best?

Her dad stood and came out from behind the desk. Wrapping her in a hug, he squeezed tight. "Something special will happen to you soon, little girl. I can feel it."

"I hope so. I could use something special."

Phoebe left the inn by the rear door and

CATHY McDAVID 325

drove the half mile to Wishing Well Springs. At the garage, she activated the automatic door opener, planning on parking next to Laurel's SUV in the empty space where Cash's truck had been.

Except his pickup was still there! He hadn't left for Phoenix. What the…

Reversing, she pulled alongside the garage to where she parked when both Cash and Laurel were home. Climbing out, she caught sight of movement and a flash of color down by the paddock. Was Cash with the horses?

If she had a lick of sense, she'd go directly into the house. Do not pass Go. Do not collect two hundred dollars. She had work waiting for her and calls to place. They had a wedding tonight, and the secret couple's personal assistant had sent two emails about Saturday's event. Instead, she hurried along the footpath to the paddock, slowing her steps as she neared.

Cash stood with his back propped up against the fence. Otis and Elvis were close by, their heads buried in the feeder. To Cash's right, the little cat sat on top of the fence post, grooming herself. The two of them were carrying on a conversation about the drawings for Burle's cabin.

The hurt clinging to Phoebe's heart loosened its grip. What kind of guy talked to a cat? None she knew other than Cash.

The kind of guy worth waiting for, a small voice inside said.

Stop it. She was done pining after him. That was what she'd told her dad and what she'd decided was for the best. Phoebe Kellerman was moving on.

"Hi. I didn't see you there," Cash said.

"Sorry to interrupt."

"I wasn't doing much. Killing time." He patted Otis's neck. By now, the cat had scampered off to her hiding place in the carriage house.

"I…um, figured you'd be long gone by now."

"Change of plans." He smiled almost apologetically. "I'm staying on through Christmas. My boss gave me the okay."

"Why?"

"You and me. I can't leave. Not until we're back to where we were before."

Despite her fluttering heart, she refused to jump to conclusions. "You want to start dating again?"

"Back to where we were pre-dating," he clarified.

"Right. Good idea."

Thankfully, she hadn't run to him and fallen into his arms. That would have been embarrassing. But Phoebe was a little wiser now than she'd been a few weeks ago. And more cautious.

CHAPTER FIFTEEN

CASH SAT ON the couch in the client seating area, watching Phoebe pace back and forth in the entryway. She stopped every two or three passes to either glance at her phone or peer out one of the tall narrow windows bracketing the front door.

Not that she could see much; it was pitch-black outside. Add to that, a light snow had been falling intermittently for the past twenty-four hours, and an overcast sky blocked out any hint of moonlight.

"They're late," she said to no one in particular.

"They'll be here," Cash answered, not moving. "They probably encountered some traffic delays because of the weather."

The secret couple and their wedding party were supposed to have arrived by now. Phoebe was beside herself with worry and agitation. She'd been scrambling morning to night since yesterday, making sure everything was perfect and every request, no matter how trivial, was fulfilled. They still had no clue as to the bride's and groom's identities and apparently wouldn't until they showed...*if* they showed.

"Why haven't they called or texted me?" Phoebe demanded, again to no one in particular.

"Weren't you just speaking to someone an hour ago?" Laurel emerged from Bellissima, stopping just short of being plowed over by Phoebe. "What's their ETA?"

"Seven thirty," she lamented. "At this rate, there's no way we can start the wedding at eight."

"Maybe they're traveling through a dead zone. Cell phone reception's iffy in the mountains, especially during storms."

"Oh God!" Phoebe's hand flew to her mouth. "You don't think they had an accident, do you? The roads are slippery and visibility is, like, zero. We should call the sheriff's office."

"Not yet," Laurel assured her and then, when the coast was clear, cut across the entryway to join Cash on the couch.

Together, they continued watching Phoebe pace. Tonight she wore a long shirt made to look like a Christmas tree, complete with ornaments, garlands and wrapped presents. Cash thought it must be uncomfortable, what with the branches sticking out on the sides, but she didn't seem to notice or care. On top of her head sat a stocking cap with a star rather than a fluffy ball at the tip. Bells adorned her boots, similar to the ones he'd come eye to eye with that day three weeks ago when she'd descended the ladder in front of him.

The outfit should have been ridiculous and on anyone else it would have been. Phoebe, however, pulled it off and managed to look adorable.

Cash had heard she was wearing a Mrs. Claus costume for the Christmas Day vow renewal ceremony. Santa would be played by the officiant. Guests were required to wear either a Santa hat or reindeer antlers. Cash would be the one exception. Phoebe hadn't been able to convince him to wear so much as a Christmas tie clasp. When she'd complained, he'd volunteered to stay home.

The two of them had found a moment to talk the other day and, for the most part, were getting along. Some residual awkwardness remained, but that was to be expected and should eventually diminish, especially when he returned to Phoenix on the twenty-sixth.

Life as they'd known it had resumed at Wishing Well Springs. Phoebe wasn't quitting, Laurel had stopped being mad at him, excavation on the mock Western town was still scheduled for early January and business was booming. Cash wasn't a failure like his father and grandfather.

He did regret hurting Phoebe and really missed their former camaraderie. When things had been good between them, they'd been really good. He wanted that kind of relationship with the person he fell in love with and married. If only she'd been willing to wait.

Enough already. No point dwelling on what would never be. They'd made their choices and were living with the consequences.

"They're here! They're here!" Phoebe ran to the front door, throwing it wide open. "Thank goodness."

Cash and Laurel pushed off the couch and reached the entryway in time to see a caravan of five black vehicles traveling the road toward the house. Twin beams of lights shot out from each vehicle, beacons in a pitch black night. In total, there were two limousines and two town cars, with an SUV bringing up the rear.

"That's quite a showing for people who wanted to keep a low profile," Cash observed dryly.

"I'll say." Laurel hugged herself against the blast of cold air coming through the open door.

Phoebe stepped out onto the porch. "Where are they going?"

Cash came up behind her. It was the closest they'd been since the night of their first and last official date. He found himself so distracted by a loose strand of hair that had escaped her star cap, he almost forgot to look at the cavalcade of impressive vehicles. A nudge from Laurel reminded him.

"They're heading to the barn."

Phoebe flew into action, fishing in her pocket for the golf cart keys. "They were supposed to meet me here first. I had an email from their personal assistant confirming."

"Maybe they're confused," Laurel offered. "It's dark outside and they haven't been here before."

That was strange. Cash couldn't recall a single wedding where the bride and groom hadn't made at least one visit prior to the big day.

"I have to meet them at the barn." Phoebe dashed outside, jogging down the porch steps to the golf cart parked in front of the house.

"Wait." Cash grabbed his jacket and her shawl from the nearby coatrack. She'd freeze to death without something warm to wear. "You forgot this."

She'd already started the golf cart and was pulling away when he reached the bottom porch step. Without stopping to think, he hopped into the moving cart, falling hard onto the seat when she accelerated.

"What are you doing?" She sent him an annoyed glare.

"Here." He shoved her shawl at her.

"I'm not… Thanks." She gathered it into her lap, her gaze remaining riveted on the road.

"Slow down," Cash hollered when she took a turn at top speed. If not for holding on to the safety bar, he would have been ejected. Icy snow pelted them. Wind stung his face, causing his eyes to water. "It's not like they're going anywhere."

"I was supposed to meet them," she repeated.

Any other wedding, Georgia Ann and the crew would be at the barn setting up. But the couple's personal assistant had insisted only Phoebe be present and, if absolutely necessary, Cash. No one else, under any circumstances. Even Laurel, though she'd signed the NDA.

"Everything will be fine," he said.

Phoebe ignored him for the next ninety seconds, which was how long it took them to reach the barn. Slowing to a reasonable speed, she bypassed the parked vehicles and braked to a stop alongside the first one. Without bothering to shut off the golf cart's engine, she jumped out and ran toward the cluster of people emerging from the various vehicles in an elegant procession. He picked up the shawl she'd forgotten on the seat, and then thought better of chasing after her. At the rate her blood was pumping, she probably didn't feel the cold.

Cash slid over into the driver's seat. Pressing on the accelerator, he parked the golf cart next to the well and the pony cart with its inflatable Mr. and Mrs. Claus and animated reindeer. He'd wait until the wedding was underway before seeking shelter.

A few minutes later, the wedding party proceeded toward the barn. He counted roughly twenty people altogether. Most had donned heavy coats and woolen scarves over their wedding finery. From this distance, and with coats obscuring their clothes, Cash wasn't sure which two people were the bride and groom. The woman carrying a bouquet could be the bride or the maid of honor, and the guy holding a manila envelope might be the groom or officiant.

As the group strolled past, Cash noticed a tall woman flanked by two men. She wore one of those funny little hats stuck to the top of her head, a short, sheer veil covering half her face. Given the way her escorts shielded her, Cash decided she must be the bride and about to marry a notorious criminal or powerful businessman. On second thought, she could be the politician's daughter and the groom a European royal as Phoebe had suspected.

Speaking of Phoebe, had she recognized the bride? If so, nothing about her usual harried actions indicated it.

He scanned the faces in the group. None looked familiar to Cash. And try as he might, he still couldn't discern the woman's face. Even so, something about the tilt of her head and her slim, graceful form struck a familiar chord with him. He must have seen her on the big screen or the evening news. It would be interesting to finally learn her identity and the groom's. One or the other obviously had money and influence.

Buttoning up his jacket, Cash hunkered down in the golf cart to wait. They hadn't set out the propane heaters—there'd be no reception tonight. The normally bright Christmas lights strung inside and outside the barn had been left off. Only the tree, visible through the large doorway, twinkled and glittered.

Was the couple really that worried about paparazzi? An intimate wedding was one thing; this had been taken to the extreme. Cash noted a broad-shouldered man in a dark navy suit, his short hair cut in military fashion. Was he a bodyguard?

Once everyone was inside, Cash left the golf cart to stand near the barn's doorway where the eave provided cover from the snow and the heated barn a modicum of warmth. From his vantage point, he could watch the wedding without being seen.

He'd been right—the woman with the funny little hat was the bride. She stood at the altar with her back to Cash and next to a gray-haired man who, while fit and trim, was a good twenty years her senior. No big deal. Cash had seen couples of every imaginable age difference tying the knot.

As she moved, now without her heavy coat and clad in a slim-fitting sparkling dress, he was again struck by a sense of familiarity. If only he could wrangle a closer look at her face.

Soon after that, the wedding started. Phoebe retreated to the rear of the barn and her usual corner. Almost immediately, she caught sight of Cash and gestured for him to remain where he was. Apparently, she was following the couple's instructions for privacy to the letter.

Cash acknowledged her with a small nod. Now that the wedding was underway, she appeared less agitated. Far from calm, however, as evidenced by her wringing hands.

Propping a shoulder on the wall, he settled in to wait. Ten minutes later, Phoebe was summoned to the altar. Already? That had to be the fastest ceremony in Wishing Well Springs' history.

The next moment, she was outside, standing beside him.

"What's up?" he asked.

A glance inside the barn revealed the bride and groom still at the altar and the guests seated in the first rows. In eerie unison, everyone's heads cranked around and every pair of eyes locked on him and Phoebe.

"In all the excitement," she said, "they forgot the rings. Apparently the bride had them specially designed as a surprise for the groom."

Unusual, but Cash didn't comment.

"They're in boxes on the seat in the last limo," Phoebe said. "Can you get them, please?"

"Sure."

"Hurry."

Cash jogged to the limo, his arms churning. The driver's-side door opened and a uniformed man emerged well before Cash got there. He explained what happened, and the man quickly located the two velvet boxes. One in each hand, Cash hurried back to the barn, expecting to turn the boxes over to Phoebe.

Instead, the bride stood at the door. Even with the veil covering her eyes, he recognized her immediately. How could he not? It hadn't been that long since he'd last seen Silver.

SHOCK RIPPED THROUGH Cash like a fault opening during a magnitude nine earthquake.

"Cash? I—" Silver floundered, confusion and accusation flaring in her eyes. "What are you doing here?"

He moved in what felt like slow motion, his limbs sluggish to respond to his brain's commands. Holding out the ring boxes, he said, "It appears congratulations are in order."

Silver took the rings and pressed them to her middle. "I don't understand. None of this makes sense."

"I own Wishing Well Springs. This is—was—my grandfather's ranch."

At some point the veil had been lifted, giving Cash an unobstructed view of her flushed features. He had to admit, she was as beautiful as ever. But he might as well have been gazing upon a mannequin for the lack of emotion she stirred in him.

"Your grandfather's ranch," she murmured as if searching her memory. "I had no idea."

Why would she? They'd broken up months before Cash, Laurel and Phoebe had decided to go into business together. And unlike Melanie and Hannah, he'd never taken Silver to

Payson. At the time, the house and barn had been sitting empty, slowly decaying until his grandfather's estate was settled. Unless she'd researched Cash online—and he sincerely doubted that, given the life she led—she probably assumed he still worked at Strategic Design or some other architectural firm.

"It's a long story." He cleared his throat. "And you're kind of busy at the moment."

"Yes, I am. Let's talk later." She pivoted and glided gracefully down the aisle. Nothing in her expression or manner indicated she'd just run into her former fiancé.

Cash couldn't say the same for himself. His heart continued to hammer as his mind grappled with the impossible. All three of his former fiancées had gotten married at Wishing Well Springs within a couple weeks of each other. The odds had to be a million to one. What next? An alien invasion? Him being elected president? He stepped inside the barn and out of the cold, stopping on the other side of the door. Phoebe rushed over from where she'd been conversing with the guests and pulled him deeper into the corner.

"Thanks for getting the rings," she whispered. "I got pulled away."

"That's Silver."

Phoebe whirled and gawked at the bride. "Silver your former fiancée?"

"The very same."

"No way!" She turned to him and then back to Silver.

"Didn't you recognize her?"

Phoebe and Silver hadn't met before, though Phoebe had watched Silver's movies and seen photos of her in magazines.

"I can tell it's her now, and no, I didn't recognize her. The veil and her hair…" Phoebe blew out a breath. "Good thing we're not allowed to tell anyone, because no one will believe us."

They quietly moved to Phoebe's corner.

"She must be a bigger celebrity than I thought." Cash considered the limos and the bodyguard and all the effort she and the groom had gone through to avoid paparazzi.

"She's not," Phoebe answered in a low voice. "But the groom is Martin Nessmith. The Oscar-winning director," she added when Cash shrugged. "They met during his last film. He was still married at the time."

"How do you know?"

"One of the guests told me. She also said that Martin's divorce was finalized only last week. They're keeping everything hush-hush for a while to avoid any bad publicity surrounding his latest film. That is why we weren't told their names and had to sign nondisclosure agreements. And why they picked an out-of-the-way place far from Hollywood. After the film's been out awhile, they're going to make a big announcement and throw a reception."

"That explains a lot."

"I swear, Cash, if I'd known Silver was the bride, I'd've said something to you."

He stared down the aisle at the bride and groom. A moment later, the officiant declared them husband and wife, and they kissed. The guests clapped and cheered, the noise echoing loudly in the mostly empty barn.

"You okay?" Phoebe placed a hand on his shoulder, their first physical contact since their falling-out. Warmth seeped through his jacket.

"Kind of weird watching your ex-fiancée marry another man."

"I can imagine. I mean, even if you don't love that person anymore, it's still gotta be strange." She removed her hand. "If things had been different, that might have been you standing there with her."

He stared at Silver, relief the only emotion he felt. When he turned to Phoebe, a whole new gamut of emotions filled him.

"Phoebe." There was much he wanted to say to her. "Can we—"

"Hold that thought. I'll be right back."

With the formalities over, she scurried off to attend to any final requests the wedding party may have. Cash remained in the corner, thinking how glad he was he'd dodged a bullet with Silver.

In all honesty, he hadn't expected her to seek him out. She'd just gotten married and was the center of attention. A guest took several photographs with their phone and then recruited Phoebe to snap some group shots. When they were done, Silver spoke to her new husband and, shocking Cash a second time, started in his direction. He stepped forward, but she motioned for him to remain there.

"Nice wedding," he said when she joined him, glowing like any new bride.

"Thanks to your wedding coordinator. Phoebe, isn't that her name? My assistant raved about her."

Cash nodded. "She's great. The best in town."

"She's a miracle worker. Martin and I appreciate all she did and, especially, her discretion."

"She can be counted on. Me, too."

"Thank you, Cash." Silver spoke in the low, sultry voice that had no doubt aided her Hollywood career and initially attracted him to her. "How long have you and she been together?"

"About two years. Wishing Well Springs was Laurel's idea, and she proposed we bring Phoebe on as a third partner."

"No." Silver laughed and ran her manicured fingernails along his arm. He didn't feel so much as a sliver of warmth. "How long have you and Phoebe been *together*?"

"We're not."

"Really? That surprises me. The way you look at each other, I assumed you were involved."

The way they looked at each other? Silver wasn't the first one to notice. Channing and Burle had, too.

Cash had no idea why, but he confessed, "We did date. Briefly. It didn't last."

"I'm sorry to hear that. She's sweet and very much your type."

"Actually, we couldn't be more different."

"Which keeps things interesting. That's what I tell Martin, anyway." She laughed again. "What went wrong with you and Phoebe, if you don't mind me asking?"

"Same as with you and me. She was in a hurry, and I wanted to wait. We have a large expansion project starting in a couple of weeks. An entire mock Western town."

"Let me guess. You're worried about money."

"The expansion is cutting into profits. I

don't feel right committing until the business is in the black again."

"Oh please." Silver's flawless brow crinkled. "From the looks of this place, you're doing very well. Why on earth would you torture that lovely girl by insisting she wait till some indefinite date?"

His defenses instantly rose. "I don't make promises I can't keep."

"But, my dear Cash, you do. You propose, which is a promise, and then you break that promise. Honestly, I've never understood that. You apparently want to get married—you've certainly proposed often enough—but then you leave the poor woman high and dry."

"You left me."

"Because you pushed me away. *And* the others. From the sounds of it, you did the same to Phoebe. The only difference is she was smarter than the rest of us and got out sooner."

Cash resisted the urge to engage with Silver. This was her wedding day. He wouldn't stoop that low.

Instead, he said, "I'm glad you're happy and that you have the career you've always wanted. It's been nice talking to you."

"I'm being dismissed. How like you. Same old emotionally unavailable Cash. You haven't changed one iota."

He wouldn't bicker with her, either. "Phoebe mentioned you and your husband are leaving right away for your honeymoon."

Silver continued as if he hadn't spoken. "You've always been so afraid of failing and losing the woman you love, like what happened to your parents, that you sabotage every relationship. Am I right? Of course I'm right."

He didn't care for Silver's attitude or her assessment of him. It struck too close to the truth.

"I realize I hurt you," he said evenly. "And you might feel inclined to take some swings at me."

"You did hurt me. But everything worked out for the best. As you can see, I landed on my feet."

"Congratulations are in order."

Hearing her new husband call her name, she smiled radiantly and blew him a kiss. "Be right there, love." To Cash, she said, "What you do with your life is none of my business. It hasn't been for a long while. But if I can offer you one piece of parting advice it's this. Don't push people away. If you do, you'll spend the rest of your life alone and miserable." When he opened his mouth to object, she raised a finger. "No, wait. I have another piece of advice. That darling woman loves you. Change your ways and come to your senses while there's still a slim chance you can win her back."

She turned and walked away from Cash and into the arms of her new husband. Cash stayed where he was, more affected by her short speech that he cared to admit.

She was right. He'd allowed his fear of failure to get the best of him in every relationship, including his short-lived one with Phoebe.

Cash's head throbbed and his chest ached. He didn't want to spend the rest of his life alone. No, that wasn't right—he didn't want to spend the rest of his life without Phoebe.

He ducked outside and stayed in the shadows while Silver, her new husband and the wedding party left the barn. If she saw him on her stroll to the parked vehicles, she didn't acknowledge him. She had eyes only for the man on her arm.

The small cavalcade no sooner drove away than the lights in the barn blinked out. Phoebe's doing—she was closing up for the night. Cash started the golf cart and drove it to the door at the same moment she emerged. Leaving the engine running, he hopped out and slid the heavy barn door shut, snapping the padlock in place.

"I saw you and Silver talking," she said, removing her shawl from the golf cart seat and wrapping it around her. "How'd that go?"

"It was interesting." He started down the road once she was seated.

"You seem upset."

"I'm not. More like processing. The conversation was enlightening."

"You don't say. Did you get the same kind of closure you did with Melanie and Hannah?"

"Not exactly."

"Care to talk about it?"

"She agreed with you and everyone else. I push people away. I'm afraid of failure. I have some serious hang-ups, thanks to my parents. What else?" He didn't tell her what Silver had said about Phoebe being in love with him and a possible second chance.

"Was that hard to hear?" she asked.

"You mean hard to hear for the fourth time in two weeks?"

"You have been taking a beating lately."

He snuck glances at her as they drove. "Do you regret what happened with us?"

"I regret the way it ended, yes."

"If we could try again, would you want to?"

She sent him a curious look. "What exactly did Silver say to you?"

"Forget it," he said. "Weddings, you know. They can make sentimental fools of anyone."

She seemed about to say more but then clamped her mouth shut until they neared the main house. "Drop me off here. I left my purse inside, and I need to chat with Laurel before heading home."

"It's late. You going to be okay?" He braked to a stop across from the porch steps. "I can wait for you. Walk you to your car."

"I'll be fine," she said.

When she started to climb out of the golf cart, he stayed her with a hand on her arm. If he didn't ask her now, he might never find the courage again.

"Silver did say something interesting. She seemed to think you—" He stopped himself before saying *love me*. "She thinks I may have a slim chance of winning you back. Is she right?"

Phoebe pulled her shawl more snugly around her. "Like you say, weddings can make sentimental fools of anyone."

"Is that a no?"

"If you have to ask, you don't know me at all." At what must be his obvious confusion, she added, "I'll give you a hint. Think about Enrico and his fiancée and his proposal on the hill."

"You want me to propose?"

She huffed. "Are you really that dense, Cash, or simply pretending?"

Climbing out of the golf cart, she walked up

the steps, leaving him to mull over her remarks in complete confusion.

His befuddled state didn't last. With the sudden clarity of a lightning strike, Cash understood and realized what he had to do. Now, if only he could find a way.

Bit by bit, a plan came together.

CHAPTER SIXTEEN

PHOEBE'S KNEES ACHED from her being down on all fours for ten minutes straight. The tree branches that had initially tickled her face and hands now scratched like tiny claws. A needle had poked her in the eye, causing stinging and tears. Tinsel clung to her hair and sweater. A broken ornament shard had driven pricks of pain into her skin when she inadvertently leaned a palm on it.

She refused to abandon her efforts, however. Not until she'd replaced the last dead bulb on the string of Christmas tree lights. One had flickered out a short while ago, causing another dozen to follow. These last few were located in the back of the tree.

Where else? That was how her luck had been running lately, from none to bad.

Groaning, she inserted a fresh bulb into an empty socket, snapping it in place. She'd been awake since five o'clock and toiling laboriously since six, the time she'd arrived at her parents' house to help her mother with breakfast. The meal had been eaten at breakneck speed, the gifts opened equally fast by nieces and nephews who were bouncing off the walls with excitement. No one lingered—everyone had somewhere else to be: the inn, their in-laws', volunteering to serve meals at the homeless shelter. Phoebe arrived at the ranch by nine, completely drained and with a full day still ahead of her.

Every crew member was there today, despite it being Christmas. They had a mere four hours total to transform the barn into a version of Santa's workshop for the vow renewal ceremony. When they finished with setup, the crew would be dismissed to enjoy what was left of the day. Those wanting extra pay were returning later to clean up and ready the barn for tomorrow's wedding.

With over two hundred guests expected, the vow renewal extravaganza was without a doubt Wishing Well Springs' biggest and most elaborate event to date. As the story had been told to Phoebe, the happy couple met when they were both in college. To earn extra money, they'd taken seasonal jobs as Santa's helpers at the local mall's North Pole Village. They'd fallen in love at first sight, seeing past the goofy elf costumes, fake ears and cartoon-ish pointy shoes. Not long after graduation, they'd married.

The couple's large extended family had planned the entire event and paid every expense, right down to the cost of live musicians, props and a portable stage for a skit featuring the many grandchildren, rented Mr. and Mrs. Claus costumes for Phoebe and the officiant, Santa hats and reindeer antlers for all the guests to wear, and travel for the out-of-town guests. One of the more creative daughters had put together a display featuring fifty photos, one from every Christmas the couple had spent together as husband and wife.

Phoebe adored the idea and was delighted to help bring the family's vision for their holiday anniversary celebration to life. *Had* been delighted, anyway. At the moment, she was having trouble mustering enthusiasm for anything.

Had Cash been serious when he'd asked about them dating again? She hadn't been able to get their conversation out in front of the house from her mind, continually replaying it in her head. She'd been too flabbergasted to ask for clarification and then afraid of embarrassing herself by appearing too eager. As a result, she'd gone a little off the deep end—not eating, not sleeping, becoming forgetful, grumpy and jumpy, and biting her nails, something she hadn't done in twenty years.

There'd been no opportunity to talk to him even if she had dared broach the subject. Whenever they weren't working or involved with holiday and family obligations—his mom had arrived late yesterday with all her dinner fixings—Cash was holed up in the attic room. Laurel had said he was finalizing the expansion drawings, the plans for Burle's cabin and a mysterious something for someone else, she didn't know what.

Could that mysterious something be the motel he'd told Phoebe about? She didn't ask, not wanting to hear the answer. If the mystery drawings weren't of the motel, she'd be disappointed. If they were, she'd get her hopes up yet again. Better to remain ignorant.

And, this was news to her, he'd started remodeling the attic room. Apparently, he and Laurel were turning it into a rental or boarding room for an employee. Phoebe wondered where Cash would bunk once that project was complete. Did he plan to commute less often to Payson in the near future? That could only mean he wasn't interested in them dating again.

Argh! Nothing was ever easy or simple with Cash. She wanted to scream and would have if she hadn't had a vow renewal ceremony to coordinate.

"Give it a rest, will you?" Laurel said from somewhere on the other side of the Christmas tree.

"I can't," Phoebe mumbled. "There's still two lights out." As if it mattered; they were in the back, so no one would notice.

"That'll wait," Laurel said.

"It won't."

Well, it would. Except she wasn't ready to emerge from her hiding place. If she stayed where she was, she wouldn't have to look at people's faces and see their concerned expressions. All the employees could tell she hadn't been herself, and she'd grown weary of deflecting their questions.

"Please, come now," Laurel pleaded. "We need you. I need you."

"Okay, okay. I'm done." Phoebe inserted the last of the bulbs. The entire light string twinkled merrily in stark contrast to her mood.

Crawling backward, she inched out from behind the tree, knocking off an ornament in the process. It fell but didn't break. She paused long enough to rehang it and then continued her arduous exit.

Out at last, she sat back on her calves, giving her throbbing knees and aching muscles a rest before attempting to stand. "This had better be important."

Laurel stood with her back to Phoebe. "You can't hide out forever."

"I'm not. I'm right here."

"What?" Laurel pivoted. "I'm talking to Cash."

It was then Phoebe noticed Laurel's phone plastered to the side of her head. "Ah."

She pushed clumsily to her feet, ignoring the cramps seizing her legs. Straightening, she brushed off the front of her slacks and picked tinsel from her hair and sweater. She had to change into her Mrs. Claus costume soon for the vow renewal ceremony. A longtime friend of the couple would be wearing a matching Santa costume. They both had parts in the skit, and he was officiating the ceremony.

According to the family's lengthy notes, part of his officiating duties would be the sharing of several cute and touching anecdotes from the couple's many years together. The couple would then exchange their own vows. Besides the live music, the usual toasts and the grandchildren's skit, the reception would include a this-is-your-life presentation. A traditional turkey dinner would be served family style.

"I swear," Laurel complained, "getting Cash

to leave the attic room was next to impossible. But he's on his way now."

Phoebe's nerves, already frazzled, crackled with anticipation.

"He's been such a curmudgeon. You two aren't squabbling again, are you?"

"We're barely talking."

Laurel narrowed her gaze. "I thought you'd made up."

"We did."

"Then what's going on?"

Phoebe hesitated. She hadn't told Laurel about Cash's do-over comment for obvious reasons. Her friend would pick apart every word and analyze the conversation to death.

"Nothing. I'm busy. Weddings, you know. Lots of them. A huge vow renewal ceremony starting in an hour."

"Did he say something? Because I wouldn't put it past him."

Phoebe clenched her teeth in frustration. Laurel's pestering wouldn't stop until she had a satisfactory answer. Might as well get it over with now rather than later.

"Sort of…" she began hesitantly.

"Tell me."

Phoebe considered carefully before speaking. She hadn't and wouldn't mention Silver—the news was Cash's to tell his sister or whoever.

Even though Laurel was Phoebe's best friend, she'd have to wait. "Someone suggested to Cash that I might give him another chance. He mentioned it."

Laurel brightened. "Are you?"

"No. And I won't unless he changes, which I'm sure he won't."

"Well that explains him becoming a hermit." She made a sad face. "He's pretty unhappy."

"I wish he wasn't." *I wish I wasn't.*

"So you won't even consider it?" Laurel asked, digging in as Phoebe had predicted.

"Cash isn't about to change. He is who he is. Take him or leave him." Hadn't Phoebe's dad said as much? "I'm not risking another heartache that's all but guaranteed."

"He's not Sam."

"I agree. Sam lied to me, saying we'd get married when he had absolutely no intention. Cash was honest from the start."

"You want to know what I think?" Laurel asked.

"Sure. You're going to tell me anyway."

"If my brother really and truly wanted to marry any of this three former fiancées, he would have. But he didn't. He let them walk away without a fight."

"Your point?"

"They weren't right for him." Laurel smiled mischievously. "But you are."

"Let me remind you that he didn't fight for me, either." Phoebe tamped down a surge of misery. "And nothing you are saying is making me feel better."

Laurel snorted. "You're your own worst enemy, girl, I swear. The two of you are. Have you any idea how hard it is being me, sitting on the sidelines and watching you wreck your every opportunity for happiness?"

"Gee, that wasn't mean at all."

"Look, I'm not one to talk. I've made my own mistakes. Which is why I can sympathize. This being in love stuff? It's not for sissies."

"You aren't joking."

"And it can be scary," Laurel continued. "Especially when we've been burned in the past. Cash watched our parents' marriage implode, and it defined him. He needs someone who understands that and can be patient with him. If that's not you, if you're unable to wait, then fine. But get over him and quit moping around like a kid who's lost their puppy."

"You're right." Phoebe squared her shoulders. "Enough is enough."

Cash suddenly appeared in the barn doorway and, like that, he stole her breath away. Stripping off his jacket, he tossed it and his cowboy hat on a nearby chair. The plaid flannel shirt he'd donned emphasized his broad shoulders and athletic frame. The two-day beard he sported turned him from boy next door to bad boy.

"Hey, you two." His chestnut eyes locked with Phoebe's.

"Ah, hi, Cash."

Laurel waggled her eyebrows at Phoebe. *You are so going to give him another chance.*

Phoebe frowned and shook her head. *I am not.*

Laurel smirked. *Wanna bet?*

"Let's get to work," Phoebe said, escaping before her will to resist completely deserted her.

With everyone pitching in, including Cash and a full crew on hand, they made their one o'clock deadline by one twenty. That was good enough for Phoebe. The immediate family had arrived and was setting up when she excused herself to change. She'd left her Mrs. Claus costume in the bride's dressing room and wanted to be out before the bride showed and required the room. Normally, she'd adore dressing up in costume—give her padding, a white wig and wire-rimmed glasses any day. But today, her heart wasn't in it.

When she emerged, tying her apron strings, she got straight to extinguishing the latest fires. She came up for air in time for the ceremony to start. One good thing: she'd been too busy to think about Cash.

Laurel joined Phoebe in her corner. "All systems go?"

"We're as ready as we'll ever be." She glanced up at the hayloft. "Is Cash in charge of the snow?" They'd rented the party machine again and, like before, particles would rain down on the couple at the end of the ceremony.

"I don't know where he is," Laurel answered. "Georgia Ann's manning the machine."

Phoebe took stock of the room, a sea of Santa hats and reindeer antlers before her. The Christmas tree glittered merrily. Fresh streamers had been added to the wreath. A foam snowman grinned jauntily from Santa's workshop. Cash, however, was nowhere to be seen. He must have left, Phoebe decided. He'd said before he'd stay away rather than wear a costume.

Her mood sunk further. His fixation with making and having money was annoying but understandable. He was a product of his past. Refusing to be a good sport? That was plain old obstinacy. Or spite. He knew this event was important to her. Yet he couldn't wear a stupid Santa hat for an hour.

Getting over him just got a whole lot easier.

The next moment, Santa emerged from the area behind the altar, looking jolly with his long white beard, red suit, black boots and generous belly. Behind him came the "groom," wearing an elf costume that resembled the ones he and his wife had been wearing the first time they'd met at their college jobs.

Phoebe had to admit, the man did look ridiculous. But his ear-to-ear grin showed he didn't mind. He'd clearly gone along to please his wife and family. He was the kind of man Phoebe wanted to marry. A man who didn't take himself too seriously. Or life. Or money.

Just as Santa and the groom took their places at the altar, recorded music started. The daughter had told Phoebe the song about Santa coming to town had been playing when the couple met. Okay, that was just too cute.

The "bride" appeared, also in an elf costume, and started her walk down the aisle on the arm of her oldest son. All the guests stood.

Something that should have been completely ridiculous was absolutely charming, and tears sprang to Phoebe's eyes.

"What would a wedding be without you crying," Laurel said good-naturedly.

Except Phoebe's tears weren't the sentimental kind. She was crying over what hadn't been and could never be.

"Ho, ho, ho, that was a good one," Santa said in a booming voice.

With the one hand, he patted his jiggling and very padded belly. With the other, he held the prepared speech, which he'd read stiltedly at first and then with growing ease. Yes, he'd stumbled over a few words and lost his place. The couple and their guests had all laughed, finding him amusing rather than annoying.

Laurel leaned in close to Phoebe and whispered, "That friend the family recruited to play Santa is overdoing it, don't you think?"

They'd reached the halfway point of the ceremony, and Santa had bellowed, "Ho, ho, ho" a half dozen times.

"Nobody seems to mind," she said, thankful she'd managed to stifle her crying jag.

Laughter had erupted regularly, along with tears, much cheering and the random sentimental sigh. Fifty years of marriage was indeed something to celebrate. Who cared if the Santa officiant bumbled and fumbled?

Next came the vows. Lenny and Charlene stood facing each other, their hands clasped. First Lenny and then Charlene recited the vows they'd written, citing the many joys and also difficulties they'd shared during their half century together. Tissues were plucked from purses to dab misty eyes, and men cleared their throats while struggling for composure.

"Now," Santa said, "I was told that Lenny and Charlene wouldn't be exchanging rings. Apparently they did that once before." More laughs followed. "Lenny must not have received the memo because he has a surprise for Charlene."

Oohs and aahs broke out when Lenny reached into the front pocket of his elf shorts and produced a ring box. Charlene's eyes widened and she gasped with excitement.

"I love you, sweetheart." Lenny slipped the ring on her finger. "I take you as my wife for another fifty years."

The sound of applause and cheers reached an earsplitting level, filling every corner of the barn.

"Aww." Laurel swallowed a sob. "That was sweet."

Phoebe wanted to voice her agreement. But she couldn't get any words past the giant lump in her throat.

Charlene threw herself at Lenny, who gave her a smooch on the lips.

"Why can't we find men like him?" Laurel bemoaned.

Yeah. Why?

Cash would never make such a grand gesture. Any gesture. He was too practical. Too logical. Too fixated with money. Too stuck in his ways. Just look at his reaction to Enrico's proposal. If he'd been even a tiny smidgeon happy for the dishwasher instead of so critical, his and Phoebe's first date would have ended very differently.

She assumed the ceremony was almost over and shook off her emotions by straightening her wig and glasses. She'd be springing into action the second Lenny and Charlene began their walk back down the aisle.

"I have the best job in the world," Santa said. "Nothing is more rewarding than making children happy. Officiating Lenny and Charlene's vow renewal ceremony…well, that's a mighty close second."

His voice had changed, Phoebe noted. All during the ceremony, he'd played a part. Now he seemed to be speaking in normal tones. He was, she realized, younger than she'd initially assumed and not a contemporary of Lenny and Charlene's.

"Meeting them today has been a tremendous honor," Santa continued. "Their love for one another… Their dedication and commitment… I have to tell you, it's inspiring. These days, you don't see a lot of couples who've been married to each other their entire adult lives." Santa started and then stopped. "Give me a second here."

Was he, too, feeling sentimental? Phoebe squinted. It was hard to tell under the voluminous beard and hair.

"I may be old," he said at last, "but I can still learn a thing or two. Too often in the past, I've focused on the superficial and missed what really matters. What's been under my nose the whole time. Who else here has had that same problem? Come on, don't be shy."

A smattering of applause broke out in the audience, and someone whistled. A few brave individuals raised their hands.

"Lenny and Charlene were lucky to have found each other. I found someone, too. Once. But I was stupid. Can you guess what happened?"

"You lost her," someone yelled.

"That's right. I did."

The audience responded with sympathetic groans and awws.

Weird. Phoebe had just been thinking the very same thing about Cash.

Santa continued. "I asked Lenny earlier when we were in the dressing room what was the secret to a long marriage. He didn't hesitate. He said to me, 'Find a woman who keeps things interesting. I did, and not a day goes by my beautiful wife doesn't surprise me.'"

More *awws* followed, and several heads nodded approvingly. A few people reached for a nearby hand to squeeze. Charlene gazed adoringly at Lenny.

"I think our Lenny here is one smart man," Santa said, "and I should follow his advice."

"What are you going to do?" a woman called out.

"Go after her," a man in the last row hollered.

Santa nodded thoughtfully. "I just might do that. Before she finds someone new. I'm kind of surprised she hasn't yet."

"Put a ring on it," another woman shouted.

A little boy sitting near the aisle whined, "Mommy, I'm hungry."

Santa bellowed another loud "Ho, ho, ho" and then said, "Enough about me. We're gathered today to celebrate Lenny and Charlene and their amazing life together. We also have some great food, which I think some of our guests are more than ready for." He lifted a white-gloved hand and held it to the side of his mouth as if revealing a secret. Except he spoke loudly. "Not sure the two of you've heard, but your kids and grandkids have put together quite a shindig."

Lenny and Charlene laughed and pretended to be embarrassed. Phoebe figured they were loving every minute.

"With that," Santa said, "I'll finish with a sentiment that Lenny and Charlene asked me to share on their behalf. There are three words stronger than *I love you*. They are *I* choose *you*. Today, Lenny and Charlene stand before you as a reminder that they choose each other over all others. To share their joys and their sorrows with. To care for. To cherish. To have a family with. To grow old with and to love forever. Don't just love your special person, *choose* them. Each and every day." Santa clapped his hands. "And with that, I now pronounce you husband and wife again."

Lenny drew Charlene close for a kiss. No sooner did they break apart than they were mobbed by family and friends from the first few rows. Chaos promptly ensued after that.

"Wow." Laurel turned to Phoebe. "Whoever they got for Santa really came through. Especially at the end."

"Funny, though…"

"What?"

"They told me the officiant was a friend. Santa mentioned just meeting Lenny and Charlene today."

"Huh. That is funny." Laurel glanced toward the door. "You need help with anything else? If not, the dress for tomorrow's wedding is waiting on alterations."

"Go on. The crew and I have this handled."

"I can track down Cash and send him your way, if you want."

Phoebe would rather not see him now; her emotions were too raw. "I'll text you if there's a change." *Which there won't be*, Phoebe silently added.

"Sounds good."

By then, guests had started filing outside where propane heaters fended off the cold. During the ceremony, the caterers had prepared the dinner service. Long tables contained towers of china plates, bins of flatware, fans of linen napkins, covered platters and a multitude of steaming chafing dishes.

Once Phoebe had congratulated Lenny and Charlene, she assisted with organizing the reception line. That task accomplished, she returned inside where the crew was hurriedly arranging dining tables and chairs.

She hadn't expected to find Santa, or whoever he was, standing alone near the last row of seats as if waiting for someone. Perhaps he was killing time until the skit.

Summoning a smile, she approached him and said, "You were very good. I'm sure Lenny and Charlene appreciated it."

"Thanks. I admit, I was trying to impress someone. Show her I'm not as dense as she thinks I am and can take a hint." He tugged off his fake hair and hat. Next came his beard. "Do you think I succeeded?"

Phoebe stared, too stunned to move or speak. She'd recognize those chestnut eyes anywhere. She saw them every day. Dreamed about them at night.

"Surprise," he said.

"C-Cash? What are you…? I don't understand."

"I asked the family if I could step in. They agreed when I told them why."

"You wouldn't wear a Christmas tie when I asked you. And now this?" She indicated his costume.

He grinned. "I was trying to get your attention."

"You did." She stared. The Cash she knew would never have officiated a wedding, especially dressed as Santa. "All those things you said during the ceremony… Where did they come from?"

"I'm in the wedding business. I've heard one or two speeches. And I have a taskmaster for a partner. She makes me read a lot."

He'd been paying attention. "It was nice. People responded well."

"I saw you crying."

She shook her head. "I might have gotten choked up for a second."

"You always cry at weddings. It's one of the things I love about you."

"Love? I usually annoy you."

"That, too." He dropped his hat, wig and beard onto a chair. When he was done, he moved as close as their padded bellies allowed. "You keep things interesting, Phoebe. Every day with you is a new adventure. Lenny was right when he told me to find a woman who isn't boring."

She felt the change between them like electricity in the air before a thunderstorm.

"Lenny's a very smart man." Cash removed her wig and glasses, tossing them onto the same chair. "And he has a lot to say on the subject of winning a woman's heart."

"Such as?" She brushed her mussed hair.

"He said most women like grand gestures. Hence, the Santa suit."

"What if I'm not most women?"

Cash chuckled and pressed a kiss to her temple. "Says the person whose job is literally helping people to make the biggest grand gesture ever."

"Hmm." She didn't immediately melt against him. She had her pride and, no, she wouldn't make this easy for him. He had to put in the work if he wanted to win her back. "What else did Lenny say?"

"That when it's right, you know it." He raised a gloved hand to her cheek. The soft cotton material caressed her skin. "You're the right one for me, Phoebe Kellerman. I'm just sorry I took so long to figure that out."

"What about your three former fiancées?"

She didn't like mentioning them, not in this pivotal moment when his actions had revealed a new side of him and given her hope for a possible future together. But she had to know for sure this time was the one that truly counted.

"That's a fair question, and one I've been considering lately." He met her gaze head-on, and in his eyes she saw a vulnerability and honesty that hadn't been there before. "I'd convinced myself that by having a successful marriage, I'd prove I wasn't broken inside. But when push came to shove, I couldn't go through with the weddings. I kept stalling and creating excuses that had nothing to do with the real reason."

"You had to fix yourself first," she suggested.

"Yeah." He chuckled dryly. "Apparently that's obvious to everyone but me."

"How do you know it's different with me?"

His tender smile was immediate and warmed her insides. "That's easy. I realized the moment

I left your house after our date that I'd made a terrible mistake."

"Why didn't you say something?"

"Fear. I needed someone or something to give me a swift kick in the butt. I got that from Silver. She told me if I didn't change my ways, I'd spend the rest of my life alone. I knew right then I was in love with you. That's why I asked if you'd consider a second chance."

"And I said no."

"What about now? Any second thoughts?"

She wrapped her arms around his waist. They didn't go all the way—too much padding. "I've loved you half my life, Cash. One argument isn't going to change that."

"I have a lot of catching up to do. Who knows, maybe we'll beat Lenny and Charlene's record."

She stood on her tiptoes and brought her mouth to his. "I'm willing to try."

Instead of kissing her, as she'd expected, he grabbed her hand and tugged her across the room, navigating between the tables and chairs.

"Where are we going?" she asked.

"You'll see."

They went out the back door, their destination becoming quickly clear. Cash was taking her to the hill. Another grand gesture? She could get used to them.

At the top, he gathered her hands in his. Behind them, the sun had begun its slow descent behind the distant mountains. Phoebe couldn't imagine a more romantic setting.

"What about the skit?" she asked, her breath coming in short bursts. "The family's expecting us."

"This won't take long." His gaze softened and she felt the love he'd expressed just minutes ago deep in her heart. "I have a very important question to ask you."

Could he...? Was he...? Her heart started dancing the way it always did around him, and her voice trembled. "What's that?"

"Will you reconsider and have dinner with me, my mom and Laurel tonight?"

Phoebe laughed at her own foolishness. What had she been expecting? A proposal?

"As it so happens, I'm free."

They kissed then. And talked. Before heading down the hill, they planned their next date and the one after that.

Phoebe couldn't have asked for a better Christmas present.

EPILOGUE

Christmas Eve, One Year Later

"How much longer are you going to be?" Phoebe asked.

Cash glanced over his shoulder at his fiancée—as of tomorrow, she'd be his wife. They'd been engaged since this past summer when he'd popped the question at her birthday dinner in front of her entire family—which had grown by one with Trudy's new baby daughter. He'd have married Phoebe on the spot—when he'd finally and fully committed, he'd committed—but, for once, Phoebe had been the one to insist on waiting.

She'd wanted a Christmas wedding. For her, there was no more perfect day to tie the knot and no more perfect place than Wishing Well Springs. And as a wedding coordinator, she had a lot of plans to put in place and tons of ideas. Plus, Laurel required several months to create a stunning dress.

They'd turned down dozens of couples requesting to reserve the barn for a Christmas wedding, giving up the premium rate. Cash didn't care. Money had become less of a priority since the vow renewal ceremony last year when Phoebe had said she loved him.

Oddly enough, she'd become more conscientious about spending, impressively curbing her impulses. These days, they agreed more often than they disagreed.

"Come here and take a look," Cash said.

She stared at the ground from the golf cart's driver's seat and grimaced. "My boots will get dirty."

"They'll clean up. And I promise, you'll be glad you did."

She gingerly hopped out onto the ground.

Crossing the open area, she cut around Otis and Elvis, who'd been tied to the hitching post in front of the mock Western town's livery stable. They were decked out in their holiday finery, wearing wreaths around their necks and green-velvet blankets on their backs. Red ribbons had been woven through their braided manes and tails. They'd been requested for a photo shoot at this evening's Christmas Eve wedding.

Cash constantly worried about the elderly horses. Neither was having the easiest of winters. The cold weather was affecting their tired and aching joints. He coddled them worse than any mother with a brand-new infant, making sure they had the best of care and most comfortable of accommodations. He'd do whatever was necessary to ensure they remained a part of the ranch for as long as possible.

Stubby had moved out of the carriage house and in with Cash. To everyone's amazement, she'd adjusted well to being an indoor cat, liking Cash's new home in the wooded foothills a few miles down the road from the ranch.

He'd bought the property, which also included a small horse setup, last March, shortly after giving his notice at Strategic Design and moving to Payson. It had been exactly what he was looking for, a diamond in the rough with potential to become a showplace.

The remodeling was to be completed in stages, with Lexi in charge of construction. After Cash and Phoebe returned from their honeymoon in Big Sur, she'd take up residence along with Stubby. In preparation, Phoebe had been moving in her furniture and possessions piece by piece for weeks now. Stubby tolerated her future roommate and the commotion she created, but allowed only Cash to pet her.

"What is it?" Phoebe asked, climbing onto the boardwalk to join Cash.

Today she wore a sweater with a jack-o'-lantern wrapped in glittering lights. Beneath it was printed "I leave my Christmas lights up as long as I possibly can. They go great with the Halloween decor." Enough of her legs showed between the boots and her skirt to catch his attention and hold it.

"This." He showed her the horseshoe they'd found in the paddock and that he'd cleaned and polished. "I'm hanging it over the door." He nodded at the peg he'd hammered in a few minutes ago. This newest building, added onto the general store, had been an impulse decision that proved to be pure genius. "For luck."

Phoebe smiled. "I like it."

The mock Western town was every bit as successful as Cash had hoped it would be. As hoped, business had tripled this year, thanks to its popularity, and had moved Wishing Well Springs up the list of most popular wedding venues in the state. They'd hired Georgia Ann on full-time and another two crew members.

They were also outsourcing all the bookkeeping and accounting tasks to a local firm. Cash didn't have time anymore for that. He was too busy with his new architectural practice. What had started at his old desk behind the partition quickly expanded until he needed his own office with a plan room and conference room and waiting area.

It had been Phoebe's idea to build his new

office in the mock Western town. Cash hadn't been sure at first, but people loved coming there for their appointments. Plus, he regularly landed new clients who'd seen his business or grabbed a brochure when attending a wedding.

"You want to do the honors?" He handed Phoebe the horseshoe.

She grinned gleefully. "Can I?"

He pushed the small stepladder forward.

She held his hand as she climbed.

Slipping the horseshoe onto the peg, she drew back to inspect her efforts. "Not crooked?" she asked.

"Gorgeous."

She turned and found him gazing up at her. "I was talking about the horseshoe."

"I wasn't."

He looped his arms around her waist, reminded of that day just over a year ago when he'd walked into the barn and caught her at the top of an extension ladder hanging that enormous wreath.

"What are you doing, Mr. Montgomery?"

"Hugging you, Mrs. Montgomery."

"We're not married yet."

"Twenty-four more hours. Are you ready?"

"Are you kidding?" She laughed. "You happen to be holding on to the best wedding coordinator in town, if not the entire state. Of course I'm ready."

"That's my girl."

He lifted her off the stool and set her on the boardwalk. "I think we need to practice for when the minister says, 'You may now kiss your bride.'"

"I'm supposed to be meeting the catering manager at the inn in ten minutes. Then we have dinner tonight for all the out-of-town guests. Thank goodness, your mom agreed to handle that. She's been a huge help. Do you think she and your dad are going to get along?"

"They both promised."

No one had been more surprised than Cash when his father had responded positively to the wedding invitation. They had a lot of burned bridges to rebuild. It was, however, the season of giving and, for Cash, forgiving.

"Channing will be here with your tux in an hour." Phoebe tried to pull away.

Cash held tight. "He can wait. The catering manager can, too." He lowered his lips to Phoebe's. "I love you, Phoebe, and I choose you. Today and every day."

"I choose you, too."

As it turned out, she was late for her meeting with the catering manager. That happened a lot with them.

* * * * *

*Watch for the next story in
Cathy McDavid's Wishing Well Springs
miniseries,* How to Marry a Cowboy,
*coming April 2021,
only from Harlequin Heartwarming!*

Get 4 FREE REWARDS!

We'll send you 2 FREE Books plus 2 FREE Mystery Gifts.

Love Inspired Suspense books showcase how courage and optimism unite in stories of faith and love in the face of danger.

FREE Value Over $20

YES! Please send me 2 FREE Love Inspired Suspense novels and my 2 FREE mystery gifts (gifts are worth about $10 retail). After receiving them, if I don't wish to receive any more books, I can return the shipping statement marked "cancel." If I don't cancel, I will receive 6 brand-new novels every month and be billed just $5.24 each for the regular-print edition or $5.99 each for the larger-print edition in the U.S., or $5.74 each for the regular-print edition or $6.24 each for the larger-print edition in Canada. That's a savings of at least 13% off the cover price. It's quite a bargain! Shipping and handling is just 50¢ per book in the U.S. and $1.25 per book in Canada.* I understand that accepting the 2 free books and gifts places me under no obligation to buy anything. I can always return a shipment and cancel at any time. The free books and gifts are mine to keep no matter what I decide.

Choose one: ☐ **Love Inspired Suspense Regular-Print** (153/353 IDN GNWN) ☐ **Love Inspired Suspense Larger-Print** (107/307 IDN GNWN)

Name (please print)

Address   Apt. #

City   State/Province   Zip/Postal Code

Email: Please check this box ☐ if you would like to receive newsletters and promotional emails from Harlequin Enterprises ULC and its affiliates. You can unsubscribe anytime.

Mail to the Reader Service:
IN U.S.A.: P.O. Box 1341, Buffalo, NY 14240-8531
IN CANADA: P.O. Box 603, Fort Erie, Ontario L2A 5X3

Want to try 2 free books from another series? Call 1-800-873-8635 or visit www.ReaderService.com.

*Terms and prices subject to change without notice. Prices do not include sales taxes, which will be charged (if applicable) based on your state or country of residence. Canadian residents will be charged applicable taxes. Offer not valid in Quebec. This offer is limited to one order per household. Books received may not be as shown. Not valid for current subscribers to Love Inspired Suspense books. All orders subject to approval. Credit or debit balances in a customer's account(s) may be offset by any other outstanding balance owed by or to the customer. Please allow 4 to 6 weeks for delivery. Offer available while quantities last.

Your Privacy—Your information is being collected by Harlequin Enterprises ULC, operating as Reader Service. For a complete summary of the information we collect, how we use this information and to whom it is disclosed, please visit our privacy notice located at corporate.harlequin.com/privacy-notice. From time to time we may also exchange your personal information with reputable third parties. If you wish to opt out of this sharing of your personal information, please visit readerservice.com/consumerschoice or call 1-800-873-8635. **Notice to California Residents**—Under California law, you have specific rights to control and access your data. For more information on these rights and how to exercise them, visit corporate.harlequin.com/california-privacy.

LIS20R2

THE WESTERN HEARTS COLLECTION!

COWBOYS. RANCHERS. RODEO REBELS.
Here are their charming love stories in one prized Collection:
51 emotional and heart-filled romances that capture the majesty and rugged beauty of the American West!

YES! Please send me **The Western Hearts Collection** in Larger Print. This collection begins with 3 FREE books and 2 FREE gifts in the first shipment. Along with my 3 free books, I'll also get the next 4 books from The Western Hearts Collection, in LARGER PRINT, which I may either return and owe nothing, or keep for the low price of $5.45 U.S./$6.23 CDN each plus $2.99 U.S./$7.49 CDN for shipping and handling per shipment*. If I decide to continue, about once a month for 8 months I will get 6 or 7 more books but will only need to pay for 4. That means 2 or 3 books in every shipment will be FREE! If I decide to keep the entire collection, I'll have paid for only 32 books because 19 books are FREE! I understand that accepting the 3 free books and gifts places me under no obligation to buy anything. I can always return a shipment and cancel at any time. My free books and gifts are mine to keep no matter what I decide.

☐ 270 HCN 5354   ☐ 470 HCN 5354

Name (please print)

Address   Apt. #

City   State/Province   Zip/Postal Code

Mail to the **Reader Service:**
IN U.S.A.: P.O. Box 1341, Buffalo, N.Y. 14240-8531
IN CANADA: P.O. Box 603, Fort Erie, Ontario L2A 5X3

Get 4 FREE REWARDS!

We'll send you 2 FREE Books <u>plus</u> 2 FREE Mystery Gifts.

FREE Value Over **$20**

Both the **Romance** and **Suspense** collections feature compelling novels written by many of today's bestselling authors.

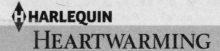